COPPER

Elise Noble

Published by Undercover Publishing Limited

ISBN: 978-1-912888-08-5

Edited by Amanda Ann Larson

Cover by Sapphire Designs

www.undercover-publishing.com

www.elise-noble.com

For Fairfax.

CHAPTER 1 - TAI

"COME ON. COME on!"

Up ahead, brake lights glowed as traffic ground to a halt again. Yes, shouting at the queue was pointless, but it made me feel better, even if the businessman in the car next to mine gave me a strange look and inched forward to get away from the crazy lady. Okay, I should have left home earlier, but I'd barely got any sleep last night thanks to the party downstairs. Who held a New Year's party on the first of January instead of the thirty-first of December? Nobody. Well, nobody except the inconsiderate idiot who lived in the flat below mine.

It was the second of January, a brand new year, a brand new start. Or so all the adverts said. Change your life. Join a gym. Stop drinking. Who wanted to be exhausted and sober anyway? For me, it was back to the same-old, same-old. Same job, same traffic jam on the M25, same lonely evenings with only Netflix for company.

And today, I had the joy of departing for a week-long trip to an exhibition in Holland where I'd be joining two of my favourite people in the world to sell our company's new product, the jewel in the crown of our offerings for the next year. It didn't actually work yet, but let's not allow a little thing like that to stop us, eh?

I'd worked for Garrett-Hart Safety Systems for over a year now. It was never my dream job, but until five months ago when I'd moved departments and met my new boss, I'd spent most of my time in the factory clipping big plastic widgets into smaller plastic widgets, and it hadn't been so bad. Landing an interesting, well-paid graduate position in engineering wasn't easy if you hadn't actually graduated. Missing my last set of exams hadn't gone down so well with the university, even though I had a really good excuse, and I couldn't afford to repeat my final year. Hence the reason why I was stuck in the second of six lanes of traffic in my nine-year-old Honda going absolutely nowhere.

My phone rang, and far from stifling my groan, I let out a huff any tantrum-throwing toddler would have been proud of. Matthew Smart, my aforementioned boss, was calling. To give you an idea of my opinion of Matthew, I'd ordered myself a voodoo doll and three dozen hatpins as an early Christmas present, printed out his mugshot from the "Meet Our Staff" page on Garrett-Hart's website, and glued it on. Every morning, I sprinkled a pinch of the herbs Praktisha in the corner shop swore warded off evil spirits over the top of the doll's head and poked another pin in. So far, zilch. Matthew hadn't suffered a single heart attack or debilitating migraine, and now he wanted to talk to me.

"Tai, where are you? We're supposed to be leaving in fifteen minutes, and Jeffery's here already."

"So sorry, Matthew. I'm stuck on the motorway. I think there's been an accident."

He tutted, and I imagined him drumming his fingers on the desk as he browsed porn on his iPad. Yes, I knew his little secret. He'd left one of his dirty movies on pause one evening while he nipped over to the printer, and now I'd never get the sight of Naughty Nadine getting impaled by a masked dude who'd overdosed on Viagra out of my head.

"If you don't get here soon, we'll miss our crossing on the Eurotunnel."

No, we wouldn't, because he'd insisted the departmental secretary book a flexible ticket. What Matthew meant was that he might miss the chance to put his feet up with a croissant and a cup of coffee in the priority lounge before we got on the train.

"I'll be there as fast as I can. It's starting to move again now."

"Just hurry up. Have you got that memory stick with the program on it?"

"Yes, Matthew."

"And all the cables?"

"Yes, and the spares."

I wasn't even sure why I needed to go to Holland. I didn't speak the language, and Matthew never let me talk to prospective clients. Mostly I was there to make the drinks and carry things, I suspected, plus my darling boss could pull his usual trick of claiming credit for everything I did right and blaming me for everything he did wrong.

Oh, how I hated my job.

My grandma had been ill for most of the last year, and I'd spent all of my spare time taking care of her, hoping she'd pull through somehow, but it wasn't to be. Her death three months ago left me hollow. Matthew had grudgingly given me an afternoon off to attend her funeral, and that was the day I decided things needed to change.

I'd started hunting for a new job, but in my three interviews, the story had always been the same—they liked my attitude, but I didn't have the right qualifications or enough experience. Not only that, I didn't trust Matthew not to screw me over with a reference because he had a vindictive streak too. Just last week, he'd bragged about blocking in a car with twenty shopping trolleys after its driver allegedly stole a space from him at the supermarket. Arsehole.

I had one interview lined up for the new year, an entry-level position at a design firm, but the competition promised to be tough. What were my chances of convincing them I was the girl they wanted?

Must try harder, Tai.

With that thought, I made a New Year's resolution: change not just my job, but all the things I hated about my life.

Like my flat. I'd rented it furnished, and the drab decor depressed me each time I walked through the door. Everything in there was either beige or brown except for the bathroom suite, which was Pepto-Bismol pink and obviously installed by a colour-blind person. Plus the faint smell of vomit permeated throughout no matter how many times I cleaned, although to be fair, that could have been drifting up from the alley below.

Then there was loneliness. I needed to get out more and meet people my own age. Perhaps I could take up a new hobby?

A sign overhead informed me the junction for Heathrow Airport was a mile ahead. My exit was the one after that, and at my current speed, it should only take me about three hours to get there. It would be quicker on foot. What would happen if I did just that?

Abandoned my crappy car at the side of the road, got out, and started walking? Knowing my luck, I'd probably get arrested. And fired.

Although would that really be such a bad thing? Getting fired, I mean, not getting arrested. Nobody wanted to get arrested, did they? Mind you, jail was probably more luxurious than my flat, and at least I wouldn't have to cook.

On the gantry above, the variable speed limit sign switched from forty miles per hour to thirty. Thirty? Hurrah—now I could go faster according to the moron in the control room. Slowly, so slowly, I crawled past a taxi broken down on the hard shoulder. The bonnet was up, and the passenger stood behind the safety barrier looking as bored as I felt while the driver paced back and forth, yelling into his phone.

Another sign for the airport, this time accompanied by a picture of an aeroplane, just in case you didn't realise what an airport was. Maybe I should skip the walking-slash-prison idea and take a plane instead? Just hop on the next flight to...well, anywhere really.

Seriously, why didn't I just do that? I had a bag of clothes, I had my passport, and I had my grandma's favourite gold necklace, which was the only possession I cared about, safely around my neck. The gold felt cool but comforting under my fingers. Tears prickled behind my eyelids, and I blinked them back. Thanks Grandma, I had a little bit of money too—after she died in October, I found she'd taken out a small life insurance policy I knew nothing about, and I was the sole beneficiary. As long as I didn't splurge on caviar or champagne, I could live on that for a few months. Who liked slimy little fish eggs anyway? I shuddered at the thought.

Stay or go? Wait—I couldn't seriously be considering leaving, could I? I was Taisiya Hermione Beaulieu, boring from the split ends of my drab brown hair to the tips of my scuffed black ballet pumps, apart from my unpronounceable name, obviously. My sole ambition in life was to get rid of it, but it didn't look likely to happen anytime soon. The last time I got involved with a man, he'd turned out to be a psycho, and I'd been avoiding them ever since. Not just psychos —men in general. It seemed like the safest option.

I straightened to check my reflection in the rear-view mirror. Yup, the hair definitely needed a cut. Just a trim, and I'd keep the same style, of course. I'd worn it this way since I was fourteen—long layers, no fringe, easy to tie back out of the way while I slaved over CAD drawings and circuit diagrams on my computer.

What would Matthew Smart say if I rang and told him I wasn't going to Holland? Oh, who was I kidding...? I'd send a text message or possibly an email. Non-confrontational, that was me.

My phone screen lit up, and since we were stationary again, I scrolled through the message.

Mum: You haven't forgotten Peony's dance recital this weekend, have you?

How could I possibly forget Peony's dance recital? I'd been dreading it for weeks, ever since Mum told me they were going to the south of France for Christmas but not to worry, we could do a turkey dinner with all the trimmings in the new year when they came back and combine it with Peony's show. Because after spending an exhausting week in Holland, driving to Cheshire on Saturday morning so I could watch the stepsister who hated me prance around on stage in a leotard was exactly what I wanted to do. And did I mention I hated brussels sprouts?

The phone buzzed again, this time with a message from Jeffery Docker, the salesman who'd be coming to Holland with us. Jeffery wasn't so bad apart from the fact he chased anything in a skirt. Except me. I'd never been sure whether to feel relieved or insulted by that.

Jeffery: Where are you? Matthew's getting pissed. His nose has turned purple.

Uh oh. That meant he was about to blow, and the traffic was still going nowhere fast. Another picture of a plane appeared ahead, taunting me. Half a mile to the airport. What if I did it? Swung the wheel to the left and abandoned my car in long-term parking, then bought a one-way ticket to somewhere hot... Or even somewhere cold. I'd never been skiing before. Exercise wasn't really my forte.

I giggled as I pictured the look on Matthew's face if I told him I was skipping the exhibition. He wouldn't just turn purple, he'd go full-on aubergine. An eggplant version of Mr. Potato Head. But what did I truly have to lose if I ran from everything? A mediocre job with disappointing career prospects and a handful of belongings left in the flat I dreaded going home to every evening.

And what would I gain if I took off? A suntan—only on my hands and feet, of course, because I didn't do bikinis—and a story to tell my children if I ever had any. Right now, the only way I'd get pregnant was by immaculate conception.

If I stayed? I might get the job I was due to interview for next week, but it was a hundred to one shot. And with more time in the evenings, I could sign up for classes or try online dating. Oh, haha, dating. Right. What about a cat? I could adopt a cat.

The countdown boards for the junction began. Three... Two... One... Time to decide. Try a new life or stick with the old one? Should I stay or should I go?

CHAPTER 2 - TAI

I JERKED THE steering wheel to the left.

"Oops, sorry," I muttered as the driver of a fancy Mercedes swerved and missed me by inches.

Mental note: must use the mirrors for more than checking my hair.

From today on, Matthew Smart could carry his own boxes of product brochures, and if he—yet again—got lost in a foreign country, he wouldn't be able to blame it on me anymore.

As I got to the end of the slip road, a strange lightness came over me. A glow. Oh no, my mistake. That was the oil warning light on my car. It had been leaking for a while now, and since car mechanics scared me a bit, I'd just been pouring more oil in and hoping the problem would disappear.

No such luck, it seemed.

Another sign materialised. Oh, joy—Heathrow Airport had five terminals, and I had no idea which one to pick. *Quick, Tai...* Two. I chose terminal two. Two was my lucky number and had been ever since Grandma taught me about the joys of BOGOF deals at the supermarket.

I pulled onto the roundabout, only to get cut off by a white van and completely miss my turn. Okay, terminal five. Terminal five was a good option as well. I headed for the long-term car park, but when I saw the cost, I almost cried. After a moment of careful consideration, I reversed out of the entrance and parked neatly in a no-parking zone on the other side of the road. As well as the oil leak, my Honda needed a new clutch and new tyres, so I figured it would work out cheaper if someone stole it. I even left the keys in the ignition to help them out.

My feet felt decidedly chilly as I rode the shuttle bus to the terminal, and not just because of the British weather. Right now, I could still turn around. Still run back to my car, drive to Garrett-Hart, and grovel to Matthew with a million apologies for being late. Sure, I'd be on coffee duty for life, but...

Tai, enough!

Before I changed my mind, or rather, regained my sanity, I typed out a quick text message.

Me: I'm really sorry, but please could you tell Matthew that I've quit?

Hmm, no, I couldn't ask Jeffery to do my dirty work. I tried again.

Me: Dear Matthew, I hereby tender my resignation, effective from...

Too formal.

Me: After a year of living hell, I've finally decided you can do your own damn job. Good luck unjamming the photocopier.

That was what I wanted to say, but...no.

Me: Matthew, I know this is short notice, but I've decided to leave Garratt-Hart. Thank you for all your help and guidance over the last year. Please accept this as my resignation, and best of luck for the future.

There, that worked.

I pressed send just as the bus drew to a halt in front of the terminal, then I quickly turned the phone off. If Matthew called me, I didn't want to speak to him. Heat from the bridges I'd just burned singed my heels as I scurried into the building. *Keep breathing, Tai.* Having a panic attack or passing out wouldn't help matters.

All around, the place buzzed with quiet activity. Businesspeople, families, backpackers, tour groups—they all drifted past as I paused inside the doors, wondering what the hell I'd done.

"Don't just stand there, lady," a teenager muttered as he skirted around me.

"Sorry."

I needed to move before I annoyed anyone else. The ticket counter. Where was the ticket counter?

"Excuse me?" I waved down a man in a hi-vis jacket. "Where can I buy a ticket?"

He pointed wordlessly at the British Airways counter, and I joined the queue. If there was one thing the British were good at, it was queuing.

Although when I reached the front of the line fifteen minutes later, I still had no idea where to go.

"Hi."

The lady behind the counter, Londeka according to her name badge, gave me a perky smile. "Can I help?"

"I need to buy a plane ticket."

"Well, you're in the right place. Where do you want to travel?"

"Uh... I'm not entirely sure."

"Oh?"

"Actually, I think I've lost my mind. I was on my way to work, but then I realised I hated my job and I hated my boss, so I kind of quit and drove here instead."

Her eyes widened, but then she held up a hand for a high-five.

"You go, girl." She lowered her voice to a conspiratorial whisper. "Between you and me, we all wish we could do that."

"Really? Because at the moment, I'm not sure whether to fly somewhere sunny or check myself into the psych ward." A groan escaped. "I don't even have sunscreen."

"Don't worry, hun; you can buy everything you need in duty-free. Flip-flops are thirty percent off this week."

My entire suitcase was filled with business attire, apart from the single pair of yoga pants, the faded T-shirt, and the comfy old trainers I'd planned to wear in the evenings. Perhaps I could dump the suits and invest in a kaftan? Or a ski suit? Or a pair of hiking boots?

"What flights are leaving soon?"

"Let's see now... If this is a last-minute thing, I don't suppose you have a visa for anywhere?"

A visa? That thought had never even occurred to me. Apart from the odd foray through the Channel Tunnel for work and one disastrous trip to Marbella with Peony, I'd avoided venturing abroad.

"No, no visa."

"Not to worry—I'm sure we can find something. How about Australia? You'd need to get a visa, but you can apply online, and it only takes a couple of minutes."

Hmm... During a sleepless night last year, I'd made the mistake of switching over to the Nature Channel. The documentary I watched on Australian wildlife had given me nightmares for weeks. Snakes, sharks, eight-legged freaks...

"Do you have anywhere else? Somewhere with less spiders?"

Londeka consulted her computer again. "Brazil?"

"Scorpions and piranhas."

And more snakes. Okay, so I had a lot of sleepless nights.

"Canada?"

"Bears."

"Not in the city. I went to Vancouver the year before last, and there's loads to do—museums, parks, botanical gardens. Ooh, and the aquarium! The otters were sooo cute, and you can apply for a Canadian visa online too."

"Isn't Canada expensive?"

Sally, who worked in the warehouse at Garrett-Hart, had gone to Toronto the year before last, and she said it nearly bankrupted her.

"Well, Vancouver's a city, so it isn't cheap. But if you stay in one of the budget hotels on the Sky Train route, you can cut down the costs. Oh, and Whistler's less than a hundred miles away if you like skiing."

"I've never been skiing."

"Perhaps you should try it? You know, with your new start and everything."

Knowing my luck, I'd fall and break my leg.

"Maybe. Are there any other options?"

More tapping away at the keyboard. "Egypt? We've got a flight to Cairo leaving soon."

I'd always wanted to see the pyramids. Yes, more Discovery Channel. But I also watched the news, and I'd seen the stories about Tahrir Square.

"Isn't there trouble with terrorists in Cairo?"

"Oh, you don't believe all that stuff in the papers, do you? Two of my friends went to Egypt last month, and they loved it. Winter sun without the huge price tag of the Caribbean, and the flight time's less than five hours."

History did fascinate me, and okay, I'd watched *The Mummy* at least ten times. Purely for the plot, of course. The idea of seeing the Sphinx and Tutankhamun's mask with my own eyes... Wow. I was really doing this. I pinched myself as Londeka carried on.

"Or there's Portugal if you'd rather stay in Europe. The Algarve. Even at this time of year, the beaches are beautiful, and you can do a day trip to Seville. And if you like golf..." She leaned forward to peer over the counter. "Oh. No golf clubs."

Even if I did play, I'd hardly have taken them to work with me, would I? But alas, my sole experience with putting was a round of crazy golf several years ago, and even then, I'd lost to a seven-year-old.

"I'm not very good at sports."

I'd been last to get picked for every team at school, although I'd become somewhat of a celebrity when I got knocked out by a hockey ball.

"Then how about—"

"Ladies, can you hurry this up?" a voice asked from behind me.

I turned to find a weaselly man in a suit glaring at me, his coat folded over one arm and one of those little wheeled cases with the matching laptop bag parked beside him, complete with monogrammed luggage straps. *MAC.* In my head, I christened him Mr. Ass Clown.

"Some of us actually know where we're going," he added.

"Sorry, I—"

"She queued up, just like everybody else," Londeka told him.

"And now there are seventeen people waiting. Are you going to help her plan her entire itinerary?"

She pointed to the words *Customer Service Agent* on her badge. "That's my job, sir. And I'll be happy to help you plan your trip too, after I've finished helping this lady."

I could have kissed Londeka. People rarely stood up for me that way. But I also saw Mr. Ass Clown's point, even if he'd been overly rude in making it.

"Don't worry; I'll grab a coffee while I decide where to go," I told Londeka. After all, I was in no hurry. "I'll come back when I've made up my mind."

"Okay, hun." She waved a hand at the café opposite. "The Coffee House has free Wi-Fi, and if you tell Marie behind the counter that Londeka sent you, she'll give you a staff discount."

"Aw, thanks."

"Don't mention it." She looked past me to Mr. Ass Clown. "Now, sir, how can I help you?"

Over at The Coffee House, I perused the delights behind the glass-fronted counter. Did I want a croissant? A chocolate brownie? A giant cookie? Good grief, if I couldn't even decide what I wanted to eat, how on earth was I supposed to choose a destination for my...my what? Escape? Fresh start? Mental breakdown?

"What would you like, ma'am?"

"A cookie. Please can I have a cookie?"

"Milk choc chip, oatmeal and raisin, salted caramel, or coconut?"

Arrrgh. "Could you just surprise me?"

CHAPTER 3 - TAI

ONCE I'D SETTLED at a table beside the window with a plain black filter coffee and a choc chip cookie, I pulled out my laptop. Half an hour later, a consultation with Trip Advisor left me more undecided than ever. The last three destinations Londeka had suggested all had their pros and cons.

Did I fancy a dose of culture in the hustle and bustle of Cairo? Or the relaxed atmosphere of the Algarve in the off-season when some attractions were closed? The scenery in Vancouver looked breathtaking but also bloody freezing.

Where should I go?

A flash of lightning against the grey sky made up my mind for me. Egypt. I'd go to Egypt. More than anything, I was sick of rain, plus it had the added bonus of being cheaper. My money would go further, so if I fell in love with the country, I could stay there longer.

The queue at the ticket desk had disappeared, thankfully, so I drained my coffee and hurried back over to Londeka.

"Made up your mind?"

"Tell me the flight to Cairo still has space?"

She tapped away at her keyboard as I slid my passport across the desk.

"You're in luck—there are two seats left. Hmm...

The one in economy is next to Mr. Always Complaining."

"Who?"

"The guy who was behind you in the queue last time. His initials were MAC, so I called him Mr. Always Complaining. Between you and me, it gets dead boring working here, so I have to make stuff up to stay awake."

"I called him Mr. Ass Clown."

Londeka properly snorted, and she didn't look at all embarrassed. "Mr. Ass Clown? Much better. Anyhow, you won't want to sit beside him, so I'll put you in business class. No extra charge."

"Really? That's so kind of you."

"It's the least I can do. You've certainly brightened up my day. Who knows? Maybe sometime I'll keep walking and get on a plane too." She studied my passport. "Uh, Tasha? Taysha? Bow-loo? Sorry, I have no idea how to pronounce your name."

The story of my life.

"It's Ty-ee-see-ya Bew-lee. Tai for short."

"Oh. It's nice. Where's does Taisiya come from?"

"Russia. And no, I'm not Russian, not even a tiny bit. Originally, I was supposed to be Tracy, but my mum watched a documentary on the Bolshoi Ballet just before I was born, and now I'm stuck with the results for the rest of my life."

"It could be worse. My mum watched *Footballer's Wives*, and my little sister's called Chardonnay."

"Wow."

"Exactly. Now, you've got an hour and a quarter before boarding, so I suggest you get yourself through security and start shopping."

I gave her a mock salute. "On my way, ma'am."

She was still laughing as I hauled my case towards the check-in desk. Were the body scanners those ones I'd seen on the news recently? The kind that pictured you naked? My cheeks burned at the thought because I desperately needed to lose a few pounds. Having to work with Matthew Smart for the last year had driven me to the company biscuit tin several times a day. Then, to my shame, I'd started bringing Oreos and Jammie Dodgers to work because Garrett-Hart only gave us digestives, and not even the good kind with the chocolate.

On the other side of the scanner, I breathed out, and the stomach I'd been holding in for the past five minutes pressed against my waistband again. Tourists wandered everywhere, clutching shopping bags filled with everything from cigarettes and spirits to electronics and perfume.

Which way to go...? Clothes. I needed clothes. Shorts, T-shirts, a pair of flip-flops. Just a couple of outfits that wouldn't be out of place in thirty-degree heat.

Forty-five minutes later, I ran out of the boutique clutching my purchases. Three pretty tops, one of which I wasn't sure I'd be able to put on again without help, a pair of white capri pants, a cocktail dress, and a pair of red stilettos that the assistant assured me made my legs look fantastic.

Dammit, Tai.

This. *This* was why I did all my shopping on the internet. Online stores didn't have overly enthusiastic staff who convinced you to buy stuff you didn't want with money you didn't have.

With fifteen minutes left until I had to trek to the

gate, I grabbed a pair of cheap sunglasses, a bottle of sunscreen, and a selection of snacks to eat on the plane. I might as well have written "I have no clue what I'm doing" across my forehead with a Sharpie.

The final call for boarding came over the tannoy as I ran towards the gate with bags bouncing around my legs. *Mental note: don't open that can of San Pellegrino for at least an hour.* Sweat dripped down my back as I handed my pass over to the lady at the desk and tried a smile.

"Am I in the right place?"

"You are. Business class? Just go straight to the front of the line."

The absolute best part of my day so far was the glare I got from Mr. Ass Clown when he realised I had a bigger seat than he did. On the plane, I couldn't resist watching as he squeezed along the aisle and took a seat right at the back, next to the toilet. *Thanks, Londeka.*

Now I had to fit my bags into the overhead locker. I was just contemplating how squashed my cheese and pickle sandwiches would get when a man stepped up close behind me.

"Here, let me help you."

"Honestly, there's no need. I'm fine here."

"I've got an ulterior motive. I can't get to my seat until you move."

Whoops.

"Oh, I'm so sorry."

His accent was a strange mix of American and British, and his eyes twinkled as he smiled. The rest of him was a mass of contradictions—his chiselled jaw, straight nose, and tousled wavy hair were boy-next-door sexy, his thick-framed glasses gave him a geeky air, but his dark beige button-down shirt and brown cords reminded me of our eighty-year-old next-door neighbour back in Cheshire. And when he reached up to stow my bags, I caught a glimpse of taut abs under a light beige jumper that matched the walls in my old flat perfectly.

Stop staring, Tai.

"Is there a problem?" he asked.

"No, no problem. I'm just not sure whether to eat my sandwiches now or later."

"You don't like the airline food?"

What food? "They give us food?"

"Drinks on the tarmac, canapés when we take off, then hot food somewhere over Europe."

"Oh."

"First time on a plane?"

"Second. The first time, all the food cost a fortune, and the only thing they had left by the time they got to us was a pot of spicy couscous or a long-life packet of cheese and crackers."

He made a face. "Budget airline?"

"How did you guess? Do you fly often?"

"About twice a month."

"Wow. Work or pleasure?"

"Both, but mainly work."

I left the sandwiches where they were—probably flattened in a bag alongside my crisps, chocolate bar, fruit pastilles, and the apple I'd bought in an effort to convince myself that I wasn't totally unhealthy. The soft leather seat sure beat being crammed into the back of Matthew Smart's Volkswagen alongside product mock-ups and his stinky gym bag.

"What do you do?" I asked my new companion.

"I'm an archaeologist. Based in the field, for the most part, but I also lecture at Oxford University and Harvard." He held out a hand. "Miles Bradley."

"Taisiya Beaulieu. Tai for short."

"Interesting. Russian?"

"It is; I'm not. You have no idea how often I've wished I had a nice, normal name that people could actually pronounce. Like yours, for example."

He buckled his seatbelt and stretched out his legs. "My name was okay until I started dating a guy called Bradley Miles."

So much information in one little sentence. Miles wasn't single. And he was gay. Why were nice guys always totally unavailable? Not that I'd ever stand a chance with someone so clearly out of my league, anyway. I was an imposter in business class, I didn't have a job anymore, and I didn't even know where Harvard was.

Still, I should have sympathised or reassured him that dating somebody with almost exactly the same name as him really wasn't that bad. But what came out was an incredulous, "Bradley Miles?"

"A mutual friend introduced us as a joke. And yes, we laughed. But after we laughed, we realised we quite liked each other, and now we've been living with the awkwardness for ten years."

"I suppose at least I'm unlikely to meet a man called Beaulieu Taisiya."

That got a laugh out of him. "Agreed. So, Tai, what takes you to Egypt? A vacation?"

"Not exactly." The whole story of me quitting my job and driving to the airport came spilling out as we trundled along the tarmac. "You must think I'm crazy."

He sucked in a breath. "Let's go with adventurous."

The engines whined, and the pilot accelerated for takeoff. No turning back. I'd made my bed, and now I had to lie in it. Except I no longer had a bed or even a freaking hotel booking for tonight. As the plane lifted into the air, I began to hyperventilate a bit, and Miles's eyes widened in concern.

"Scared of flying?"

"No, I'm nervous because I've just left everything I've ever known."

"And if you did it so easily, I'd hazard a guess that you weren't enjoying life that much."

"No, I wasn't."

"Look upon this as a new opportunity. A chance to become the person you want to be."

"But I don't know anybody in Egypt. I'll be completely on my own."

"And you also won't have people criticising you because you're not doing things their way."

"I've got no home. No job."

"No commitments."

"Are you always this optimistic?"

"Truthfully? No. I'm channelling my boyfriend."

His boyfriend was a lucky guy. Miles seemed nice, far nicer than the maniac I'd dated before I moved to the south of England. Even after we split up, Paul had stuck around like chewing gum on a sock.

"Have you been to Egypt before?" I asked.

"I've lost count of the number of times. There are so many unexplored archaeological sites there, just waiting for somebody to dig beneath the surface. Do you have *any* plans for your trip?"

"Nope. Is Cairo nice?"

"Cairo's busy. If you want to relax, I'd suggest heading south or east."

"South or east? What's there?"

"In the east, you've got Sinai. Sharm el-Sheikh and Dahab. Sharm's touristy—nice beaches and a lot of bars."

"I'm not really a bar-hopping kind of girl."

He looked me up and down. "I didn't think so."

Of course he didn't. Going by appearances, I was a hobo who'd been dragged along by a car for a mile or two, whereas even in fifty shades of beige, Miles still came across as distinguished rather than dull.

"How about Dahab?" I asked, desperate to change the subject away from my appearance. "What's that like?"

"Scuba diving, windsurfing, nice restaurants. Did you know that Dahab is Arabic for gold?"

"I don't speak any Arabic at all."

"Don't worry; almost everyone speaks basic English. Dahab's a laid back little town. I think you'd like it."

"I've never tried any water sports. I'm not sure I'd be very good at them."

"What happened to your adventurous side?"

"It's snoozing."

Miles laughed. "You could just get some R&R on the beach, but if you'd rather take in the country's history, how about heading down the Nile to visit Luxor? There's plenty to see in that area—the Valley of the Kings, the Valley of the Queens, the Temple of Hatshepsut, Karnak Temple. And Luxor's got an excellent mummification museum."

"Doesn't seeing mummies freak you out? I mean,

they're dead."

"I find them more fascinating than anything else. They're part of the Egyptian culture. The ancient civilisations were both primitive and advanced in ways we've barely begun to understand. And speaking of mummies..." He pointed at the in-flight movie options scrolling up the screen on the back of the seat in front. "How do you fancy joining me for an instalment of Tom Cruise?"

"Uh, I actually preferred the Brendan Fraser version."

"Shh! So did I."

The food came out, and I couldn't have asked for a better travel buddy. Miles ate my tomatoes, I ate his olives, and we laughed and drooled our way through the movie. I learned a little more about him—he was British, but his boyfriend was American, so he'd based himself in Virginia for the last decade. And I may have confessed how dysfunctional my family was. When the plane landed in Cairo, I was sad to disembark.

"Sorry to leave you on your own, but I have to dash to a meeting," he said. "I'll call my driver and have him arrange for a friend to take you to a good hotel. Don't worry; it won't be expensive."

"There's no—"

"Yes, there is a need. What kind of man would I be if I left you to fend completely for yourself?"

"Thank you."

Miles tucked a straggly lock of hair behind my ear. "You've done an incredibly brave thing, Tai. Promise you'll remember to focus on the positive."

My eyes began to prickle. It had been so long since anybody helped me like that—not because they wanted something in return, but just to be nice.

"I promise."

He handed over a business card, thick cream cardstock printed with his name—*Dr.* Miles Bradley—and his phone number.

"If you decide on Luxor, I'd recommend staying at the Winter Palace. The old part's expensive, but the Pavilion block behind is cheaper, and it's got a good view of the gardens. And if you pick Dahab, try the Black Diamond hotel. A friend of mine owns it, and if you mention my name at the desk, they'll give you a discount."

A discount sounded good, but I still couldn't decide.

Time on the beach to rest after the year from hell, to take stock of my life and plan for the future, sounded like a dream. I might even get brave enough to go in the water—who knew? But after watching *The Mummy*, nosing around ancient temples appealed too. I'd only ever seen those places on TV, and the idea of walking in the footsteps of those who lived thousands of years ago blew my mind.

"I think I'll sleep on it."

"Good plan. And if in a week or two, you fancy scraping around in the desert, we'll be digging east of Luxor. You could join us for a few days if you get lonely."

"Really? That would be amazing."

"Really. It's not the most luxurious accommodation, but my team's a friendly bunch."

"But if I go to Dahab, I'll be miles away."

"Not as far as you might think. There's a ferry that runs between Sharm el-Sheikh and Hurghada, and it's quite a scenic trip." He checked his watch. "I'm sorry, but I've got to rush."

"Thank you. For the advice, for the offer, for everything."

"You were welcome to the olives. They're nasty little things." He bent to kiss me on the cheek. "Until we meet again, Taisiya Beaulieu."

I carried on waving as he strode towards the exit. Today, the first day of my new life, had certainly been interesting. Now I was in a foreign country, complete with impractical shoes and a warm cheese and pickle sandwich, with yet another decision to make.

Fantastic.

CHAPTER 4 - TAI

A HUGE POSTER on the wall caught my attention, a stunning photo of a sandy valley at sunset framed by smaller pictures of colourful hieroglyphics and camels trekking through the desert and mysterious men with scarves around their faces. *Visit the Valley of the Kings*, the caption read. It all looked so intriguing, I made up my mind on the spot.

Luxor. I'd go to Luxor.

At least, I would as soon as I found my suitcase.

The baggage carousel wheezed like asthmatic bagpipes as I approached, and I momentarily panicked that my bag had ended up in Abu Dhabi or Slovenia or Japan, but after a minute, my little black case trundled towards me, and I heaved it off the belt. Boy, it seemed heavier than I remembered, or perhaps that was because I had my haul from duty-free to carry as well.

Outside the terminal, I was pleased to see Miles had kept his word. A man in a white dress held up a hastily written sign with *Tie Puwlee* written on it, and I assumed that was meant for me.

"Hi. Are you my driver?"

"Mrs. Tai?"

"Miss Tai, yes."

"I'm Ahmed. We go to the hotel?"

"Yes, a hotel. Do you know a good one?"

"We have many good hotels in Cairo. How long you stay?"

"Just one night. I want to go to Luxor tomorrow."

"Luxor?" He beamed at me and pointed at his chest. "I come from Luxor."

Super. Perhaps he could help me? "Uh, I don't suppose you can tell me how to get there?"

"For a tourist, the best way is the night train."

In the dark? "What about the day train?"

"No, they don't allow tourists to take the day train."

"What? Why not?"

Ahmed shrugged. "Rules. But the night train is much nicer. It has beds."

"Really? So I wouldn't need a hotel at all?"

"No hotel. You want to go to the station?"

Why not? If I went to a hotel tonight, I'd only have to pack up and take the exact same train tomorrow. Far better to get the journey over with so I could relax properly.

"You're sure it's safe?"

"Yes, very safe. My brother lives in Luxor. I'll call him to pick you up."

"I don't want to put you to any trouble."

"No trouble. He drives a taxi too, and also runs a chicken shop."

"A chicken shop?"

"You know...the chicken?" Ahmed mimed eating with a knife and fork. "Fresh chicken. You like chicken?"

"Yes, I like chicken."

"I will tell him. The train station?"

"Yes, please."

If Ahmed hadn't come with me, I'd have given up

and stayed in Cairo forever. The sheer number of queues was bewildering, the departure boards confused me, and please say the train had air conditioning because, at that moment, I was melting from the heat.

Luckily, the man at the counter accepted my British money. Ninety pounds for the trip, and considering Garrett-Hart had spent two-hundred pounds on a trip to Birmingham for me last month and I'd had to sit on the floor the whole way, that seemed remarkably cheap.

Ahmed wheeled my suitcase as he led me first to the bank, where I got a fat wedge of Egyptian pounds, and then to a snack stand, which thankfully sold Pringles. There was nothing like salt and vinegar flavoured reconstituted potato products to calm a girl's frazzled nerves.

"Is it too late to go home?" I asked Ahmed when the time came for me to board. Nerves had kicked in. It was one thing getting on a nice, safe British Airways flight and quite another travelling across an unknown country by train.

"You don't want to go home. Once you visit Luxor, you will want to stay forever."

"And you've spoken to your brother?"

"He will be waiting."

I'd never been on a sleeper train before, and being honest, I didn't have high hopes. If Britain couldn't provide comfortable trains that ran to a timetable properly, what chance did Egypt have? But to my surprise, the cabin was clean, although basic, and we left Cairo right on time. We even got food—vegetable stew, fruit, and bread—and it tasted far better than the packet of Twiglets and overpriced mineral water I'd have bought in England.

Darkness soon fell, and after I'd eaten, I stretched out on the tiny bunk and tried to get some sleep. Tried being the operative word.

What the hell had I done?

The first part of the trip had been kind of exciting, but now reality hit. I hadn't even told my mother what I was doing, and if she couldn't get hold of me, she'd report me as missing to the police. Did I mention Mum was a total drama queen? I figured I should probably call her before she overdosed on Valium. Plus I needed to give my landlord notice, although after he took six weeks to fix my broken toilet, I also wanted to let him stew for as long as possible. He'd already informed me he'd be keeping my entire security deposit due to a tiny Nutella stain on the living room carpet. What sort of idiot put cream shag pile in a rental property, anyway?

I so nearly turned my phone on, but the thought of seeing the inevitable angry messages from Matthew stopped me. When I took a sick day three months ago, he'd insisted I send him documentary evidence to prove I was genuinely ill, and I'd had to snap a picture of my cystitis medication and email it to him so he'd stop calling me. Today's little stunt had undoubtedly given him apoplexy, although I harboured a secret hope he'd stroke out because of that.

No, I'd call later. Today was Tuesday, and Mum had a yoga class in the evening, followed by a Rotary Club meeting tomorrow. Realistically, she wouldn't notice I'd vanished until Thursday, which bought me some time.

I thought I'd never sleep, but as the train sped south through the Nile valley, the gentle rocking motion helped me to nod off. Today might have been crazy, but tomorrow was a new day, and I had to make the most of it.

Just after six o'clock in the morning, I awoke to a glorious sunrise over Luxor. Beautiful reds and oranges faded into green. I'd expected desert everywhere, but instead, I saw fields and palm trees.

Soon afterwards, the train slowed, and I brushed my teeth at the tiny basin in my cabin then chugged down half a bottle of mineral water. Although the train was air-conditioned, one glance outside told me I was in for some serious heat, and I was still wearing yesterday's work clothes, so I felt pretty yucky. As soon as I got to a hotel, I'd take a shower, but first, I had to find Ahmed's brother Mohammed.

"Tax! Tax! Tax!"

The shouts came from all sides.

"Where you want to go?" a man asked.

"You need hotel? Cheap room, very clean. Just five minutes down the street," said another.

"Sorry, I'm looking for someone."

"Who? Who you look for?"

"Uh, Mohammed."

"I'm Mohammed."

"Really?" He seemed kind of old to be Ahmed's brother. Like, around sixty.

"Yes, Mohammed. You want to visit perfume shop?"

"No, thank you."

"They give you good price."

Touts swarmed around me like wasps on a Mars

bar. Where the hell was the right Mohammed? I backed away, and I was about to hit the wall when a young guy elbowed his way through the crowd and waved a sign with *Thai* written on it in my face. Close enough.

"Are you Mohammed?"

"Miss Tai?"

Oh, thank goodness. "Yes."

"Ahmed told me to look after you well. You need somewhere to stay?"

"Yes, I do. I only booked this trip at the last minute. Someone suggested the Pavilion at the Winter Palace?"

"Very nice hotel. How long you stay?"

"I'm not sure yet. Maybe a week? Or longer if I really like it here."

"Then you will stay for a year. You should rent an apartment."

Mohammed held his hands out for my bags, and I relinquished them gratefully before following him out of the station. Yes, I'd been right about the heat. Barely seven o'clock, and sweat was already running down my back.

"I'm not sure I need a whole apartment. I mean, that's got to be expensive."

"No, is cheaper. My friend has a nice place he rents out to tourists."

"Really?"

"A double bedroom, bathroom, living room, kitchen. And it has a garden with sunbeds."

I didn't need a double bedroom but having a kitchen did sound attractive. That way, I could save money by cooking some meals myself instead of going to restaurants all the time. But a hotel would come with a housekeeper and a laundry service and hopefully a concierge who could help me out when I needed to find my way around.

Decisions, decisions...

Outside, Mohammed stopped next to a rusty blue and white car that had to be three decades old. Would that make it as far as wherever I needed to go?

"You get in."

He held the door open, and I almost had a heart attack when I looked in the back seat.

"Uh, Mohammed? There's a chicken in here."

A live freaking chicken. It stared out from a tiny bamboo cage and squawked a bit.

Mohammed beamed at me. "Yes. It's a gift. Ahmed said you like chicken."

Yes, but only when it came shrink-wrapped from Tesco.

"But what am I supposed to do with it?"

"Make sandwich. Or soup. Or put it on pizza."

Oh, flip. I felt sick. Logically, I knew chicken came from actual chickens, but I'd never been quite so close to one before. And now it stared at me as if it knew what we were talking about. A little scared, a little pissed off.

"The chef at the Winter Palace makes excellent pizza," Mohammed continued. "I supply chickens to the whole hotel."

The chicken looked at me beseechingly, and I considered turning vegetarian. The thing had a face, for crying out loud.

"What if I don't want to eat it?"

"You don't want my chicken? Is good chicken."

Now Mohammed looked crestfallen. He'd driven all the way to the station to pick me up at stupid o'clock in the morning, and now I'd insulted him by refusing his chicken. I managed a weak smile.

"Of course I want the chicken. It looks, uh, lovely."

Good grief. What the heck was I supposed to do? As the engine coughed and rattled into life, the chicken pecked at the bars in a vain bid for freedom. Poor thing. Was it a girl? The boys had big red combs on their heads, didn't they? This scrawny thing didn't have much of one.

Okay, the sensible solution would be to accept the chicken, find the concierge at the hotel, and beg him to take it away. Then I could avoid eating any meat for the whole of my time in Egypt and stop worrying. Simple, right? That was a good plan.

The chicken clucked at me, reminding me of grandma's old friend Betsy, who'd died last year when she suffered a heart attack playing bingo, God rest her soul. She was a soap opera fan, and she'd made that exact same sound whenever *Coronation Street* came on the telly. For a moment, I considered the possibility of reincarnation. A man outside Tesco had shoved a pamphlet about precisely that in my hand last week, although I'd wedged it under the leg of my wobbly desk at work rather than reading it. Could I really consign Betsy to the stockpot?

She clucked again. Oh dear.

What other choices did I have? Mohammed said the apartment came with a garden, didn't he? Perhaps I could rent the place and put her outside for a day or two while I considered my options. She might even lay eggs, although in this heat, they'd end up hard-boiled before they hit the ground. But I'd still be stuck with a freaking chicken. What did they even eat?

"Where do you want to go, Miss Tai?" Mohammed asked. "Do you want to go to the hotel, or shall I show you the apartment?"

Deep breaths, Tai. Why didn't I pick Portugal?

CHAPTER 5 - TAI

BETSY CLUCKED AT me, and I couldn't send her to the stockpot. I just couldn't. Besides, since I'd moved out of home, I'd learned to appreciate having my own space. As a child, I'd shared a room with Peony, and she'd always griped if I so much as breathed on her belongings. That didn't stop her from borrowing my stuff without asking, of course, but my parents just shrugged and lectured me on the importance of being tolerant. Ten-year-old me had dreamed of becoming a lawyer for the sole reason of suing Peony for the return of my limited edition My Little Pony glitter castle, which had mysteriously disappeared. A whole freaking castle. To this day, I didn't know what she'd done with it.

Aaaaaand breathe.

"Could we look at the apartment, please?"

Mohammed gave me a toothy grin in the rear-view mirror. "I'll take you there right away, Miss Tai."

The streets were a maze, and I wasn't sure I'd ever find my way out of town again. I'd be stuck there forever, stranded with just a chicken for company. Most of the houses were made of grey bricks—squat, ugly little boxes—and the apartment buildings all looked...unfinished. Concrete pillars at the top sprouted steel rods like mutant spaghetti, and the top floors didn't have walls, yet the bottom floors were occupied, complete with satellite dishes and washing hung out on the balconies. We bumped over potholes that could have housed a small family with room to spare and finally pulled up outside a wonky wall with a wooden gate set into it.

"We're here," Mohammed announced.

This? This was the apartment? I almost told him to turn right around and take me back to the Winter Palace, but Betsy ruffled her feathers, and I shut my mouth. How bad could it be? At least it didn't have Peony in residence.

A man Mohammed's age scurried out of the building next door and unlocked the gate, throwing it open before he turned around to beam at us. At least everyone in Egypt had been friendly so far. Smile in London and everyone backed slowly away because they thought you were crazy.

"Welcome back," the guy said, holding out a weathered hand for me to shake. "I'm Sayid."

"Tai."

"Come in, come in. I show you the rooms. Very nice apartment."

I didn't want to leave Betsy to roast in the car, although I'm sure she'd have been delicious, so I lifted her little cage out and set it on the ground just inside the gate. She scratched around through the bars, looking for food. All I had left was half a tub of Pringles, and I was pretty sure chickens weren't supposed to eat those.

"Here we have the sunbeds..." Sayid waved one arm to the left, gesturing at a pair of sunloungers on a postage-stamp-sized lawn. Three spiky palms provided little in the way of shade. More plants sprouted from a collection of terracotta pots, and a table and chairs sat under a pergola beyond. "There are towels in the closet, and the Wi-Fi works outside."

I followed him through a set of double doors that opened onto the terrace and found myself in a lounge. Oh. Oh! It was actually quite pleasant. Far nicer than I thought it would be from the outside. A squashy two-seater sofa, a beanbag, and a sort of hammock thing hanging from the ceiling all surrounded a low table, and there was even a flat-screen TV on the wall and colourful rugs on the floor. And an air conditioner, thank goodness. The bedroom was clean but basic with a big bed and a good-sized wardrobe, and Sayid proudly pointed out that the bathroom had hot water. The kitchen came with a hotplate, a microwave, a toaster and, apparently, ants.

"You must put any open food in the fridge," Sayid explained. "Or they eat it."

Okay, ants. At least they weren't cockroaches. Or mice. Grandma once had mice in her flat, and they ate everything from an Easter egg to my phone charger.

The place was twice the size of the flat I'd left behind, and when I nervously asked Sayid about the rent, only a tiny fraction of the price.

"And I live right next door," he said. "So if you have any problems, just call and I fix them. My wife will clean once a week, and my cousin waters the plants."

Wow, it even came with staff? I did some rapid calculations. If I rented the apartment for a month and ate cheaply, I'd spend less than five percent of my savings plus get a free suntan. And a chicken.

"Is this a safe area? I mean, for a girl on her own?"

Sayid pointed at another door off the terrace. "There's an Australian girl staying too. She's been here for over a month already and all is good."

So I wouldn't be completely alone either. Phew.

"I'll take it."

I only hoped the Australian girl liked Betsy.

After I'd handed over rent money to Sayid and taken Mohammed's business card in case I needed a taxi later on, I slumped onto the bed. Hard to believe it was only a day since I'd left England, but now I was on the other side of the world, and I felt drained. Still, I was a free woman. What did I have to do today but take a shower, find some food for Betsy and me, and lie in the sun?

I found out the answer to that when I tried to open my suitcase. The lock on the little brass padlock had jammed tight, and no matter which way I wiggled the key, the sodding thing wouldn't open.

How else could I get at my things? The journey had taken its toll on my hair, and I desperately needed my bottle of shampoo. I rummaged through the drawer in the kitchen for scissors, but all I found were table knives and a blunt bread knife. I contemplated trying to saw through the fabric, but firstly, I'd probably end up cutting off a finger, and secondly, I wouldn't have a suitcase anymore. No, I needed to get the padlock off, but how?

There was nothing for it—I'd have to go next door and ask Sayid for help. He did say to call any time, right?

I knocked on his gate. Waited. Knocked again. Just

as I was about to give up, the latch rattled, the gate opened an inch, and a woman my age peeked through the gap.

"Is Sayid there, please?"

She didn't answer, just smiled and beckoned me inside. Two small children played in the gravelly dirt beside the house, one with a hula hoop and the other with a football. Behind them—hallelujah—half a dozen chickens scratched around.

"Can you tell me what chickens eat?"

No answer, but Sayid popped out of the house two seconds later.

"My wife is Nabila. She doesn't speak English. You want to know about chickens?"

"Yes. Ahmed gave me the chicken as a gift."

"You want to eat it?"

"No! I need to feed it." How did I end up in these messes? "Is there a shop nearby?"

"Five Egyptian pounds, and I get you the food."

Well, that was almost too easy. I was beginning to like Egypt.

"And I'm having a small problem getting into my suitcase. I don't suppose you've got a hacksaw?"

"A hacksaw?"

"A small saw for cutting metal?"

"You need to cut the metal?"

"The padlock on my suitcase. I need to get it off."

"Ah!" Sayid nodded enthusiastically. "I know a man. Ten minutes."

He disappeared inside. What should I do? Just wait? Or go back to the apartment? I figured Sayid knew where I was, so I headed next door to release Betsy from her tiny prison. If Sayid's chickens were loose, that suggested they weren't too good at flying, so at least I could let her stretch her legs.

She'd only strutted halfway around the garden when Sayid came back with his friend in tow, an elderly man carrying the biggest pair of bolt cutters I'd ever seen. He could have broken into Fort Knox with those. Thirty seconds later, the padlock lay in little pieces, and he held out his hand.

"Baksheesh."

What did that mean? Payment? Of course, he wanted payment.

"How much?"

"Fifty pounds."

That seemed kind of steep at first, but then I converted it into English money in my head, and it was only two or three pounds sterling. And when my colleague Janice locked herself out of her house last year, the locksmith had charged her almost two hundred quid.

"Here you go."

I handed over the cash and got a huge smile in return, and better still, Sayid appeared with two plastic dishes and a bag of birdseed for Betsy. One more item checked off my list.

And another huge item added.

Once Sayid and his friend had left, I unzipped my suitcase and gasped in horror because unless I'd suddenly grown facial hair and a pair of testicles, this wasn't my freaking bag. Oh, it was identical from the outside, but—I held up a pair of Calvin Klein boxer briefs—these clothes definitely weren't mine. Nor was the fancy silver razor, the Armani cologne, the board shorts, or the expensive-looking camera.

Oh, rats. I cursed under my breath, and Betsy waddled up to the door, head tilted to one side.

"It's okay, girl. Just another cock-up on my part, that's all."

I didn't know what was worse—the fact that I'd accidentally stolen a man's luggage or that he probably had mine and was at that moment thumbing through one of my romance novels while wondering what idiot needed three squeezy stress balls and a pair of Garfield pyjamas. Oh, heck. What if he found the mini dartboard with Matthew Smart's stupid grinning face stuck to it? He'd think I was a lunatic, and with good reason.

I tore off half a fingernail as I frantically searched through the pockets for a luggage tag or a business card, something—anything—that would identify the suitcase's owner, but there was zilch. Zip. Now what? The airport. I should call the airport. They must have a lost property office, mustn't they?

But to do that, I'd have to turn on my laptop to find the phone number, something I'd been avoiding because I knew Matthew Smart would have sent me an email, and I really didn't want to read it.

Dammit, I *needed* one of my squeezy stress balls.

Sayid had helpfully sellotaped the Wi-Fi password to the wall by the door, and I groaned out loud once I'd tapped it into my laptop. Forty-seven emails since yesterday morning, and like a moth to a flame, I couldn't stop myself from opening my inbox. Spam, spam, spam, and there it was...

Sender: Matthew Smart
  Subject: Where the hell are you?

But wait—what was the message below it?

Sender: Ren Fontana
Subject: Luggage

No way... Hold on—this case may not have had a luggage tag, but mine did. Yes, it had fallen off months ago, but I'd stuffed it into the outside pocket. I quickly opened the email.

Hey Tai,
Seems I've made a mistake and picked up your suitcase, and I'm hoping you have mine? Drop me a message, and we can get this sorted out.
Ren

Oh, thank goodness. I did a happy dance, then realised I still had no clue where my bag actually was—in Cairo, most likely—and Matthew Smart's email continued to taunt me.

Hi Ren,
Yes, I've got your bag, and I'm so, so sorry. I'm in Luxor at the moment. Whereabouts are you?
Tai

I jumped into the shower before I got tempted to open my ex-boss's tirade, and thankfully Sayid had left a hotel-sized bottle of shower gel in there so I could wash. Deodorant was a problem, but then I spotted Ren's can of Axe lying in his open suitcase. He wouldn't mind, would he? Heck, he probably wouldn't even notice. It was just a couple of squirts.

A couple of squirts that left me smelling like a bachelor on the prowl.

Rowr.

Did I have an email yet? Please say I did.

Luxor? Nice. I always wanted to visit Tutankhamun. I'm kitesurfing in Dahab. Want to send the bags by courier? Or if you can wait a few days, I could fly down with your stuff.

Ren

Dahab? Oh, for goodness' sake. I should have gone there instead, shouldn't I? Then I wouldn't be stuck in this apartment with only a chicken, a cocktail dress, and a stranger's fancy camera for company. How would I go about arranging a courier? Did this street even have a name? Worse, Ren's suitcase was unlocked now, so what if somebody stole his belongings en route?

Could I manage with what I had for a few days? I had money, so I wouldn't starve, and surely I'd be able to buy some toiletries and a T-shirt or two somewhere? Yes, I'd cope.

I'd also feel terribly guilty making Ren fly hundreds of miles to deliver my suitcase when he'd planned to spend the week kitesurfing, whatever that was. But he had offered...

Dammit, why did decisions have to be so difficult?

CHAPTER 6 - TAI

THE THOUGHT OF trying to arrange a courier filled me with dread. Visions of Ren's suitcase travelling north on a truck and ending up in Giza or Cairo or even Alexandria danced through my mind, and where would *my* luggage end up? Probably in Aswan. I really didn't want to travel all the way to Dahab, not when I'd only just arrived in Luxor and rented an apartment. And Ren *had* offered to come. He wouldn't have done that if he didn't mean it, would he?

Before I chickened out—sorry, Betsy—I quickly typed an email.

Ren,
    That's very kind of you to offer. If you're sure you don't mind flying to Luxor, I'd be happy to wait a few days for my things.
    Tai

That decision meant I needed to go out and buy some basic toiletries and a map of the area at the very least. And chocolate, because after the day I'd had, I deserved that much.

Outside in the garden, Betsy had eaten half of her birdseed and started scratching around in the dirt. I followed her as she walked around the corner of the apartment and found the garden continued. Someone had strung a hammock up between two leafy trees. Were those mangoes peeping out from among the foliage? To my left was another bijou terrace with double doors in the corner. A third apartment? When I peered through the glass, I saw a bedroom smaller than my lounge, furnished in pink rather than blue, empty and still. Yes, it was another apartment, but unoccupied.

I carried on and walked around the whole building, only to jump out of my skin when my new neighbour flung open her front door. Well, not so much jump as fall. I stumbled backwards, arms windmilling, and landed not-so-gracefully in a heap on a sunlounger.

"Sorry, didn't mean to scare you."

The girl was my age, blonde and pretty with sparkling green eyes and a figure I could only dream of. She carried a yoga mat in one hand and a chocolate bar in the other, but she dropped both to help me back to my feet.

"It's fine. Totally my fault for not seeing you sooner."

And also for being so nervy. Uprooting myself from my entire life had left me feeling strangely unsettled.

"Are you staying next door?" she asked.

"Yes, for a month, hopefully."

"I planned to stay for a week, but I've been here for five now, and I still don't want to leave. There's so much to see."

"You don't need to go home?"

"Where's home? I've been travelling the world for three years now, going wherever I want."

"Wow, really? Where have you been?"

She ticked off on her fingers. "I started in Central America—Costa Rica and Honduras. Then I went to Russia, but it was bloody freezing, so I flew to Cape Verde, then Tunisia, then Algeria, and now here."

"I've only been to Europe."

"Really? I'm thinking of heading to Oman next."

"What about work?"

She pointed at her chest. "Digital nomad. I can work from anywhere. Duh—I haven't even introduced myself. I'm Tegan."

"Tai."

"That's Vietnamese, right?"

"In my case, it's short for Taisiya."

"I think I'll stick with Tai—at least that's easy to remember. You're here on holiday?"

"More or less. I guess so."

"You're not sure?"

"I suppose this was more of a daring escape."

"Escape from what?"

"My job, mainly. But also my family, my ex-boyfriend, and life in general."

Tegan giggled. "You've come to the right place. Sun, sand, and...well, there's no sangria, but we have Sprite. Do you want something to drink? You must be parched if you've been travelling this morning."

"What about your yoga?"

"I can do that later. Wanna split the chocolate with me before it melts?"

"I'd love that."

Tegan, it turned out, only did yoga so she could eat chocolate. The offsetting principle, she called it. Usually, she did the yoga then rewarded herself, but with the sun so strong in Egypt, she ate the chocolate first then left the wrapper out to guilt herself into finishing a dozen sun salutations. That seemed like a pretty sensible arrangement to me. Not that I ever did yoga. Or exercise in general. I'd joined a gym last January, but after I dropped a weight on my foot and fractured my toe, I cancelled the membership and began buying stretchier clothes instead.

We'd just settled down with peppermint tea when Betsy wandered around the corner.

"Uh, I think one of Sayid's chickens has escaped," Tegan said.

"No, that's my chicken."

She stared at me.

"It's a long story."

She kept staring.

"Okay, so it started in Cairo when I accidentally mentioned to Sayid's friend Mohammed's brother Ahmed that I liked chicken..."

I told Tegan about Betsy, and by the end, she'd doubled up with laughter.

"I think I like you. And I like animals too, so Betsy's in no danger from me."

"How *is* the food around here?"

"Better than you'd think. Sometimes I get a funny tummy, but that's actually quite good because it stops me from putting on weight." She wrinkled her nose. "Too much information?"

Yes, definitely. "A little."

"Sorry. Anyhow, you can find almost anything to eat. Indian, Chinese, Italian, Lebanese. All the big hotels have restaurants, and you can just go in to dine. And if you're on a budget, there's good local food too, or you can cook yourself. Just don't drink the tap water."

"No tap water. Got it."

"Bottled water costs pennies, anyhow."

"Where can I buy it?"

"There's a supermarket at the end of the street. Want me to show you?"

"Yes, please. There was a small technical hitch with my luggage, so I also need toiletries and maybe some clothes. And a map."

"Okay, so toiletries are easy. Everywhere sells those. There's not much choice in Western clothing, but a few places sell secondhand stuff. And I've got a spare tourist map."

Life was much nicer with a friend to help, and I hadn't had a proper one of those since my childhood bestie, Valerie, moved to Michigan with her family when we were both fifteen. While I'd drifted through the remaining years of secondary school with only casual acquaintances, she'd quickly fitted in, joined a sorority at college, and married a football jock last year. She didn't invite me to the wedding, and our contact had dwindled to the occasional email. Probably I should let her know I wasn't dead, but...

"Lunch. Let's go for lunch," Tegan said. "Then we can do your shopping."

Could she be the friend I'd been looking for?

"Sounds good to me. Where do you want to go?"

Tegan checked her watch. "The café up the road should still be serving falafel. They make it fresh every morning."

"Falafel for breakfast?"

"Yup. That's how it works around here."

By the end of the afternoon, I had a full belly, shampoo, conditioner, deodorant, soap, a toothbrush, and toothpaste. Tegan had offered to cook, and we'd traipsed around the souk, buying vegetables from one stall, bread from another, and chocolate cake from a shop that wasn't much more than a handcart. Clothes, however, remained a problem. I'd picked up an *I Love Luxor* T-shirt, another with a picture of Tutankhamun on it, a baggy pair of harem pants, and flip-flops.

Oh, and did I mention the harem pants were gold? I felt like MC Hammer.

"Perhaps we can have another look tomorrow?" Tegan suggested. "It's a shame we're not the same size, or I could lend you something."

"Yes, tomorrow. I don't think I can walk any further today."

A passing carriage driver overheard me. "Hey, you want a ride? Only thirty pounds."

This was so much easier than the UK. "We'd love a ride."

I was halfway into the carriage before Tegan grabbed my arm. "Tai, what have I been telling you all day?"

Ah, yes. I was meant to haggle. Arguing over the price felt really weird—I mean, it wasn't as if I'd do that in Tesco.

"Twenty-five pounds?"

"Fifteen," Tegan said, still holding me back.

"She said twenty-five," the driver said.

"Yes, because she's new here. But we both know

that's too much, don't we?"

"Okay, twenty pounds."

Tegan nodded, and now she smiled. "Twenty."

Boy, there was still so much to learn in Luxor.

Our little apartment block came with a barbecue, and thankfully Tegan knew how to light it. Before long, we had kebabs cooking, plus baked potatoes wrapped in tinfoil buried in the embers at the side.

"You need to sit by the Nile one night and watch the sunset," she said. "It's beautiful. Or take an evening trip on a felucca."

"What's a felucca?"

"A little sailboat."

"This is a whole different world to the one I just left."

Evenings on the outskirts of London consisted of wondering whether to eat an out-of-date lasagne or walk to the supermarket; watching mind-numbing reality TV marathons; and having stare-offs with the neighbour's cat, who'd taken to sitting on my tiny balcony at odd hours ever since I gave him a piece of hamburger last year. In Luxor, I hadn't even turned the television on yet.

But I did have to look at my emails again. After dinner, I retreated to the comfort of my air-conditioned bedroom and turned on my laptop. Sure enough, Ren had replied.

Tai,

I'll be there Monday or Tuesday. Nice dartboard, by the way. Your ex?

Ren

I groaned out loud. He'd been through my stuff? That asshole had been through my stuff? Yes, technically I'd looked in his bag too, but I didn't feel the need to comment on his choice of aftershave. Still, he was flying to Luxor with my suitcase, so I couldn't afford to be rude to him.

Ren,

Thank you. I'm staying at...

Hold on, where even was this?

I tiptoed barefoot to Tegan's door and knocked, unfortunately catching sight of myself in the glass while I waited. Even in the dark, the stupid gold trousers hurt my eyes.

"What's up?" Tegan asked.

"The guy's supposed to be bringing my stuff on Monday, but how do I explain where I am? Does this apartment have an actual address?"

"Oh, just get him to tell the cab driver we're next to Sayid with the pool table."

"The pool table?"

"It's out the back of his house. His mates come over to play most nights. How's your game?"

"I've never played pool in my life."

"Well, there'll be no shortage of people offering to teach you."

Back in my apartment, I finished my message.

Ren,

Thank you. I'm staying in an apartment next door to "Sayid with the pool table." Apparently, the taxi driver will know where that is.

Tai

As I hit send, I scanned down the rest of the emails I'd been trying not to read. Now the HR department at Garrett-Hart was trying to reach me too. Should I reply? At some point, I probably should, but I'd been so utterly miserable working at that place, I figured they deserved to stew for a while. They already had my resignation letter. Er, text message.

Before I could resort to apologising or allowing myself to be walked all over yet again, I turned the laptop off.

Screw Garrett-Hart. I was going to sleep.

"I think those look better," Tegan said. "Don't you think they look better?"

"Uh..."

Tiredness had caught up with me on Thursday morning, and I hadn't woken up until nearly noon. Since nobody seemed to do anything in a hurry around here, I'd eaten a leisurely lunch with Tegan before we tried shopping again. Tried being the operative word. If Ali Baba had lived in the sixties, he'd have definitely picked out these trousers. Whether they were better or worse than the gold pants was debatable.

But my desperation for clean clothes wasn't. Apparently, Sayid's wife's cousin ran a laundry service, but he'd gone to Faiyum for a wedding and wouldn't be back for two days.

"The orange and yellow flowers match the sunset," Tegan said, clutching at straws.

At least I'd be able to fade into the background again.

"I'll take them."

They'd go nicely with my lime-green hoodie and my new *I visited King Tut and all I got was this lousy shirt* T-shirt. I'd started a countdown to Monday in my head. Three-and-a-half days to go until I got my yoga pants and underwear back.

"So, what are we doing tonight?" Tegan asked as we walked home to our apartments.

"Hiding."

"No way. How about we go to the Fellah's Tent?"

"What's that?"

"The hotel on Kings Island has a big marquee out the back, and every week, they hold a party in it. A buffet, dancers, a snake charmer, magicians. And you can meet Cleo the camel."

"Snakes? I'm not so keen on snakes."

"It's really well behaved. He keeps it in a basket."

"Or camels."

"Have you ever actually seen a camel?"

"On TV, and that's quite close enough."

"They also have about ten different kinds of dessert."

Hmm...

"What are the other options?"

"We could go to a restaurant. Or buy food from the supermarket and cook it ourselves then go next door to play pool. Sayid usually has at least a dozen people over, and there's always tea and shisha."

"I've never smoked shisha. Knowing me, I'd end up having a coughing fit."

"Then just drink the tea. If you're planning on

sticking around for a few weeks, it's a great way to meet people."

She did make a good point, but ugh, networking. At work, I'd always found it a necessary evil.

The Fellah's Tent sounded fun, apart from the snakes and possibly the camel, and if there was a buffet, I'd be sure to find something I liked to eat. Going to Sayid's would be more convenient, but with a smaller gathering, I might actually have to talk to people.

Gah. The thought of being social left me cold despite the heat.

CHAPTER 7 - TAI

I'D MOVED TO Egypt for a change, hadn't I? To live dangerously? Then I shouldn't keep picking the safe option, or I'd spend the rest of my life as boring old Tai Beaulieu.

"Let's go to the Fellah's Tent."

Tegan beamed at me. "You won't regret it, I swear."

"Just promise you won't let any snakes near me."

"The snake charmer invites people up onto the stage instead of walking around the audience."

"What if nobody volunteers?"

"People always volunteer. Tourists mainly. Hey, we might meet some hot guys."

I shuddered involuntarily. "I don't want to meet a guy."

"Don't freak out. I'm not suggesting you choose a wedding dress. I mean a hookup. Tourists are the best because..." She clicked her fingers. "Poof. A week later, they're gone. On a plane back to England or Germany or France." Her voice turned wistful. "Nobody talks dirty like a Frenchman."

Tegan was the kind of girl I'd once aspired to be. Confident and daring, she knew what she wanted and she went out and got it, whether that was a man for the night or a temporary home in a new country. As a teenager, I'd dreamed of travelling the world with

Prince Charming at my side, but my ex, Paul, had pretty much put me off relationships for life. Although you couldn't fault his commitment. Even a restraining order hadn't stopped him from trying to kill me.

Yes, I'd tried dating again afterwards, although not exactly by choice. Grandma had insisted. I could still hear her voice now, telling me I shouldn't waste my life because of one mistake. The first man she set me up with—and I use the term "man" loosely—had been the thirty-year-old son of one of her bingo buddies. He'd spent two hours in a pizza restaurant telling me how much better his mum cooked, and when it came to splitting the bill at the end, he said that as I'd eaten two more dough balls and one more polenta chip than him, I should pay an extra one pound thirty-seven. Yes, he counted the freaking dough balls then got his calculator out and worked out how much each one cost. For a brief moment, I'd actually hankered back to Paul, and he'd been insane.

Date number two, who grandma had met in the doctor's waiting room, patiently explained in excruciating detail over dinner how an alien race was trying to take over the country by installing its citizens as members of parliament. Although that would have gone some way to explaining the crackpot laws and regulations they came up with on a regular basis, I wasn't quite convinced by his tale of oversized cockroaches stuffed into human skin. When the leftovers arrived wrapped in tinfoil, I'd almost offered it to the weirdo to make a hat.

So you see, I was better off single, even if that meant getting lost in Luxor and having to remove spiders from my bedroom by myself.

"I'm not looking for a hookup," I told Tegan. "Or in fact any sort of man at all."

"You're into women?"

"No! Not that there's anything wrong with that, but I just want to enjoy my travels for a while."

"Okay, so no snakes and no men." She scrunched her lips to one side. "How about wine?"

"Can we get wine in Egypt? I thought it was a dry country."

"The big hotels all serve alcohol. Sometimes it's good, and sometimes it tastes like paint stripper."

"Perhaps we should stick to soft drinks, then."

"What happened to your sense of adventure?"

"It's a finite supply, and I already used up this week's quota."

The Fellah's Tent was a huge marquee set amid the lush tropical gardens of a five-star hotel. According to Google, a fellah was an Egyptian peasant, but there were none of those in sight, just gaggles of tourists and a cluster of smiling waiters. A small stage at one end of the tent hosted the acts, and thankfully, the snake had behaved itself and was now safely back in its basket. The dinner buffet spanned six tables, an endless array of barbecue dishes and, oddly, pizza. No, I didn't eat the chicken.

"Did you know that before this place was called Kings Island, it was called Crocodile Island?"

The speaker was Dale, a tour guide for Hot Sun Holidays, and I might have been more interested in what he had to say if he hadn't directed every single comment at my chest. Not that I was showing any actual cleavage, but when Tegan had popped out to get us lunch while I fed Betsy and took a shower, she'd come back with two Big Macs—because the McDonald's empire knew no bounds—and a T-shirt a couple of sizes too small advertising Camel Towing Services with the slogan *When it's wedged in tight, we'll pull it out.*

"I thought you could wear it around the apartment," she said. "It's your size, and it was cheap."

But because everything else I owned was dirty, and the laundry guy still wasn't back, I'd been forced to wear it to the party. Dale should've learned to make eye contact rather than sniggering. That would've been the polite thing to do.

Thankfully, Tegan saved me the trouble of shaking my head in response to his question.

"Why?" she asked. "Was there a crocodile?"

"Yeah, but it died."

"So did the kings."

"Er, yeah, I suppose. Can I get you ladies another drink?"

I shook my head because what I really wanted was for Dale to stop talking. He'd sat down at our table uninvited half an hour ago and proceeded to regale us with endless anecdotes that he punctuated with laughter, except none of them were funny. While the food and entertainment had been good tonight, the company had sadly been lacking, but since Tegan had been drinking the paint stripper, she giggled along anyway.

"I'd love another drink. Have they got any more of that red?"

"I'll have a word with the suma...the somal...the

wine waiter."

Who wasn't actually a sommelier, he was just an Egyptian in a galabeya who knew the difference between red and white. When Dale walked off, I leaned in closer to Tegan.

"Doesn't he understand the concept of personal space?"

"Dale? Nope. He's sleazy with everyone. But he also buys drinks, which is great when you're on a budget."

"So this is like a trade? Bad conversation in exchange for wine?"

"Exactly. And if you want to visit the Valley of the Kings or the Temple of Hatshepsut, smile sweetly through dessert, and he'll let you tag onto the back of one of his tour groups."

"I think I'd rather pay for a ticket. And speaking of dessert, I fancy some of that chocolate cake. Do you want anything?"

"The strawberry mousse. Think that counts as one of my five-a-day?"

"Definitely."

"Look, the whirling dervish is about to start."

I thought the whirling dervish sounded like a cartoon character, but it turned out to be a man wearing a colourful skirt who spun around and around as musicians tapped out a beat on their drums, and I had to applaud him. Why? Because I was the girl who'd broken her ankle as a nine-year-old trying to turn a pirouette in Peony's pink satin ballet shoes. Her wails of anguish that I'd scuffed one of the toes had eclipsed my howls of pain.

I tried to push memories of home out of my head as I queued for dessert. So far, I'd successfully avoided my emails after my conversation with Ren, and while I knew I'd have to read them eventually, today was not that day.

"Here, ma'am." A waiter handed me a plate.

"Could I have two plates?"

He passed me another. "You are very hungry."

"Oh, they're not both for me."

"Is okay, we don't mind you eating lots of food. Is good food."

"No, really…"

"Please." He just smiled and waved a hand at the dessert table. "Help yourself."

Okay, so maybe I picked out some banoffee pie as well as the chocolate cake, but the other plateful was definitely for Tegan. Except when I went to walk back to the table, Dale was already seated, and Tegan made a frantic "keep away" motion with her hand behind her back. What was the problem? Honestly, I didn't want to find out if it meant listening to Mr. Skeevy again, so I snagged a passing waiter.

"Please could you take these plates to that table over there?"

"It would be my pleasure."

With Tegan's dessert on its way, I decided to do the adult thing and hide in the bathroom, a tactic that had worked well for me at Garrett-Hart when Matthew Smart went on his I-need-somebody-to-blame rampages. Hopefully, Dale would be gone when I finished, and we could escape back to Sayid's.

Cartoonish hieroglyphics decorated the walls in the ladies' room, everything from a pharaoh washing his hands above the sink to a peasant girl dancing with a goat. Next to the toilet paper, a guy in an ornate headdress played a trumpet. Did they even have trumpets in those days? The distinctive smell of an incense stick drifted in my direction as I cleaned up, then I crept back along the hallway.

And I so, so nearly made it outside.

The door was within touching distance when I caught a glimpse of Dale's red T-shirt heading in my direction, and yes, I panicked. Old Tai might have brazened it out, but when it came to the choice between fight and flight, post-Paul Tai ran every time. In today's case, into a dusty hallway marked with an Arabic sign I couldn't read. What looked like old storage rooms opened off either side, and I ducked into the first and hid behind a stack of chairs. Dammit, we should have gone to play pool at Sayid's, then I could have been home in bed by now.

How long should I wait? I checked my watch and saw it was half past nine. If Dale was going to use the loo, he couldn't take more than five minutes, surely? Dust tickled my nostrils, and I was about to sneeze when I heard footsteps in the corridor. Uh oh. I pinched my nose and cursed inwardly as the steps stopped right outside. Was it Dale? Had he found me? How the heck was I supposed to explain why I was in there? Hmm... Perhaps I could play the "I got lost" card if I acted ditzy enough?

But it wasn't Dale. Low voices began talking, two of them, both male. One British and one American by the sound of it.

"What did you think of dinner?" the Brit asked.

"Overcooked. What was that meat?"

"Goat, I think."

Goat? Yeuch. I thought it was beef. Dinner

threatened to repeat, but I swallowed it back down, relieved at the same time that Dale hadn't come back to bug me and it was just two fellow tourists having a chat instead. Even so, I didn't want to have an awkward conversation about why I was hiding in a storeroom. Best to stay put.

"It was too damn spicy."

"Next time, try the shawarma stall by the entrance to the thouk. He always gets the thpices just right."

Hmm, I'd have to remember that. Shawarma was lamb, that much I knew from Tegan.

"I fly back to the US tomorrow. The buyers want to talk in person."

"For the Ramesses cartouche?" the Brit asked. He spoke with a London accent, slightly posh, and every so often, he lisped an *S* the same way I used to when I wore a brace on my top teeth.

"And Ay's mask. Now all you have to do is deliver them."

"It's in hand."

"How long will it take?"

"My contact's pleased with progreth. He thinks a fortnight, maybe a month."

"Good. Keep this moving along, because I want everything wrapped up before summer. Nobody wants to be stuck here when the temperature hits a hundred."

"The dry heat here isn't so bad."

"It is when you're from Minnesota. Have you checked over the arrangements for shipping?"

"Everything's looking good. Thay, how's the hotel this time? Did they fix the air conditioning?"

"Better. And they got a new coffee machine, so at least they're not serving instant at breakfast anymore."

The men walked off along the corridor, but I didn't dare to move for at least five minutes after their voices had faded, just in case they'd stopped nearby. Why did I always get myself into these situations? It was like I'd taken out the Sharpie again, and this time, written *trouble magnet* on my forehead.

"Where have you been?" Tegan asked when I got back to the table.

"Hiding from Dale. What was all that hand-waving about?"

"He was planning to ask you out for dinner, and I figured you'd rather avoid that conversation."

"You were right about that. Has he left now?"

"One of the women in his tour group drank too much, and he had to escort her back to her room."

Which suggested he might be coming back at some point. "I'm super tired. Do you mind if we head home?"

"Aren't you gonna eat dessert?"

"I've lost my appetite."

"Okay, sure. Let's go."

I even managed to make a mess of walking out of the hotel. Today really wasn't my day. One moment I was strolling along the path to the front of the building, the next, I'd tripped over a step and sprawled across the grass. Worse, it was still damp from being watered so now I had grass stains on the knees of my white capri pants and see-through patches on my mostly white T-shirt. This was one of those days I regretted getting out of bed in the morning.

"Are you okay?" Tegan asked, giving me a hand to get to my feet.

"I'm fine. No serious damage." Except to my pride, obviously.

Tegan began picking up the contents of my handbag, which lay scattered across the path, and I grabbed a stray tampon from under a bush and stuffed it into my pocket. My knees hurt more than I cared to admit, but I plastered on a smile for show.

"Hey, what's this?" she asked.

"What's what?"

"This." She waved a card at me. "I thought you said you weren't into men."

"I'm not." When she held her hand still, I took a closer look. "Oh, that's the guy I sat next to on the plane. He's an archaeologist digging near here, and he invited me to visit if I wanted a day out."

"You're smiling when you talk about him."

"Because he was nice to me, but don't get your hopes up. He's gay."

"Aww. Never mind. Are you going?"

"Going where?"

"To visit his dig."

"Uh, I don't know. I haven't really given it any thought until now. He probably only asked to be polite. You know, the way you meet someone on holiday and say you must catch up when everyone gets back home, but you've got no intention of actually doing so."

"And if they do turn up at your house, they're an axe murderer?"

"Something like that."

"But inviting you to an archaeological dig is different. I hear academic types always love to talk about their work, and you might get to see some real treasures. Like a tomb or something."

"Can't I see those here? In the Valley of the Kings?"

"Only a few of the tombs there are open at the

moment, and you're not allowed to take photos inside them. Why don't you call him and see if we can both visit?"

Knowing me, I'd probably fall into an excavation pit and break my leg, and what if Miles didn't really want us to come and only agreed out of politeness? I'd feel horribly guilty. Then again, if he hadn't been serious about me visiting, why had he mentioned his dig at all? I could be passing up on a great chance to find out more about Egypt's history because I was too much of a coward to make a phone call.

"I suppose I could."

Oh, what the heck... I'd try calling Miles. Live dangerously, eh? The worst he could do was say no, and if he hesitated, I wouldn't push him.

CHAPTER 8 - TAI

OF COURSE, CALLING Miles meant turning my phone on again, and when I plucked up the courage to do so the next morning, I was up to 427 unread emails and twenty-six text messages. Probably most of the emails were junk, but when I saw the number, I was tempted to just delete the email app altogether. My finger hovered over the button. What if Ren needed to get hold of me?

Dammit, I had to check. I wouldn't read the actual messages, just the subject lines in case there was a problem and he'd decided to take my suitcase to Saudi Arabia or something.

Spam, spam, spam... Boy, there were an awful lot of African princes around at the moment. Wakanda? I was pretty sure that wasn't even a real country. Hold on, why was Peony emailing me? I didn't even know she had my address—I certainly hadn't given it to her. The subject line said *Are you dead?* following on from three simple *Where are yous?* sent by Mum. And there was another stroppy directive from Matthew Smart: *Call Victor Andrews NOW!*

Victor Andrews was the big boss at Garrett-Hart. What did Matthew plan to do when I didn't follow his order? Add "or else" to the end of it?

There was nothing from Ren, but I did feel a tiny bit

guilty for leaving Mum in the dark for so long, and I wanted to avoid her calling the police and having them waste time looking for me. I fired off a quick email to keep her from worrying or planning my funeral.

Hi Mum,

I'm absolutely fine, but I came to the realisation that I really hated my job, so I quit and decided to take a last-minute holiday. No need to worry. I'll be back soon.

Tai.

I wouldn't be back soon, but if I told her that right away, she'd freak out and beg the British embassy to send psychiatric help or something. Far better to manage her expectations and extend my trip by a week at a time. With any luck, she'd forget I existed in a month or two.

After I'd sort of dealt with my emails, I took a deep breath and dialled Miles's number. He'd be awake at nine o'clock, right? Or maybe he was a night owl, late to bed and late to rise? What if I woke him up? Perhaps I should call back la—

"Hello?"

"Uh, hi. You probably don't remember me, but we sat together on the plane on... What day was it? Uh, Tuesday, and—"

"Tai?"

Wow, he *did* remember me. "Yes."

"Where did you end up?"

"In Luxor."

"Good choice. At the Winter Palace?"

"Not exactly." I gave Miles the short version of the

Betsy saga, and of course, he chuckled. "So I'm sort of stuck for now, although I quite like the apartment. How's your archaeology going?"

He paused for a second, but when he spoke again, the excitement in his voice was palpable. "Good. Great, in fact. We've made some exciting discoveries in the last few days."

"Does that mean you're busy at the moment? I was wondering whether it'd be possible to visit. If you've got too much on, that's no problem—I can go to the Valley of the Kings instead."

"The Valley of the Kings is always worth a visit. Seti the First's tomb is closed, as is Horemheb's, which is a shame because they're the best decorated, but Thutmose the Third should be open. The hieroglyphs on the ochre background are unusual rather than spectacular, but it's at the back of the Valley and the stairs up to the entrance deter the regular day-trippers, so it's less crowded. Then there's Ramesses the Fourth and Merenptah... Listen to me—I could talk about Egyptology all day and bore you to death."

"No, no, it's interesting. What about Tutankhamun? Isn't that the most famous?"

"Yes, but it's also the smallest and quite plain. They moved all the good stuff to the museum in Cairo."

"So I should avoid that one?"

"It's still worth a look, and since you're staying in Luxor, you'll have time to visit the Valley more than once. And of course I can show you around our site too, or at least the parts that are safe. We *are* a little busy right now, but how does Thursday sound?"

"This Thursday?"

"Or later if you prefer?"

"No, this Thursday's perfect." It wasn't as if I had to check my busy schedule, was it? "Would you mind if I brought a friend? She's staying in the apartment next door."

"I don't mind at all. I'll send my driver to pick you up. We're out in the middle of nowhere, and the average taxi driver'll get lost. Where are you staying?"

"Uh, next door to Sayid with the pool table? The place doesn't seem to have a proper address."

"Ah, the famous pool table."

"You know where it is?"

"Everybody knows where it is. Six o'clock?"

"In the evening?"

Miles laughed. "No, in the morning. It's cooler before the sun comes up. The heat isn't so bad at this time of year, but we'll have some walking to do. Make sure you wear comfortable shoes."

Darn it—after quitting work, I'd just begun getting used to my morning lie-ins, and now I'd have to set the alarm again. At least it was only for one day, and I didn't need to pretend to be nice to Matthew Smart for eight hours afterwards.

"Okay, six in the morning. Great."

"I'll have the coffee waiting."

With our archaeological adventure organised, the next task on my list was a visit to the supermarket. The cupboard was bare, and even the ants were scratching around for something to eat. Maybe I could check out that shawarma stand by the souk too? Was it open this early?

When I opened the door, it seemed as though Tegan was thinking along the same lines. She'd just raised one hand to knock, and she held a shopping bag in the other.

"Do you want anything from the market?" she asked.

"I'm just going myself."

"Awesome—group outing. I gave Betsy fresh water, by the way. Has she got any more corn?"

"I need to get some from Sayid."

"Or the souk. It sells everything from bananas to shoes to table lamps, so someone's bound to have chicken feed."

Perhaps unsurprisingly, considering my experiences of Egypt so far, the guy who ran the shawarma stand had a cousin who sold animal feed, and while we munched on breakfast sandwiches, he dispatched a nephew to pick up a bag for me. At first, I wondered why a small child wasn't in school on a Friday, but Tegan reminded me that the Egyptian weekend ran Friday to Saturday.

"There'll be kids everywhere later. They ask for sweets, but if you hand any over, two children become twenty."

"So you never give any out?"

"No, I do, but it costs me a fortune."

I'd just made a mental note to buy a bag of cheap sweets when the man at the next table turned around. The shawarma place wasn't much more than a hole-in-the-wall, but there were a bunch of cheap plastic lawn chairs grouped around tables on the pavement outside.

"If you go to the supermarket next to the mosque, they sell giant bags of fruit candies, so it doesn't work out that expensive. Sorry, I couldn't help overhearing."

A fellow Brit, and this one was rather handsome in a boy-next-door sort of way with chocolate brown hair, soft brown eyes, a friendly smile, and a giant sandwich filled with lamb, houmous, and salad. He caught me looking at it and grimaced.

"I made the mistake of ordering a large portion."

I'd considered that, but now I was glad I'd picked the smaller size. "Thanks for the tip. Are you here on holiday?"

"Sort of. I guess."

"That sounds like a definite maybe."

He paused, the corner of his mouth twitching as if he wasn't sure he wanted to elaborate. But after a moment, he came to a decision.

"I came to Luxor for various reasons, one of them being that I just split up with my girlfriend. My brother's a tour rep out here, and he insisted I take a break before I did something stupid."

Oh my gosh! He was suicidal? We'd had a talk on this at work, probably because everyone who worked at Garrett-Hart felt so bloody miserable all the time. Encourage the person to talk, the lady had said. Ask open-ended questions, and don't worry about getting the answers—just listen.

"Uh, how are you feeling now?"

He burst out laughing, which wasn't quite what I'd expected.

"Damn, I should have phrased that better. I'm not planning to top myself. But I may have contemplated punching my personal trainer after I caught the pair of them...together."

Phew. Thank goodness, and at least his brother had cared enough to help out. I couldn't imagine Peony bothering. In fact, when I was having all the trouble with Paul, she'd accidentally given him my new phone number, which meant I'd received three hundred text messages and a hundred and forty-seven phone calls in two days and had to change it *again.*

"So this is more of a sanity break?"

"That's a good description."

"I'm on one of those too. Not because of an ex-boyfriend, but I just quit my job."

"She's free as a bird," Tegan told him, and I willed her not to mention Betsy. Explaining the chicken to Miles had been embarrassing enough, but this guy was right here, and his smile did funny things to my insides. "I'm Tegan, by the way."

"Russell." He flashed her a smile, then turned to me and raised an eyebrow.

"I'm Tai."

"Are you two in Luxor together?"

"No, we just met. Tegan's staying in the apartment next to mine."

"Apartments, huh? I'm at the Winter Palace."

"You're not staying with your brother?"

"I was, but he lives in a houseboat on the river, and it's barely big enough for one. After three nights of sleeping on the floor and listening to him snore, I couldn't take it anymore, so I switched to somewhere with a proper bed."

Snoring. Yet another problem that Paul had suffered from. On its own, it wouldn't have been too big of a deal, but he'd absolutely refused to admit he did it, just like he refused to admit that setting up a camera in my bedroom without my knowledge was just a tiny bit intrusive. I caught myself balling my fists up under the table at the thought of him, and I forced myself to relax. Russell wasn't Paul.

"How long have you been in Egypt?" I asked.

"Almost two weeks now."

"How much longer will you be here?"

"Officially, I've taken a sabbatical from work, so up to three months. How long I stay depends on how much I find to do around here."

"There's plenty," Tegan said. "You could ride a camel, or a horse, or sail in a felucca, or visit the museum, or go to a temple... And if you'd rather veg out, there's loads of restaurants. Why don't you do something with Tai? You're both on your own here."

I glared at her, but she just grinned. Which part of yesterday's "no men" talk hadn't she understood?

For his part, Russell looked somewhat alarmed too. Poor guy. He'd only come out to get breakfast, and now Tegan seemed intent on meddling.

"Tegan, I'm sure Russell has got better things to do."

She smiled sweetly. "Do you?" she asked him.

Great. Now she'd backed him into a corner. If he said yes, he had better things to do, he'd sound like he was insulting me, and he seemed like too much of a gentleman to do that. And if he said no, he'd have to take me on a pity date.

Russell's gaze darted from side to side as he eyed up possible escape routes. Honestly, I wouldn't have been surprised if he'd legged it. A man literally running away from me would have been par for the course in my screwed up life.

But he didn't. "I suppose we could take a trip on a felucca. Or go camel riding. My brother's bound to have a tour group we can join up with."

Oh, nice move. He'd avoided the dreaded date

scenario, and I could avoid being alone with a potential axe murderer. Unless...

"Your brother's not called Dale, is he?"

"No, Finn. Why?"

"It doesn't matter." I tried for a smile, but it didn't come out right because what I really wanted to do was strangle Tegan. "Yes, either of those sounds great."

"Tomorrow?" His tone said *better get it over with.*

"Sure, tomorrow."

"Which do you prefer?"

Sitting six feet off the ground on a swaying, smelly, bad-tempered beast didn't seem at all appealing, but if I went on a boat, there'd be no escape if I hated every moment. I choked on a piece of pitta bread as I imagined diving into the murky waters of the Nile and swimming to shore, but Tegan thumped me on the back, and Russell passed me his untouched bottle of water before I could die of food-related embarrassment.

Both of the options were awful, but since Russell had offered, I couldn't very well turn him down, could I? And I may have hated camels, but a watery escape appealed even less. When I was eleven, Mum signed Peony and me up to do our lifesaving certificate at the local swimming pool, and my darling sister had nearly drowned me in the process. Ever been abandoned flailing in the deep end wearing a pair of polka dot pyjamas? Let me assure you, it's as bad as it sounds. The lifeguard wasn't one of those Baywatch types either. No, he was a greasy-haired grouch six years older than me, and he'd told the entire school about my inadequacies by the time registration finished on Monday morning.

With my history, it seemed sensible to avoid the River Nile, especially in male company.

"Uh, camel riding sounds fun."

Russell's wan smile said he shared my lack of enthusiasm, but Tegan clapped her hands together.

"It totally does. Great choice."

"Do you want to come too?" Russell quickly offered.

Now she faked disappointment. "Wish I could, but I have to...do...uh, something. Why don't you pick Tai up tomorrow? We're staying next door to Sayid with the pool table. Do you know where that is?"

"My brother's told me about him. I can find out." How come everyone knew Sayid? Was a pool table really that exciting? "Ten o'clock?"

Did I have a choice? "I'll be ready."

"Then I guess I'll see you tomorrow." Russell abandoned the remains of his shawarma sandwich and backed away. "Nice meeting you."

He practically sprinted down the street, dodging a guy with a donkey on the way, and I dug my fingernails into my palms to stop myself from shaking Tegan. Everything about Russell's body language said he'd only agreed to her stupid plan out of politeness, and I didn't want to go either.

"Why on earth did you do that?"

"Russell likes you."

"No, Tegan, he likes eating breakfast in peace."

"But he looked lonely, staring at the passers-by."

"He was probably just thinking. I do that all the time myself."

"That's great—you've got something in common."

Besides our shared dislike of camels? I wasn't sure a mutual tendency to space out was the basis for a deep and meaningful relationship, or even a two-hour date, but I did feel slightly envious of Tegan's ability to find the silver lining in every storm cloud.

"How do you always stay so positive?"

Her face fell, just for a second, but it was long enough for me to glimpse something she normally kept hidden: pain. Then her smile quickly ratcheted back into place.

"Because if I focus on the negative, it'll poison me from the inside out."

"You sound as if you're speaking from experience?"

"Once upon a time, I wanted to change the world, but it changed me instead." The smile was still there, but now it seemed forced. "So, camel riding... Ever been before?"

Ah, the old subject change. Whatever had happened to Tegan, she didn't want to talk about it, but I'll admit to being curious. What made her leave home to travel the world as a digital nomad?

"I rode a fairground horse once. That's the closest I've got."

"Just remember to hold on, and you'll be fine."

CHAPTER 9 - TAI

JUST HOLD ON, and you'll be fine.

Tegan's words echoed in my head as my camel lurched to its feet the next morning, and I gripped the handle thing on the front of the saddle so tightly my knuckles turned white. Why had I ever chosen this ahead of a boat? Drowning would have been preferable to sitting high up on a pissed-off, moth-eaten autonomous creature. The thing had already tried to spit at me when I got near.

"You won't let go, will you?"

The small child responsible for my well-being held up a frayed piece of rope, the other end of which was attached to the camel's head.

"Very safe. She's a good camel."

"Does she have a name?"

"Melania."

I snorted a laugh, and Russell looked somewhat alarmed by the noise. What were the chances of blaming it on the animal?

"Melania? Like the American First Lady?"

The child nodded proudly. "They are both very beautiful."

Never had the saying about beauty being in the eye of the beholder seemed more appropriate. Melania the camel might have been a prime specimen—although I had my doubts—but she'd get kicked out of a state dinner for sure.

"What's mine called?" Russell asked. He'd clambered on board before me, and his four-legged freak stood quietly while Melania threatened to dump me onto the ground if I so much as breathed wrong. "Donald?"

"Yes, Donald Hump," his guide said, looking vaguely disappointed. "How did you know?"

"Just a lucky guess."

A scrawny looking kitten ran past, and Melania leapt sideways. Good grief. If I made it to the afternoon without landing headfirst, I deserved a fancy cocktail and a slice of chocolate fudge cake, although I suspected in Luxor, I'd have to settle for a glass of Sprite and a knockoff Twinkie.

"How about the cat?" I asked. "Nicole?"

Had the Pussycat Dolls been big in Egypt?

"No, Michelle."

"Michelle?"

Russell was one step ahead of me. "Michelle Pfeiffer. Catwoman. The original and best. Am I right?"

His guide nodded. "Very smart man. We go now?"

"Lead the way."

Russell's brother wasn't with us, but he'd arranged for us to tag along with a group of German tourists who all seemed to be more enthusiastic about the outing than we did. Donald and Melania ambled along at the back, and they obviously liked each other because they walked close enough for Russell and me to bump knees.

"I'm so sorry about this," I said once we'd got a few hundred yards along the road. "Tegan can be a bit pushy."

"Pushy? I thought she'd frogmarch us here if I didn't agree."

"If you want, we can just head back. Melania makes me nervous anyway."

Russell sighed. "We might as well see it through. My brother keeps telling me to be more spontaneous."

"You took leave from your job and came to Egypt. That was spontaneous."

As if on cue, a ringing phone interrupted our conversation, and Russell glanced at his fancy watch.

"Uh, that's my PA. One moment..." He fished a Bluetooth headset out of his pocket and stuffed it into his ear. "Janet? What's up?"

I took in our surroundings as Russell muttered about testing protocols and client satisfaction. The streets got bumpier, the houses smaller and further apart. Town gave way to country, and I saw the magic of the Nile Valley. The river was the lifeblood of the thousands of people who lived along its banks. Farmers diverted the water to grow their crops, locals used it for washing and transport, and tourists sailed serenely on mini cruise ships.

As I watched, a trickle of water flowed down a shallow irrigation channel formed out of mud baked hard in the sun. Primitive yet effective—I could imagine peasants doing exactly the same thousands of years ago as they produced the crops to feed the army of workers who'd built the pharaohs' tombs.

"Clever, isn't it?" Russell said, jerking his head towards the water.

"Have you finished your call now?"

At least he had the good grace to look sheepish. "Sorry about that."

"I thought you took a sabbatical?"

Three months, that's what he'd said yesterday.

"Yes." He paused for a moment. "Officially I did, and if you ever meet my brother, I'd appreciate you sticking to that story."

"You're still working, and he doesn't know?" Suddenly, Russell's living arrangements made more sense. "That was the real reason you moved to the Winter Palace, wasn't it?"

"It wasn't only my brother. The HR manager started reminding me daily that I had five years' worth of accrued holiday, and my mother's been begging me to take time off for ages. She reads too many self-help books, and I told her that if I got another email about executive burnout or eye strain or RSI, I'd change her Wi-Fi password."

"Did she stop?"

"Nope. She started coming over to the office in the evenings with lectures and casseroles."

"The evenings? You were still working in the evenings? Weren't you exhausted by then?"

"Not so much exhausted, but I've been getting a lot of headaches lately. I got glasses for VDU use, which helped a tad, but I'll admit I need the occasional break from my computer screen."

"What do you do?"

"I'm a software engineer."

"You write programs? Apps?"

"Occasionally, but I'm more on the testing side now. We've got a gap until our next big project starts, and it was easier to come here for a while than listen to the constant nagging. My family, my colleagues, my doctor..."

"Your ex-girlfriend?"

"Honestly? A bad break-up seemed like an easier way to explain this trip than admitting I'm a workaholic on the verge of a relapse. It may sound callous, but I wasn't quite as bothered by the split as I made out. Yes, being cheated on stung, but I just cancelled her credit card and couriered her belongings back."

"Sometimes it's easier to be on your own, huh?"

"Exactly. No offence."

"None taken. Most of the time, I feel that way myself."

"And yet here we are..." He took a hand off the rope to gesture around us. "Side by side, riding hell-beasts because it's easier than arguing with people we care about."

That summed it up perfectly. "Yup. Reckon you'll last the full three months?"

"Unlikely. You really don't have a significant other waiting for you at home? I know your friend said you were free as a bird, but it's hard to believe you're single."

What? Why? Did I look needy or something? I was so busy puzzling over the answer that I spoke without thinking, and oh boy, did I ever put my foot in my mouth.

"No boyfriend, not since the last one went to prison."

Oh, dammit. I clapped a hand over my mouth to stop any more word vomit from escaping, but it stunk of camel, and I gagged. Marvellous. This date couldn't be going any better.

"Did you just say prison?"

"Uh, no, I said Plzeň. It's a city in the Czech

Republic."

Thank goodness I'd listened in geography at school.

"No, you didn't. Prison? What did he do?" Now it was Russell's turn to backtrack. "Sorry, I shouldn't have asked. None of my business."

"He turned into a bit of a stalker, and when I tried to break up with him, he went kind of crazy."

The mere memory of that final night made me shudder. Even in the heat of the desert, a chill ran through me.

"Are you okay?" Russell asked.

"I just don't like thinking about it, that's all."

"Then let's discuss something else. How long do you plan to stay in Egypt?"

"I'm not sure. I still have to pinch myself to believe I got here in the first place."

"Have you seen much of the place yet?"

"Not really. So far, all I've managed to do is adopt a chicken, make some terrible wardrobe decisions, and get bored to death by a lecherous tour guide. Who wasn't your brother, by the way."

"Dale?"

"How did you know?"

"You mentioned his name yesterday."

Oh. Right. "Yes, well, he talked for too long and kept brushing his hand along my leg under the table. I wanted to stab him in the eye with a fork."

What was I even saying? Musing about grievous bodily harm would hardly be attractive to the opposite sex. Not that I particularly wanted to endear myself to Russell. No, not at all, but he'd been nice so far, and I felt oddly comfortable in his company.

"Okay, so no stalking, no talking. Anything else I

should avoid if I want to keep my vision?"

"Uh, that's it, I think."

"You think?"

"I'm sure."

"So, Tai, what happened to make you run to this little corner of paradise? You said something about quitting your job? And where does the chicken come in?"

"I don't know what came over me, but I couldn't take it any longer. My boss, he used to complain about everything I ever said or did, and..."

I found myself telling Russell about Matthew Smart and his blame game, about my parents and Peony, the Betsy incident, and Tegan, and it was surprisingly cathartic to talk. Was this how people felt when they went to a therapist? Relieved? Lighter inside? Like their ass was on fire? Oh, hell. I'd been so busy unloading on a virtual stranger, I hadn't noticed how badly Melania's saddle was rubbing on my backside. It may have looked like a giant cushion, but it felt as if sandpaper was being gently dragged over the delicate skin of my behind.

"How much longer?" I whispered to the guide.

"Twenty minutes."

"Everything all right?" Russell asked.

I may have dished some of the dirt on my painful past, but confessing to an admittedly nice man that my bottom most likely resembled a side of beef was a step too far.

Instead, I gritted my teeth. "I'm fine. Just a tiny bit embarrassed that I've been talking about me for ages."

"I don't mind. When I'm in England, I volunteer at the Samaritans every Thursday, so I'm actually used to it."

"The Samaritans? That's... That's..."

Selfless? Kind? Generous? Dammit, I'd come on this camel ride determined not to like Russell much, but he was making it very difficult.

"Our company offers all employees two days off per year to help in the community, and I decided I should lead by example."

"Your company?"

"I own it with three friends. Truthfully, I wasn't expecting to enjoy the volunteering lark, but it felt good to give something back, so I carried on." He gave a wry smile. "Plus it gets me out of the office for one evening a week."

"Maybe I should try something similar when I get home?"

"I can send you the details if you like."

"Yes, I think I *would* like."

Apart from Satan holding a flaming torch to my bum, today hadn't been nearly as bad as I'd imagined. I grimaced as Melania bounced over a small hummock, then forced a smile when Russell looked at me.

"Give me your email address, and I'll dig out the information." He paused. "You're different to how I thought you'd be."

"Is that a good thing or a bad thing?"

"Good." Another pause. "Look, it's just an idea, but maybe we could help each other out. My brother and your friend seem determined to make us go out and have 'fun.'" He took his hands off Donald's rope to make little quote marks with his fingers. "And neither of us is keen on the idea. Perhaps on occasion, we could tell them we're going out together?"

My heart did a funny little jump. Was Russell asking me on a proper date?

Er, no.

"That way, I could get some work done," he continued. "And you could relax on your own."

Ah, so this would be more of a strategic alliance. And one that left me feeling mildly disappointed.

"But where would I go?"

"The Winter Palace has a great pool area, and they'll bring you anything you want to eat or drink on my room service tab."

That was actually a pretty good offer. The garden at the apartment was nice, but it didn't have much shade, and a swimming pool would be lovely in the heat. Plus it might get Tegan off my back. I did like her, but she could be slightly overwhelming at times. Russell seemed more...chilled.

I smiled through the agony of my burning ass. "Deal."

We reached across and shook on it, and Russell's hand felt firm. Dry. Not like my sweaty palms. Then Melania jumped sideways, and I clung on for dear life again.

"Deal," Russell said.

"Ohmigosh! What happened?" Tegan asked.

"Er, nothing. Nothing at all."

No way was I gonna mention my plot with Russell.

"Then why are you walking like a salty old cowboy?"

"The camel may have been a little uncomfortable."

She spun me around and gasped. "Did your period

start? Or... Or..."

There was blood coming through my clothes? Oh, rats. This was even worse than I thought. "No, that's saddle damage."

"Strewth. Okay, get out of those trousers. We should check the damage."

We? This wasn't a group freaking activity. "I'll check it myself in the bathroom."

"Do you need a first aid kit? I've got one in my room."

"Please."

Inside, I fetched a chair to stand on so I could see in the mirror above the sink, then gingerly peeled down my not-so-white capri pants. Wow. It looked as if someone had taken a cheese grater to my skin. How on earth did Bedouins ride across the Sahara without being crippled at the end of the day? The damage extended all the way down my thighs.

Cowering under the shower, I felt as if I was being attacked by a swarm of wasps, and a smear of Tegan's antiseptic cream left me whimpering. My next challenge? Finding something to wear. It had to be those flipping gold harem pants. They were the only thing that was both loose and clean-ish, and who cared about style when I was in this much pain?

Out in the garden, Tegan had been busy too.

"I borrowed these from Sayid for you."

"These" turned out to be a car inner tube and a child's paddling pool. "What for?"

"I figured you could sit on the tyre thing. You know, to keep the weight off the sore bits. And if it all gets too much, we can fill the kiddie pool with cold water to numb the area. Is it really bad?"

"I'm not sure how I'll be able to ride in a car or go to a restaurant for the next few days."

Tegan pointed at the rubber donut.

"Oh, brilliant, so then everyone'll think I've got haemorrhoids."

"Well, the good news is that you'll only have to face Sayid and his family tonight. He's invited us over for dinner. And the laundry man's back, so after you've told me about your date with Russell, we can get our clothes cleaned today too."

Clean clothes... Back in England, I'd taken them for granted, but I'd come to realise just what a luxury they were. Still, I didn't remotely feel like going out for dinner when all I wanted to do was take a handful of painkillers and lie down. On my front.

Perhaps I could make an excuse? Tell Tegan I had to stay at home and check my dreaded emails? Or should I put Plan Russell into action? Before we parted company, he'd given me his contact details with the agreement that we'd cover for each other whenever the need arose.

"Did you tell Sayid why you needed the donut?"

"I just said you had a camel-related injury. He probably thinks you fell off and bruised your coccyx."

Which was marginally better, I suppose. So, three choices... Should I brave an evening with Sayid and his family? Send a message to Russell? Or dig through the horrors waiting in my inbox, a task that was long overdue?

Chapter 10 - Tai

WELL, RUSSELL DID say to message him whenever, didn't he? There was no time like the present to try out the new arrangement, and a dip at the Winter Palace seemed a better option than squirming uncomfortably on a plastic lawn chair while Tegan played pool. Perhaps I could float around in my flipping donut?

"I actually have plans tonight."

Tegan raised an eyebrow. Of course she did because so far, I'd shown the social skills of a hedgehog. But she quickly put two and two together.

"With Russell?" Her hands flew to her mouth. "That's awesome!"

"I just have to call him and confirm." Please say he hadn't changed his mind... "Any chance you could drop my dirty washing off with Sayid's cousin if you're taking yours?"

"Sayid's *wife's* cousin. Sure—just shove it in a bag before you go."

Inside, I turned on my phone and cringed at the number of missed calls. Over a hundred now, and although most of them were from my mother, Peony had rung as well, plus Matthew Smart. And Janice, who was the MD's secretary and one of the few people I liked in my former workplace, Garrett-Hart's HR manager, and at least ten people whose numbers I didn't recognise. A niggly little voice told me that I really should start dealing with the mess, but the worse it got, the more I wanted to toss my phone into the Nile and go back to good old-fashioned letter writing.

Dear Mum,

Just a quick note to let you know I'm still alive, and despite the fact that I'm "a bit dull," as I overheard you telling Peony's ballet teacher, I've managed to make two new friends in one week. Will I be coming home soon? No, I don't think so. Egypt's a haven for me. A new beginning. An escape. For the first time in years, I haven't felt an overwhelming sense of hopelessness from the time I wake up to the moment I crawl into bed at night. Life here doesn't revolve around the demands of an unreasonable boss, and then there's the added bonus of being able to walk down the street without looking over my shoulder for Paul.

You remember Paul? He was the "polite boy, such a gentleman" you encouraged me to date once you found out his dad was a wealthy lawyer who drove a Bentley and sponsored the local theatre's production of Swan Lake. And when I confessed Paul made me uncomfortable, you convinced me it was all in my imagination because "men just don't get obsessed with girls like you." I was stupid back then. Ever since I was a little girl, competing against a stepsister who was prettier and more popular than me, I only wanted your approval.

Instead, I got scars.

And now? Now, I've got a chicken. She's called Betsy, and she makes me smile. So you can keep your lectures about etiquette and that ridiculous lace tablecloth you gave me last Christmas—I'm having fun here, and I don't intend to stop.

Tai (your other daughter).

That was what I wanted to say, but I never would because I'd used up almost my entire quota of bravery getting on the plane at Heathrow. No, I'd take the easier approach and bury my head in the sand—luckily, there was plenty of that to spare in the desert.

My last little bit of courage went on making a phone call to Russell.

"Russell? Hi, it's Tai. From, uh, the camel."

"I wasn't expecting to hear from you so soon."

"Sorry. It's just that Tegan wants me to go and play pool tonight, and I'm feeling a little unwell after this morning."

"Same here. Motion sickness? I've got pills for that."

I seized on his suggestion because it was better than having to explain that my ass looked like steak tartare. "It's mostly worn off now, but I'd rather sit in peace than make small talk with the neighbours."

"And you want to do that at the Winter Palace?"

"If you don't mind?"

"We had a deal, right? Just give me fifteen minutes to talk to the concierge."

I tried walking to the Winter Palace, but I didn't even make it to the end of the road before Mohammed honked the horn on his ancient Peugeot and shuddered to a halt beside me in a cloud of dust.

"Where you want to go?"

"Oh, I'm fine walking."

"Is no problem. I take you anywhere you want."

"But…"

Never mind. It was easier to accept his offer than to argue, even if I hated myself for giving in as soon as I climbed into the back seat. In a moment of clarity, I realised I'd spent my whole life avoiding confrontation, from taking piano lessons to please my mother, to accepting Paul's dinner invitations, to staying silent in the face of Matthew Smart's endless criticisms. Funny how taking a step back revealed a truth I'd never wanted to see, wasn't it?

My throbbing ass was a testament to my weakness as I climbed out of Mohammed's car at the Winter Palace. Every time we bounced over a pothole, I'd cursed myself.

"Shall I wait?" Mohammed asked as I handed over twenty pounds.

"I'll walk back."

"Why do you want to walk? Is a long way."

"Because I like walking. The exercise is good for me. Uh, here…" I handed over an extra ten pounds before I staggered into the hotel. "Here's a tip. I'll call you next time I need a ride."

Not brilliantly handled, but at least I hadn't backed down completely. This was progress.

Inside the Winter Palace, the concierge pounced on me before I got the chance to fully take in the old-world opulence of the lobby. Decorative white stone columns, red velvet curtains, gilt, chandeliers…

"Can I help, ma'am?"

"I'm here to see Russell… Russell…" Too late, I realised I didn't even know Russell's surname. "Uh, just Russell…"

"Mr. Wise?"

Probably. "Yes?"

"He have a phone call this evening. He say to show you the restaurant and the swimming pool. We also have a library and a changing room at your disposal."

So this really *was* just a hands-off business arrangement. Russell had said as much, so why did I feel disappointed that I wouldn't see him? *Dammit, Tai.* As soon as I had that thought, I wanted to smush it to the bottom of my brain because I absolutely hadn't come to Luxor to get confused over a man. They only caused heartache and stress and occasionally hospital or court visits.

No, I'd enjoy a quiet evening by the pool together with Russell's generosity, and not spend my time rehashing memories of an embarrassing shawarma sandwich followed by a dodgy camel ride.

"Do you have a drinks menu?" I asked the concierge. According to the badge he wore, his name was Ashraf, and he'd stuck five little gold stars along the bottom as if he worked in McDonald's and not a posh hotel. At least he'd got the "service with a smile" part down pat.

"Certainly, ma'am. I'll bring it right out."

CHAPTER 11 - TAI

SUNDAY MORNING, AND I wanted to celebrate with another of the Sahara Sunset cocktails I'd been drinking last night. Why? Because I had clothes. Clean clothes! If I'd known a bag of laundry could make me feel so happy, perhaps I'd have taken more pride in the ironing back in England. Finally, I could change out of the Camel Towing T-shirt I'd worn again because it smelled the least whiffy.

And not only did I have the clothes, but I felt extraordinarily proud of myself for managing to follow Sayid's directions to pick them up. Along the street, turn left at the clump of three palm trees, walk for six houses, maybe seven, take the alley beside the villa with the red metal gates that may or may not have a donkey tied up outside, keep going past the plant nursery—which turned out to be a few dozen pots in a poorly tended yard—and go through the white archway. A faded wooden sign in squiggly Arabic probably said "Laundry," but I couldn't be sure. Should I make an effort to start learning the language? It looked beyond complicated, but if I planned to stick around in Luxor, speaking some of the lingo might help. I could find an online class or something, but that would involve turning my laptop on, and every time I pressed the power button, a horrible nausea washed around in my stomach.

I'd picked up Tegan's laundry too, all three bags of it, because when I got back from the Winter Palace last night, I'd found a Post-it note stuck to the door.

Tai,
Met a guy last night at Sayid's. Italian stallion!!!
Back tomorrow. Pls can you pick up the washing???
T
P.S. Hope you had fun with your British hottie ;)

At least one of us didn't have trouble getting what she wanted. I hadn't even seen Russell last night. No, I'd enjoyed a delicious pizza beside the pool, plus a slice of cake, then settled down with a romance novel I'd found lurking at the back of the hotel's library, hidden behind an Agatha Christie mystery and an out-of-date travel guide to Lower Egypt. The concierge had let me bring it home to finish, and Tegan's absence meant I'd get peace to read another chapter or two today, in between giving the apartment a tidy and going out to buy food. And I really should deal with my emails. The problem was only going to get worse, and I also needed to contact Ren Fontana to see when he'd be arriving with my case. Tomorrow or the day after, he'd said, and I couldn't wait to have clothes that fitted properly again, even if it was mostly business attire. I'd repurpose what I could and sell the rest.

And if I had more clothes, I wouldn't have to trek to the laundry so often. The thin handles on the oversized bags cut into my hands, and I'd twisted an ankle as I dodged a pile of horse poop on the way.

But now I was back. Phew. The gate clanged shut

behind me as I dragged the four bags into the garden, up the path, and towards the apartments.

"Next time, I'm hiring a caleche," I muttered to nobody in particular.

"Next time?"

What the...? I spun around to see a dark-haired man lying on my sunlounger, feet crossed at the ankles, shading his eyes from the sun with my borrowed copy of *The Dastardly Duke*. Bare feet, plaid shorts, and a white polo shirt with a pair of aviators tucked into the unbuttoned neck. He looked me up and down with the lazy intensity of a well-fed lion, and I couldn't decide whether to scream, run, or stand my ground because that was my book and my terrace, dammit.

If I screamed, would anyone even hear me? Tegan's apartment was still in darkness, and I didn't know if Sayid was home. I opened my mouth, but all that came out was a croak.

"You must be Tai?" the stranger said in response. His accent was American, disturbingly smooth with a hint of a drawl.

"How the heck do you know that?"

"Because only somebody who's lost her luggage would wear those gold pants. I know desperation when I see it, baby."

And I knew rudeness when I heard it. Too late, I noticed the little black suitcase parked outside my apartment door. "You're Ren? But... But you're not supposed to be here yet."

"A buddy was coming in this direction, so I hitched a ride for part of the way. I emailed you."

"Uh, I haven't checked my email for a few days."

He didn't tut, but his expression said he wanted to.

"What's the point in having it if you ignore it?"

"I'm on holiday, okay? I'm allowed to have peace."

"You're cute when you get defensive." Betsy chose that moment to wander around the corner, no doubt curious about the raised voices. "Hey, lunch is here."

"Betsy is *not* lunch! She's my pet."

Betsy ran at him, squawking, and I had to admit she wasn't a bad judge of character.

"Who keeps a pet chicken?" He sidestepped, laughing. "Seriously?"

"Are you always this much of an asshole?"

"So they say."

Well, at least he was honest. "Look, Mr. Fontana, I'm very grateful to you for bringing my case, but I have things to do today. I'll just fetch yours, and then you can get off my sunlounger and leave."

"No need to rush. I don't have anywhere to be. And the sunloungers are communal—Sayid said so."

"I'm sorry?"

I was beginning to get a really, really bad feeling about this.

"Figured since I travelled all the way here, I'd stick around for a week or two to get some culture, yadda yadda yadda. Sayid gave me a good deal on the empty apartment." Ren waved his hand behind him. "This is where you're supposed to welcome me to the neighbourhood."

I had many regrets in life. Like pretending to be Batgirl and falling off the back of the sofa when I was seven, because my broken wrist led Mum and me to the hospital where we met Peony and her father in the accident and emergency department. A&E for a twisted flipping ankle. All she'd done was stumble out of a pirouette. I had actual broken bones, and somehow she still garnered more sympathy. Then there was the temporary job I'd taken one summer, waiting on rich folks in corporate hospitality at a charity football match. Paul had been on one of my assigned tables, we realised we went to the same university, and the rest was history. I regretted hiding away in the library at school, never learning how to put on make-up properly, and spending my birthday money on a junior chemistry set instead of magazines. I regretted thinking I could make it in a male-dominated career, eating too many takeaways, and avoiding difficult conversations. Because all that had led me to where I was now, in the garden of a cobbled-together apartment in Luxor, where I added yet another regret to the list—not sending Ren's bloody suitcase to Dahab by courier.

"Wouldn't you prefer a hotel if you're only staying for a week? That way, you wouldn't have to cook."

"I enjoy cooking." He glanced at Betsy again. "Wait until you try my barbecue sauce."

Wait. What? Was he offering to cook? Because that... No, he couldn't bribe his way into my good books.

"What if I said I didn't like barbecued food?"

"You'd be lying."

He said it matter-of-factly, with just the smallest hint of a smirk curling at one corner of his lips. That was the moment I knew Ren Fontana was going to drive me completely insane if I didn't do something about his ridiculous plan to stay, and quickly.

Where were my keys? I fumbled in my trouser pocket, shoved open the door to my apartment, hauled his suitcase outside, and dumped it by the gate.

"How dare you tell me what I do and don't like? Get off my sunlounger, put my book down, and leave me alone."

"*Your* book? It says it's the property of the Winter Palace hotel." He flipped the page and began to read. "'The Duke of Rochester loosened the ties on Lady Elizabeth's girdle, leaving her a quivering mess of indignation. Her bosom heaved at his sheer audacity, but she didn't stop him when one gloved hand stroked the porcelain skin of her collarbone. A gasp left—'"

I snatched the *Duke* from him and slammed it down on the table. "Go and find a different apartment."

Now he stared at my chest. "Camel towing? Your shirt says you have a sense of humour, but I'm not seeing it."

Deep breaths, Tai. What was the penalty for murder in Egypt? The temptation to smother Ren Fontana with a laundry bag was almost irresistible.

"Would you like me to call you a taxi?" I asked through gritted teeth.

"Nah, but you can tell me where the nearest supermarket is. I'll get the stuff for dinner. Is your friend coming back?"

"Did you not hear a word I said?"

"Yeah, I just chose to ignore it. Maybe I'll pick you up a little something from Sayid on the way back because you definitely need to relax more, sweetheart."

"Something from Sayid? What are you talking about?"

"A few grams of hash?"

"Huh?"

Ren started laughing again. "You honestly don't know Sayid deals the best hash in Luxor?"

"Hash? As in hashish?" The blood drained down to my feet, and since my heart was still pumping in anger, I ended up giddy. "Sayid deals drugs? Are you sure? I mean, how do you know? You only just got here."

"I'm good at finding things out."

"*Drugs*?" Was that why the world and his dog knew who Sayid with the pool table was?

"Don't freak out, babe. It's herbal."

Tegan picked that moment to arrive back. The gate clanged, and she skipped up the path, grinning until she saw Ren and me toe to toe. Then her happiness evaporated under the midday sun.

"What's going on?" She swivelled to face Ren, eyes narrowed. "Who are you?"

"This is Ren. He's brought my luggage, and he's also trying to rent the third apartment from Sayid."

"Nice." Tegan checked him out, and her smile came back. "How long are you staying?"

"He's not. Did you know Sayid sells hash?"

"Oh, sure. Do you want some? I might have a bit left."

"Tegan, drugs are illegal."

"It's only pot. It's legal in Amsterdam."

"We're not *in* Amsterdam."

"I know. It's much sunnier here."

Ren's stupid smirk grew even cockier. "And there aren't so many hookers."

Never in my life had I wanted to kick a man in the testicles quite as much as I did at that moment.

"Stop being so...so..."

"Truthful? Factual?"

"Just go and find a hotel far, far away. Somewhere like Yemen."

"You haven't tried my pineapple-marinated chicken yet. One bite of that, and you'll be begging me to stay."

"You can cook?" Tegan asked.

"My mom's a chef."

"Really? And what do you do?"

"I'm a property scout."

Tegan slid her sunglasses up to the top of her head, no doubt so she could study our unwelcome visitor better. "What's one of those?"

"I advise companies on the best locations for their capital projects. Corporate headquarters, new factories, research and development facilities, that sort of thing."

"Which company wants to come to Luxor?"

"None of them. Right now, I'm on vacation. Or at least, I will be once Tai stops yelling at me."

"Sorry about that. She gets a little uptight sometimes."

"I do not get uptight." They both stared at me. Okay, so with my feet planted, my hands on my hips, and steam practically curling out of my nose, I was the very definition of uptight, but only because Ren Fontana had made me that way. "Usually."

"Relax, Tai. Is that my laundry?"

"Uh, yes."

"Thanks for picking it up. Why don't you take a shower while I show Ren around?"

Since he refused to leave, that seemed like the best option. Tegan was fond of hookups with shallow foreign men, and the American idiot certainly fitted the bill. They'd be perfect for each other. And if he was busy with Tegan, Ren wouldn't be free to irritate me.

"Fine. I'll do that."

"Want me to buy you anything for lunch?"

"I might go out this afternoon."

"With Russell?"

"Maybe." Would it be taking advantage of his kindness to hijack his room service account two days running? "Don't let Ren near Betsy. He's already threatened to barbecue her."

Tegan didn't hold back on the tutting. "You can't touch Tai's chicken."

"I'll cut your balls off with nail scissors if you do," I added, feeling braver now I wasn't alone with a virtual stranger.

"Your nail scissors aren't big enough."

"I can—" Hold on a second. Something about the way he said that made me pause. Like he was stating a fact. "You went through my *toiletries*?"

Ren shrugged. "Bet you went through mine." He rolled off the sunlounger and sauntered over to my suitcase, and before I could stop him, he'd opened it. "Here." He tossed me one of my squeezy stress balls. "You look as if you could use this."

I hurled it back at him, aiming for his head, but the asshole caught it single-handed. As he reached up, his shirt rode over his hips, gifting me a view of tanned abs and two deep grooves of muscle leading to the good bits. *Don't look, Tai.* Ren was dangerous to a girl's sanity, an incubus come to life.

"Point proven," he said.

"Just leave me and my chicken alone."

"Hey, I'm only trying to help."

I dragged my gaze upwards to liquid amber eyes. "I don't need your help."

"But do you need my culinary skills?" Now his smile turned lethal. He used it as a weapon to break down my defences. "Life's too short to keep arguing. Peace offering—I'll cook you anything you want."

This chance was too good to pass up. "Really? Anything?"

Now his expression turned wary. "As long as I can find the ingredients."

"Then how about a double chocolate fudge cake?"

"Does that mean you're joining us for dinner?"

"Maybe. I'll think about it." I wasn't going to give him an easy victory. Bribery with dessert could only get him so far. "I'll probably go out."

Before he could attack me with pheromones, I backed inside, hauling my suitcase and laundry along with me. Now I had a decision to make. Did I give in and have dinner with Ren and Tegan? Or should I pick the safe option and escape to the Winter Palace again? Staying here promised to be excruciatingly awkward, but if I went to the hotel, I risked outstaying my welcome with Russell, and I actually liked him.

Choices, choices... Why did they always have to be so difficult?

CHAPTER 12 - TAI

NO, I COULDN'T call Russell again. Not so soon. I hid inside my apartment, contemplating my options while Ren and Tegan went to the supermarket. Should I pretend to go out anyway and find a café somewhere? I still hadn't come to a decision by the time they arrived back and lit the barbecue. Smoke drifted in through the open window, followed by cursing, then the worrying aroma of... Oh, surely he wasn't ...?

He was. That...that asshole! I threw the door open and stomped outside.

"You're cooking chicken."

"I thought you were going out?"

"Well, clearly I didn't."

"Good thing I bought plenty of food. D'you want a leg or a breast? I'm more of a leg man myself, although I can still appreciate a good—"

"Don't you have any scruples?"

"Huh?"

Tight-lipped, I pointed at Betsy scratching around in the dust. Every so often, she threw Ren a dirty look. "You could be cooking her cousin."

"She doesn't know that."

"Hello? She can smell it."

"Okay, what does a freshly roasted human smell like?"

"How should I know? I'm not a freaking cannibal."

"So to carry on with that analogy, I'm guessing Betsy isn't all that familiar with KFC. But if you don't want any proper food, I can make you a salad."

"What happened to the cake? You can't put your money where your mouth is?"

"Have patience, Taisiya. Good things come to those who wait."

Wow. He'd actually pronounced my name right. Miracles did happen.

It was only once I'd stomped back inside, slammed the door so hard the glass rattled, and flumped back on the bed that I realised I'd never told Ren my full freaking name. So how did he find it out?

That question preyed on my mind until dinner. I hadn't written my full name on my luggage tag or included it in my emails to him. Was it anywhere in my suitcase?

"Tai came on impulse," Tegan said to Ren as we hung out on the terrace, waiting for the food to cook. "Didn't you?"

"Sorry?"

"I was just telling Ren that your trip here wasn't planned."

"Er, yes. No, it wasn't."

"So you've got something in common."

"What?"

"Well, Ren only came because of your suitcase."

And I sincerely wished he hadn't bothered. "Fantastic."

"Isn't it funny? How we come from three different walks of life, and yet we all ended up here in Luxor?"

"Hilarious."

"Tai, are you okay? You seem sort of..."

Tegan shrugged, and I didn't know whether to mention the name thing. Perhaps I'd told Ren and somehow forgotten? He rose from the sunlounger he'd dragged over and poked at the barbecue again. The smoke had dissipated, and I had to admit, the smell of meat was making my mouth water, even if I did feel awfully guilty about that. How smart were chickens? Did Betsy understand that one of her feathered friends was currently going crispy on the outside?

"I'm fine. It's just been a long day."

Tegan's face said she wasn't exactly convinced by my brush-off, but she let it pass. And I didn't want to get all accusatory, not when I had to live next door to Ren for who knew how long.

"Well, here's something that'll help you to feel better," Tegan said. "Ren made you vegetable kebabs. You know, so you don't have to eat one of Betsy's buddies."

"And chocolate cake, as requested," he said, dropping back onto the sunlounger and grinning like a catalogue model on a cheesy photo shoot. Were his teeth even real?

"Thanks."

The kebab thing was actually kind of...unexpected. But that didn't excuse his earlier behaviour.

"The cake fell in the middle," he said. "I haven't cooked properly for months."

"Why not?" Tegan asked.

"No kitchen."

"Because you've been travelling for work?"

"Partly. That and I'm renovating my house."

"How far along have you got?"

Ren made a face. "It's got walls and a roof that's mostly watertight. Work got in the way, and then my builder tore a ligament climbing out of his swimming pool and everything fell behind."

"Whereabouts do you live?" she asked.

"Small-town Virginia, USA."

"I pictured you as more of a city guy."

"Lived on the outskirts of DC for a while, but I always wanted more space. A house rather than an apartment. How about you? Where in Australia are you from?"

"Near Perth."

"Met a guy from Perth once. A bureaucrat. Came hiking with a group of us one weekend and kept bragging that he knew snakes, then got bitten by a copperhead."

Snakes scared the crap out of me. When I was little, a boy in my class kept a corn snake as a pet. Terry Stevenson, his name was—the boy, not the snake. Anyhow, he brought the freaky thing to school in his pocket one day, and it bit him on the thigh in biology then escaped into the lab. Everyone got evacuated, and we had to stand outside in the rain for two hours while they caught the flipping thing—everyone except Terry, that was. He got taken to the hospital to get the wound checked out instead. I couldn't help shuddering, and Tegan giggled.

"Snakes aren't that bad. If you keep out of their way, they keep out of yours. Mostly."

That wasn't entirely true. "I saw on TV once that somebody in Australia found a python in their toilet. And it's not only the snakes. What about the spiders?"

"Okay, I'll concede those are a problem. That's

another good thing about Egypt, actually. Have you noticed? There are hardly any spiders."

"Just mosquitos," Ren said.

"Even those aren't so bad. In Honduras, I got eaten alive, and they have Zika virus there too. Russia was the best for the lack of bugs, but only because they were probably frozen alive like everything else on the continent."

Ren raised an eyebrow. "Honduras to Russia? That's quite a culture shock. Where else have you been?"

Tegan listed off the places she'd mentioned to me before, the ones that made me feel utterly inadequate because they were all more exotic than an exhibition centre in mainland Europe or a Holiday Inn in Plymouth, which was about the breadth of my travel experience. Costa Rica, Cape Verde, Tunisia, Algeria. Sun, sea, and a completely different way of life. But while my stomach dropped lower into my flip-flops, Ren's eyebrow quirked even higher.

"Interesting. Why those particular countries?"

Tegan shifted a little in her seat. "Uh, I wanted variety."

"Do you go home often?"

"Not really."

"No family?"

"Not that miss me."

"Friends?"

Tegan ignored his question. "Do you have a big family back home in Virginia?"

"No, just me. How was life in Perth? Did you go to the beach much on the weekends?"

"Occasionally."

"I'm surprised you'd pick this place over Australia, spiders or no spiders. Don't you miss it?"

Why was Ren so nosy? Tegan was clearly reluctant to talk about home, and whatever had happened to make her leave was her business, not his.

"Is the food ready yet?" I asked. "I'm starving."

My interruption did the trick. Ren went back to the barbecue, and soon we had platefuls of chicken, bread, and in my case, vegetables and some sort of cheese that seemed to be an Egyptian version of paneer. And while I hated to admit it, Ren hadn't done a terrible job. The barbecued food was expertly browned on the outside, and he'd made a sauce that added the perfect mix of spicy and sweet. And the cake wasn't bad either. The middle barely had a dip in it, and the chocolate sponge was light and fluffy. Better than my paltry efforts in the kitchen.

He nodded towards my empty plate. "Want another piece?"

Yes, but if I kept eating like that, even the baggy gold pants wouldn't fit anymore. "No, thanks."

"In that case, why don't we go next door? Sounds as if there's a crowd around there again."

All evening, we'd heard the sounds of laughter and chatter coming over Sayid's wall, accompanied by some sort of twangy Middle Eastern music. Did I really want to join the party? Not one bit, but at least if Ren had something else to keep him occupied, I wouldn't have to talk to him. Hopefully, I could just hide in a corner then sneak off at the first available opportunity.

"Great idea. Why don't you go on ahead, and we'll clear up here?"

"What kind of man would I be if I left you two

ladies with the dirty work?"

One who knew how to take a hint?

How many times had I dreamed of being one of those take-charge girls unafraid to voice her opinion? Once upon a time, I'd stuck up for myself more, but dealing with Paul and the aftermath had left me tired. Tired of fighting, tired of life.

So I helped Tegan to wash up the dishes while Ren dealt with the remains of the barbecue, then I found a scarf to wrap around my shoulders to combat the slight chill that came when the sun went down. By English standards, it wasn't cold, not at all, but I must have been getting used to the heat because now when the temperature dropped below twenty-five, I began to wonder whether I should put a jacket on.

"Ready to go?" Ren asked.

How much did property scouts earn? Because he'd worn a thin T-shirt, a light grey one that must have been two sizes too small judging by the way the fabric stretched across his chest and arms. Couldn't he afford clothes that fitted? Or did he just prefer looking like a tanned version of The Incredible Hulk, about to burst out of his shirt at the first hint of danger?

"If I must," I muttered under my breath.

A rolling cloud of smoke hit me in the face the instant we walked through Sayid's gate. Sweet and sickly, strawberries mixed with watermelon and a hint of mint. At least it wasn't cannabis. I had to be thankful for the small things.

"Tai!" Sayid hurried over to me, his white dress blowing in the breeze. "Do you want shisha?"

I quickly shook my head. "Nuh-uh."

"What about nuts? Would you like nuts?"

To this day, I don't know why I did it. When Sayid said "nuts," my eyes strayed downwards towards Ren's package, and worse, he *freaking caught me*. That cocky smirk told me he knew he had nothing to be ashamed of, and I wanted to sink into the ground and die. The only thing that kept me from turning around, walking out the gate, and catching a cab straight to the airport was worry over what would happen to Betsy if Ren was left to look after her.

"No, I don't want any nuts, thank you. In fact, I'm not feeling so good. I might just go home."

But Tegan grabbed hold of my hand. "No way! You'll feel better once you've played a game of pool."

"I'm not sure about that," I mumbled, but it was too late. Twenty minutes later, I was bent over the pool table, embarrassing myself further. Fortunately, it turned out that hash wasn't the only frowned-upon substance Sayid dealt in, and I had a large glass of something questionable yet definitely alcoholic inside me. Yes, my throat still burned, but the pain was worth it.

"How do you even get it in the hole?" I asked as my ball careened off the sides of the table without hitting anything it was supposed to. Tegan had obviously had practice at both pool and Sayid's parties because she wielded her cue like a pro while taking the occasional drag on a funny-looking cigarette.

"Allow me to demonstrate," Ren said from far too close to my ear.

Oh, hell no!

He stretched over me, touching me in way too many places. Hip. Back. Shoulder. Arm. Hard in all the wrong ways. His hands wrapped around mine, and before my body could catch up with my mind and yell at him to get off, he helped me to pot a red and stepped back, grinning.

"There. That's how you do it. Now you try."

No. No, I didn't want to try. After Paul got arrested and I went to stay with Grandma, one thing she'd said always stuck with me. Give a man an inch, and he'd take a mile. Paul took a hundred damn miles, and I'd never let that happen again. Right now, I wasn't sure what Ren's game was, and I wasn't sure I wanted to find out either. Nor did I want his body plastered against mine.

Confrontation and I didn't mix well, so I did the only thing I knew how to do: dropped the pool cue and walked towards the gate, giving Sayid a halfhearted wave on the way.

"What's wrong?" Tegan called after me. "Ren, what did you do to her?"

"Nothing. I didn't do anything. Just helped her out with a pool shot."

"Tai? Wait up!"

But I didn't. I should have trusted my instincts and stayed at home in the first place, well away from arrogant Americans who liked to take liberties.

Phew. The door slammed behind me, and I collapsed onto the couch. Okay, so I'd embarrassed myself slightly, but that was still better than dealing with Ren. First he was rude, then he was pushy, and taken with alcohol, he made the wrong parts of me go all hot and tingly. The man left me off-kilter, and the more time I spent near him, the less I knew what to say or how to act.

"What did I say?"

Oh, dammit. I swivelled to find Ren standing in the doorway, one hand on either side of the door jamb. The flipping thing must have bounced back open instead of latching shut.

"Go back to Sayid's, would you?"

"No, I won't. I've obviously upset you, so I apologise, but unless you tell me what I did, I'll probably do it again because I'm a dick that way."

Fine. He wanted to know? Then me and whatever alcohol I just drank would tell him.

"You insulted me. You threatened my chicken. You exploded into my life, and now you're taking it over. And how did you know my name?"

"Your name? You told me."

"No, I told you my name was Tai, not Taisiya."

He looked puzzled for a moment. "Then I guess Tegan must've mentioned it."

Oh. "You were talking about me?"

He shrugged.

"Why do you ask so many questions?"

"Just curious, I guess. I thought women liked men to take an interest in them."

Not this one. Not anymore. When Paul first started hanging around, I'd been flattered. I'd answered his questions, and he'd taken all those bits of information he learned and used them to make my life a living hell.

"Trust me; they don't. Didn't you see how uncomfortable Tegan was earlier when you started interrogating her?"

"How well do you know Tegan?"

"There you go again."

"Come on, babe. How long you've known Tegan isn't exactly a state secret."

"So? What does it matter to you?

"Show and tell, Taisiya. You first."

Congratulations, Ren. You just leapfrogged Matthew Smart to take the number three spot on my list of most annoying people. And considering Paul and Peony headed up the leaderboard, that was saying something.

"How come you're always so frustrating?"

"Years and years of practice."

Gah! Part of me wanted to push Ren out of the door and lock it behind him, but *my* curiosity got the better of me.

"I met Tegan when I came to Luxor. I've known her for less than a week. Now spill. Why did you want to know that?"

Another shrug, and I itched to smack him. *Me.* Before I came to Luxor, I'd been a confirmed pacifist.

"Ren, you promised."

"It might be nothing. But then again..."

"Are you secretly a politician? Because you're really good at not answering questions."

"Tegan's Australian."

"I already noticed that."

"And what backpacker travels from Honduras to Russia to Cape Verde? They're not exactly near each other, nor are they typical tourist destinations."

"Maybe she wanted to experience different ways of life?"

"It's possible." But his tone said he didn't think it was likely. "The main thing that little collection of countries has in common is that none of them has an extradition treaty with Australia."

"Wait a minute... What are you saying?"

"That's it. That's all I'm saying."

"Are you suggesting Tegan's done something bad?"

"I'm saying that I'd be wary before I decided to trust her. And I'm only telling you that because... Never mind."

"What?"

Ren backed out the door, his earlier smile replaced by a frown. "Goodnight, Tai. And I really am sorry. I didn't mean to upset you earlier."

He vanished, leaving me alone save for a truckload of confusion. Was he serious? Was Tegan hiding something? Or was Ren the one with a secret, using Tegan's vacation habits to drive a wedge between her and me and further his own hidden agenda?

And more importantly, did I even want to know the answer to that question?

CHAPTER 13 - TAI

"TAI? IT'S RUSSELL. From the Winter Palace?"

He said it like I might not remember, but how could I forget? It wasn't every day a guy gave me free rein with his room service tab.

"How are you? Did you have a good weekend?"

Monday morning, and I'd survived twenty-four hours with Ren Fontana, but the urge to shove both him and his suitcase out of the gate hadn't diminished one little bit. What was all that stuff about Tegan last night? Chances were, Ren was only stirring, but now my curiosity had been piqued and I'd begun to wonder where Tegan came from and why exactly she'd left Australia to travel around that strange selection of countries. I'd googled them on my phone last night, and Honduras wouldn't be at the top of my travel bucket list, that was for sure. First, it had the world's highest murder rate, second, it had a region called the Mosquito Coast, and third, since the last presidential election, everyone had been arguing with everybody else, at least according to Twitter.

And then Tegan had gone to Costa Rica, but she'd skipped Nicaragua which lay in between? That made no sense. I decided to ask a few questions, but subtly, because right now, Tegan was one of the only two friends I had in Egypt. I didn't want to upset her by suggesting a lack of trust.

But she hadn't made an appearance so far this morning, and now I had Russell on the phone as I tried to relax on the terrace.

"My weekend?" he said. "Well... There was a security alert at one of our biggest clients, and the colleague who's covering for me got taken to hospital with suspected appendicitis."

Thank goodness I hadn't invited myself over last night. "That's terrible! Did you get the problem fixed?"

"Yes, yes. Quite enjoyed the challenge, actually. But it took me all of Saturday night and most of Sunday, so when my brother turned up yesterday evening, I could hardly keep my eyes open. And of course, he guessed I'd been working."

"Was he really annoyed?"

"He was about halfway through his lecture when I accidentally told him a female friend kept me awake for the whole night."

"What female friend?" I felt an irrational stab of jealousy, then realisation dawned. "Oh. Don't you think that's moving a bit fast?"

"It's not as if it actually happened."

"No, no, of course not. But he'll think I'm a loose woman."

Loose woman? I'd been reading too many historical romance novels.

"In my brother's world, sleeping with a woman on the first date is perfectly normal. Waiting a week is positively restrained. And speaking of my brother, he mentioned stopping by for a drink tonight, so if you're free..."

"You want me to come over?"

"Dinner at eight?"

An opportunity to escape from Ren? I hadn't seen him yet that day, but the walls between our apartments were disturbingly thin, and he'd woken me up at six thirty in the morning with a rendition of "Born in the USA" as he showered.

"At the Winter Palace? Sure."

"Excellent. Would you prefer to eat inside or out by the pool?"

Hmm... The gardens were beautiful, but the promise of air-conditioned luxury won out.

"Is inside okay?"

"I'll book a table. Do you want me to send a car and driver too?"

That was too much. "No, I'll be fine getting there on my own."

I'd barely finished the conversation when Tegan appeared behind me, carrying a plate of pastries.

"Was that your boyfriend?"

"Russell isn't my boyfriend."

"You've been out with him three times now."

"Tegan, one of those times, we literally interrupted his breakfast."

"He likes you."

"No, what we have is more of..." On second thoughts, I didn't want to tell Tegan about my arrangement with Russell, not when Ren had raised question marks over her character. "We're just friends. Are those cinnamon whirls?"

She held out the plate. "Here. Ren went out early and picked them up from the bakery."

Of course he did. Part of his charmy, smarmy campaign to make every woman in Luxor fall at his feet. Well, this girl would be staying firmly upright.

"Thanks." I bit into the flaky pastry, and I might have moaned. "This is yummy. I can't believe I had to come all the way to Egypt to taste food this good. The supermarket back home only sells dried-up, mass-produced things that taste like cardboard and sugar."

"Funny how people from wealthy countries look down on places like this, isn't it? Just because they don't have money. But they're rich in so many other ways—fresher food, a better sense of community, a willingness to help strangers."

"It'll be tough to leave."

"So you're planning to stick around for a while?"

"I'm not sure yet. How about you? When do you plan to go home?"

"Home? Home is each new place I travel to."

"I meant back to Australia."

"Not for a while. Probably a long time. I'd rather see the world."

"You said you were thinking of Oman next?"

"Maybe, but I hear it's very modern. Not much at all in the way of history. China's another option."

"China? What about the language barrier?"

Tegan half smiled, half grimaced. And if I wasn't mistaken, there was a hint of apprehension in her emerald eyes. But before I could probe any further, a door slammed, and Ren appeared around the corner of the building. Good grief.

"Did you forget to get dressed?"

He gestured at his board shorts and flip-flops. "Nope."

"What about your shirt?"

"It's hot."

"We're in a conservative country." All the men seemed to wear dresses, or at least jeans and shirts. "Do you seriously think it's a good idea to go out like that?"

"I'm not going out." He dropped onto the nearest sunlounger, and too late, I realised he had a book in his hand. *The Princess and her Rock Stars.* What the...?

"Did you take that out of my room?" Yes, it had the same dog-eared corner as the copy I'd brought with me from England.

"You left it out here on the table last night. I figured I'd better take it inside in case it rained."

"It rains here once every four freaking years." Or so the guy who ran the fruit stand at the market said.

Ren just shrugged. "Do women really like this stuff?"

Well, I wouldn't have bought it otherwise, would I? "Give it back."

"You're eating your breakfast. Don't worry; I'm a fast reader."

"You're also an asshole."

"Yup, that too."

If he carried on like this, he'd overtake Peony on my top-ten list of irritating people, especially now that I'd removed the email app from my phone and blocked her number. Ren Fontana made me want to throw things. At his stupid smug face.

"Fine, read it." He'd give up after half a dozen pages. I knew he was only doing this to annoy me. "You might learn something."

"I've already learned something. That it's cute how defensive you get over your choice of reading material."

Ugh. "Just leave me alone."

Ren would *not* ruin my breakfast. Pig. But when Tegan asked if I wanted to join her for coffee at the stall in the market, I was only too happy to get away from the arrogant American Idiot-with-a-capital-*I*. Why couldn't he take the hint that he wasn't wanted and go back to Dahab or the United States or anywhere else but Luxor?

It wasn't until later, after we'd got back and I escaped back into the sanctuary of my apartment, that I got curious and searched for Oman and China on my phone. Guess what? Neither of them had an extradition treaty with Australia.

I wasn't sure what to make of that.

After dealing with Ren, dinner with Russell was positively delightful. The dining room at the hotel was opulent if a little tired, and there was even a man in a tuxedo playing classical music on a grand piano in the corner. Another world compared to the street outside.

And the food tasted delicious. There was no pork because it was a Muslim country, and chicken was still off my personal menu, so I opted for lamb with pea-infused mashed potatoes and carrots while Russell went with fish. Somebody in that kitchen knew how to cook.

"Thank you for coming," he said. "I know it was short notice."

"Honestly, it's fine. I didn't have anything else on." Dullest life on earth, that was me. "And I wouldn't want you to get into trouble with your brother."

"Normally, he's not quite so bad, but our mother

called and gave him an earful yesterday. Apparently, she read an article saying scientists have found a correlation between time spent behind a computer screen and glioblastoma."

"Glio-what?"

"Brain cancer. I looked up the article, and it was obviously written by a charlatan."

"Can't you tell her that?"

"No, because I wrote an app that screens my calls and automatically diverts her to voicemail. And even if I answered, she wouldn't believe me."

"Wish I had that app. I uninstalled the email on my phone and blocked my sister's number, but I send my mum to voicemail manually. I did re-record the message to tell her I was fine, though."

Only because I didn't want her to call the police. It was funny how that little knot of tension that usually tugged at the base of my neck had loosened now that I wasn't constantly waiting for the next call chastising me for something or other.

"Want me to install it for you?" Russell asked.

"You'd do that?"

"Sure. Although you've given me an idea—I could write an extension that allows you to personalise a greeting for different callers."

"Wouldn't that be complicated?"

"I like a challenge."

"Do you sell the apps you write?"

He paused for a moment. "It's just a hobby. And with your email, you could probably set up rules to send messages you don't want to see to a separate folder rather than uninstalling the app completely,"

"Oh, I don't want to read *any* of my emails, so it's

not a problem."

"No email?" He breathed in sharply, as if the concept wasn't one he could bear. "Each to their own, I suppose. How are you enjoying Egypt so far?"

"Mostly, it's great. I mean, the change in culture takes some getting used to, but the locals have been really friendly, and it's fun exploring."

"But you said mostly—what don't you like?"

"Well, I found out my landlord deals drugs..."

"Sayid? My brother says he's harmless."

"He's always been nice, I suppose. But I also have a new neighbour, and he's driving me round the bend."

"In what way?"

"First, he laughed at my gold pants."

"Those baggy ones?" Russell looked as though he was struggling to keep a straight face himself. "Uh, I'm not really sure what to say to that."

"Okay, I admit they're ridiculous, but... Wait a second. You've never seen me in the gold pants."

"Uh, the concierge at the hotel may have mentioned them."

What were the chances of the ground opening up to swallow me? "Well, at least you're not laughing, because you're tactful. Ren isn't. Not one bit. Like this morning, when he borrowed my book without asking and made fun of it."

Yup, he'd stretched out on the sunlounger and laughed as he read lines aloud until I threw a glass of water over him. Not something to be proud of, I agree, but Ren Fontana rubbed me up the wrong way. Kind of like a balloon on hair, and I ended up all charged and crackly.

"Perhaps you could just avoid him?"

"Believe me, I'm trying. But enough of me griping..." I didn't want to ruin dinner by being a Moaning Minnie. "I'm thinking of taking a trip this week, and—"

Russell's phone buzzed from its spot beside his plate, and he swiped a finger over the screen then rolled his eyes.

"Now my brother's not coming over, after all. It seems the girl he met on a tour of Karnak temple this afternoon trumps the need to browbeat me with Mother's wisdom." Russell gave a sheepish smile. "Apologies. It seems I got you here under false pretences."

"Oh, it's fine. I don't mind at all, and the food's amazing. And the air conditioning."

The smile turned into a grin. "Good, then I won't feel too guilty. Sorry, what were you saying before my phone cut you off?"

What *was* I saying? Uh...got it.

"Just that I'm going to visit an archaeological dig on Thursday. A...well, he's not really a friend, but I sat next to a professor on the plane to Cairo, and he invited me."

"I'm sure you'll find it fascinating. I'm reading a book on the history of the area at the moment, and Thebes was at the forefront of Egyptian culture for thousands of years, especially during the eighteenth dynasty. Did you know the ancient Egyptians called it Waset?"

So Russell had an interest in history? Perhaps he'd like to come along? Purely for educational reasons, of course. I'd have to ask Miles if it was okay, obviously, but he'd been fine with me bringing Tegan. And although I didn't believe that rubbish about the brain cancer, some time outdoors might do Russell good. Should I invite him? Or would that seem weird?

CHAPTER 14 - TAI

THE MUSIC IN the Winter Palace changed to something more upbeat—was that Chopin? The pianist's fingers flew over the keys in a blur, and it struck me that he was wasted there in Luxor playing to an audience of twenty, most of whom were focused on their food. He should have been on a stage somewhere, dazzling a crowd with a full orchestra behind him.

But back to the dilemma at hand. I came to the realisation that I'd enjoyed this evening's dinner, and it had been a long while since I could say that about time spent with a man. Russell was kind and knowledgeable, and his quiet, easy company was a pleasant antidote to being bothered by the American Idiot. I'd look forward to exploring Egyptian history with him if he wanted to come.

"What are you doing on Thursday?"

"I don't have anything planned. Much depends on whether there's a crisis back in London. Why?"

"Me and Tegan are going to visit an archaeological dig, and the person running it said they've made some exciting discoveries. I just thought that if you were free..."

"You're inviting me along?"

I nodded, then forced myself to stop biting my lip. *Bad habit, Tai.* "I'd have to check with the professor in charge, but I think he'll be okay with it."

A slow smile spread over Russell's face. "Yes, I think I'd like that. Is it nearby?"

"The middle of nowhere, apparently, but there's a driver coming to pick us up from Sayid's at six."

"Six in the evening?"

"No, six in the morning."

Russell sucked in a breath, and his smile faded to a slight curve, something I could empathise with.

"You're not a morning person?" I asked.

"I'm a geek, Tai. Sure, I moonlight as a businessman, but underneath, I'm still the guy who stays up all night wired on caffeine then falls asleep over my keyboard as the sun rises."

"Do you want to change your mind? I won't be offended."

Just surprisingly disappointed. The petals on that little bud of happiness that had formed when Russell accepted my invite turned brown and crispy around the edges. Then plumped up again when he shook his head.

"No, you've intrigued me now. I'll drown myself in coffee before I leave the hotel."

The tempo of the music slowed again, this time to a melancholy tune that tugged at the ribbons of my soul. I'd heard it before, but I couldn't remember where.

"You like this?" Russell asked. "It's Albinoni's 'Adagio in G minor.'"

"Yes, I—" A shudder started in my belly and ran through every limb as I recalled where I'd last heard the piece. With Paul. Back before I realised he was unhinged, he'd taken me to a posh restaurant where it was playing in the background. He'd kissed my hand, then insisted on holding it across the table while the poor waiter tried to work out where to put our food. "Sorry. The song itself is beautiful, but it brings back bad memories."

"Someone you lost?"

"No. Well, yes, but I wanted to lose him."

"The stalker?"

"Yes."

Russell leaned forward, elbows on the table. His brown eyes shimmered in the light from the candle flickering in its old-fashioned glass-and-brass holder, and then he smiled. Not the polite, reserved smile I'd been getting until now, but an achingly sweet grin.

"Do you dance, Tai?"

"What? Why?"

He nodded towards the room behind me, and I turned to see a handful of couples on a tiny wooden dance floor, turning in time to the music. Tonight, this place... It was as if I'd stepped back a hundred years to the haughty traditions of the British Empire, so formal and ridiculously elegant. I was glad I'd made an effort and put on the cocktail dress I'd bought on impulse at the airport, even if Ren had given me an incredulous look as I'd hurried out the gate in it earlier.

"The best way to ease the burden of bad memories is to replace them with new ones."

"You sound as though you speak from experience?"

A tiny shrug, then he held out a hand. "Join me?"

"Do you know how to dance?"

"One of the benefits of my ridiculously expensive private-school education."

His hand felt cool compared to my sweaty palms, and I let him lead me over to the parquet floor. What was this? Russell taking pity on me? An attack of nostalgia? Or was this business dinner turning into more of a date? Right now, I didn't know, but I also didn't want to overthink things.

Russell positioned my left hand on his shoulder, settled his right hand onto my back, and then took my other hand in his. He radiated confidence, whereas my legs had turned into overcooked spaghetti noodles and my heart was trying to crawl up my throat.

"I should probably mention that my dancing experience is limited to a year of ballet when I was younger, and I fell over on stage in the one and only show I performed in. My sister's the dancer in the family."

"Don't worry; I've got tough toes. Just follow my lead."

Between Russell's gentle guidance and murmured instructions, I managed a passable waltz then came close to murdering a quickstep. But it was enjoyable. Not once did he make me feel inadequate, and if my stupid red stilettos hadn't rubbed blisters on my heels, I could have carried on all night.

"You're giving up?" Russell asked.

"I have to, or I won't be able to walk tomorrow. But thank you. I honestly didn't think I'd have this much fun."

Russell had kept his distance all evening, making sure to leave a small but significant gap between the two of us as he twirled me around. Either he wasn't interested in anything more than dancing, or he sensed that I'd had a difficult past and wanted to respect that. I knew which option I was hoping for, and when he guided me back towards our table with a hand on the small of my back, I allowed myself a tiny smile. I'd missed sharing that closeness with a man, even if I did appreciate taking things slow. With Paul, I'd jumped in far too quickly then faced the consequences.

"I'll have the staff call you a car," Russell said, reaching out to tuck a stray lock of hair behind my ear the way Miles had on the plane. Two very different men, both of whom had touched my life in different ways. Russell didn't make a move to sit down. A snap of his fingers, a few whispered words, and the maître d' scurried off. "It's late, and you need to get home safely."

"What time is it?"

"Almost midnight."

I hadn't noticed until that moment, but we were the last couple left in the restaurant, and although the pianist was still smiling, he probably wanted to go home before he fell asleep at the keys.

"Thank you. I..." What to say? I didn't want to come across as too needy when I still wasn't sure of Russell's intentions. "I had a great time."

"So did I. It wasn't quite how I'd imagined this evening going, but I'm glad my brother stood us up."

A giggle escaped. "Ah, your mysterious brother."

"He does exist, I swear. It wasn't just a ploy for me to get a pretty girl to have dinner with me."

Pretty? Russell thought I was pretty? But I'd always been the plain one.

"Maybe your mum's right and the computer screen's made your eyes go funny."

"Don't put yourself down, Tai. Somebody ruined your self-confidence, and I'd like to see you get it back."

What was I supposed to say to that? I opened my mouth. Closed it again in a passable imitation of a goldfish. Then a waiter saved me by popping into our field of view.

"Mr. Wise? Your car's ready."

"Wise," I repeated almost to myself as the waiter melted away. "That seems appropriate."

"It's actually pronounced Vice. W-e-i-s-z. But I've given up trying to explain that."

"Unpronounceable names. Something we've got in common."

"Besides an interest in history and a desire to be left alone by do-gooders? Yes."

That hand came back, and Russell guided me towards the lobby. I half wished he'd switch direction and head for his bedroom instead, but the moment I had that thought, I chided myself for being harebrained. Apart from paying me the odd compliment and a very chaste dancing lesson, he hadn't shown any interest in me outside of simple friendship. Either he was extraordinarily reserved or there was nothing there.

A battered white car waited by the front of the hotel, and the driver leapt out to open the back door as we approached. Russell's hand dropped to his side as he stopped a foot away from me.

"Do you want me to ride back with you?"

"No, I'll be fine. It's only a five-minute trip."

"Well, goodnight."

That was it. "I'll text you about Thursday."

"Let me know you get back safely?"

"Sure. Of course."

He retreated into the hotel as the car pulled away, and I felt oddly bereft. It was only a meal with a sort-of friend, for crying out loud. What was wrong with me? I'd come to Egypt to escape, not to get tangled up with a guy again. After Paul, I'd vowed never again to get into a position where a man could hurt me, and I needed to keep that promise.

Dinner. That's all it was.

The cab dropped me off outside Sayid's, and when I tried to pay the driver, he waved me away.

"Already on Mr. Wise's account." He gave me a toothy grin. "Even the tip. Mr. Wise very generous."

"Okay, if you're sure."

"Goodnight, Miss."

I tapped out a text as I walked through the gate, careful not to let it clang shut and wake the others.

Me: I'm back. Thank you again for dinner, and you didn't have to pay for the cab.

I tripped up the step to the terrace, only to clutch at my chest when I saw the silhouette of a man sitting at the table in front of my apartment. The phone flew out of my hand, and Ren caught it.

"What the hell are you doing here?" I demanded.

"Waiting to check you got back safely."

"You almost gave me a heart attack."

"Why are you so jumpy?"

"Anyone would freak out if there was a stranger sitting in the dark outside their door."

"It's not dark." He pointed at the candle in front of him, and I noticed one of my books was beside it, splayed open. "You should be more aware of your surroundings."

"Are you seriously reading that?"

He scrunched his mouth to one side, the flickering flame highlighting the peaks and valleys of his face. Eyes that had changed from amber in the sun to a dark, antique gold. A straight nose, almost too delicate for the rest of his features. A five o'clock shadow—a.m. not p.m.

"I thought it would be shit, but it's weirdly addictive."

My cheeks heated as I recalled the content of *The Princess and her Rock Stars*. How far through had Ren got? A little over halfway, by the look of things, which meant he'd read the rather graphic threesome between the lead guitarist, the drummer, and sweet, innocent Melody. Oh, hell.

"Uh, I-I-I wouldn't know. It's not like I've ever gone to bed with two men at once."

Ren chuckled, soft and irritating. "I meant rock music."

Oh. "You're such an asshole."

"Noted. But perhaps you should try the three-way—it might loosen you up a bit."

If I'd been a goldfish with Russell earlier, now I turned into a stranded carp. "You... You..."

"Hey, don't knock it till you've tried it."

My fists balled up in a reflex reaction. Ren Fontana made my blood run hot. Boiling even. But then I thought back to how I'd felt when I read that scene, and some of that blood ran south and pooled where it absolutely shouldn't have. I clenched my thighs together and willed my pulse to steady.

"Have... Have *you* tried it?"

The legs of the chair scraped over the flagstones as Ren got up slowly, deliberately, every movement smooth and controlled. He was the calm to my washing-machine-on-spin-cycle. Then he leaned in close, close enough that I swore I felt the brush of his lips on my earlobe.

"What do you think, Taisiya?"

CHAPTER 15 - TAI

ON ANY NORMAL day, the air conditioner in my apartment was perfectly adequate. But it was no match for a nightmare. And although I woke shuddering with one traitorous hand wedged between my legs, I still classed it as a nightmare because it had starred a man I most definitely shouldn't have been thinking of that way. Eight hours later, I could still feel his lips on my ear, the suave git. Still hear the whisper of his words as he wound me up. Had Ren had a three-way? Probably. He most likely made both women do all the work.

After I slammed the door behind me last night, I'd tossed my phone onto the sofa, which was a dumb thing to do because now I needed to drag myself out of bed so I could fetch it and text Miles. Except before I could tap out a message, I had to read the new one I'd received. Last night, from the time stamp. At two a.m.

Russell: Tai, will you come for dinner with me again?

So soon?

Me: Did your brother reschedule?

While I was on my feet, I put the kettle on to boil because even though I'd been in bed for ages, it was a restless sleep and I didn't feel refreshed. Caffeine would help with that. This morning's stupid thought? I bet they served filter coffee at the Winter Palace.

Me: Hi Miles, just wondering if it's possible to bring another friend to the dig on Thursday? He's British too, and he's very interested in the history of the area. Tai.

A single one-word answer came back: *No.* For one nerve-racking, horrifying second, I thought it was from Miles and I'd need to have an awkward conversation with Russell, but then I realised it was Russell who'd replied.

No.

No, his brother hadn't rescheduled? Then why...? Did he want to see me for another reason? A *date* sort of a reason? My pulse sped up, drumming a heady rhythm of fear and excitement as I checked Russell off against my list of past disasters. He had money, which meant he wasn't using me because he'd run out of food while he waited for the next instalment of his student loan to arrive. I didn't currently have a washing machine either. Russell didn't seem the type to ask the dull girl out for a bet, and most importantly, he didn't give off the slightly creepy, intrusive vibes that Paul had left behind him like a dog shedding hair. Just in case, I peered through the glass panel in the front door. No over-the-top bouquet or confectionery or gift voucher for a couple's massage waiting on the doorstep, thank goodness. And although I hadn't checked my email recently, I was fairly sure I wouldn't find a shaky video of him jerking off to a photo of me he'd snapped when I wasn't looking.

No, today there was just my copy of *Rock Stars* propped up against the citronella candle on the table. If any man in my life right now was behaving inappropriately, it was Ren Fontana.

Me: Yes, I'd love to come for dinner. Tonight?

Hmm... I scrubbed "love" out and replaced it with "like" before I hit send. Paul had left me paranoid about giving off the wrong signals.

Russell: Tomorrow? My brother wants to watch a bad action movie with me on his boat tonight.

Miles: Sure, that's fine. The jeep's got plenty of space.

Phew.

I fired off a quick thank-you to Miles then caught myself smiling as I replied to Russell.

Me: Tomorrow's good. Shall I meet you at the hotel again? And everything's sorted for Thursday morning.

Russell: I'll come to you. Seven o'clock? Think we'll both need an early night.

Me: Perfect :)

Well, almost perfect. I still had today to get through, which meant buying groceries and a trip to the laundry—all the glamorous stuff. Oh, and trying not to kill Ren. That might be the biggest challenge. Since he was nowhere to be seen, I slipped outside and retrieved *Rock Stars*, and no, I didn't care whether he'd finished it or not. Ren could find his own damn reading material. *The Chauvinist's Guide to Chivalry*, for example.

I was done being nice.

"Where's Ren?" I asked Tegan over lunch.

I said I was done being nice, not nosy, okay?

"Who knows? He went out really early. Like, before

five."

"But he was awake until after midnight."

Tegan shrugged then helped herself to a banana. We'd decided on a simple lunch that didn't involve cooking—pastries and fruit with lumpy white yogurt that didn't taste of an awful lot.

"He doesn't seem to sleep much," she said.

"Really? Uh, how do you know? You haven't...?

Because that could be super-awkward.

"What? Spent the night with him? I wish. He just doesn't seem interested. Sure, he flirts and stuff, but nothing more. Still, it's probably for the best."

"Why? Because he's so full of himself?"

"No, because I strongly suspect he'd ruin me for all other men, and there's also an element of shitting in my own backyard. But enough about Ren—what's happening with you and Russell? If you know Ren was still up at midnight, you must've come back late."

"Not much happened. We had dinner. We danced. It was nice."

"You danced. What, like at a club? I thought you were going to the Winter Palace?"

"The Winter Palace has a dance floor. And a pianist. Russell taught me how to dance the waltz."

"That's...that's...kind of old-fashioned, don't you think?"

"Yes, but he seems to be a real gentleman, and I like that about him."

And being old-fashioned was far better than being pushy. I thought back to last night, to how Russell had held me gently and oh-so-chastely. Almost reverently. Whereas Ren struck me as the type who'd leave bruises, both on a girl's skin and her heart.

And the thought of being that girl scared me. Even if Paul hadn't done his worst, hadn't broken my spirit, I'd probably still have stuck to the safe options. A night in front of the TV instead of speed dating. Korma instead of vindaloo. A black dress instead of red. The fact that I'd ended up in Egypt on this crazy adventure still puzzled me. I blamed it on a momentary loss of sanity.

"Well, each to her own," Tegan said. "Are you going out with him again?"

"On Wednesday. For dinner, but he didn't say where."

"Lucky you. I've got a ton of work to catch up on before Thursday. At least there's a bit of cloud today so I can sit outside."

"Want me to take any of your clothes to the laundry guy?"

"Would you mind? I'll love you forever."

After lunch, Sayid turned up with a tiny wooden house for Betsy so she'd have some shade, and he wouldn't accept a penny in payment, even though he did rib me about keeping dinner as a pet. He'd made the chicken house himself out of an old crate, by the looks of it, and Betsy waddled in and out in between scratching in the dirt and begging for snacks—grapes, tomatoes, sunflower seeds I bought from the supermarket... No, she wasn't spoiled in the slightest.

Those two days, carefree hours spent pottering around my apartment, lying in the garden reading and daydreaming of Russell while Tegan beavered away on her graphics tablet, and all with no sign of Ren—those days reminded me why I'd escaped from England in the first place.

The sun shone, the world went on quietly beyond the gates, and the sweet-acrid scent of whatever Sayid was smoking drifted over the wall whenever I needed a reminder of my rebellion. Life was good. Short-term, the future looked rosy, and long-term? Well, I didn't want to think about that part just yet.

"I hope you like Italian," Russell said when I showed him into my apartment.

Pizza? As a student with a discount card, I'd practically lived on the stuff when I wasn't making ramen noodles in a mug. But I wasn't sure Domino's was quite what Russell had in mind, so I just nodded because I hated to sound like a heathen.

"Very much. Where are we going?"

"Treviso at the Sonesta Hotel. Which'll be a welcome relief after last night."

"How was the movie?"

"Loud. I'm not really one for guns. There's quite enough violence in the world without perpetuating it through stereotypes. And my brother insisted on smoking Sayid's finest while he gave me a second-hand lecture from Mother on how I should get out more. Honestly, I sometimes wonder how we're even related."

"He sounds like he'd get on well with my stepsister and her holier-than-thou attitude. The only good thing about going on holiday with her is that nobody talks to me. She scares them all off."

"Then they're missing out."

"Were you always this sweet?"

"No, I learned it at school."

"Your fancy private school?"

"Indeed. Being sweet was on the timetable along with Latin, cello lessons, and teaching us to speak with a plummy accent. Sadly, my brother spent most of the time in detention."

"And you were always well-behaved?"

Russell flashed me a grin. "No, I was just too smart to get caught. Shall we walk or get a cab? The Sonesta's only ten minutes away on foot."

"Then let's walk."

He offered me his elbow, and I looped my arm through his. Not quite hand-holding, but it was a start. And he'd dressed smartly in flannel slacks and a collared shirt. I only had the one cocktail dress with me —strange, huh?—but I'd found a maroon shift dress in my work things and worn that with a pair of low heels comfortable enough for an evening stroll.

The sun dropped below the west bank of the Nile in a spectacular show of pinks and oranges and yellows visible between the hotels as we walked parallel to the water's edge. Taxis sputtered past, and the drivers of at least twenty caleches with their jingling brass medallions stopped to see whether we wanted a ride, seemingly incredulous when we said we'd rather walk.

"Here we are," Russell said. "Aside from the Winter Palace, this is my favourite place to eat in Luxor."

And it didn't disappoint. No pianist, but good food and better company made it hands down the best date I'd ever been on. Russell was a whole different kettle of fish to the boys I'd been out with in the past. It was as if I'd graduated from a class I didn't realise I'd taken and gained access to a whole different pool of men. In just two short weeks, being abroad had begun to change me, and I liked the person I was becoming. Adventurous Tai, always up for new experiences and willing to take a chance on the scary things in life, such as talking to guys who were way out of her league.

When Russell walked me back at the end of the evening, new Tai leaned in a little closer outside the apartment gate, looking up, smiling, and hoping, hoping, hoping for a kiss.

And I got one.

Well, a peck on the cheek, but it was better than nothing, right? Rome wasn't built in a day and all that. Better to take things slowly and lay a solid foundation than have everything topple over into a messy heap at the end. Or worse, end up in freaking court. Again.

"See you tomorrow morning?" I asked, taking a step back.

"I look forward to it."

"You've got your shirt on inside-out," Tegan whispered.

"What? Oh."

See? This was why I didn't get up early in the mornings. At least she noticed before Russell arrived, or that could have been embarrassing. I scooted inside to change as an engine purred outside the gates. Ten to freaking six. My eyes kept closing all of their own accord.

The only saving grace was that Russell looked like I felt. Slightly rough around the edges, and he clutched a Thermos flask of coffee as if his life depended on it.

"Morning."

"Yes," he mumbled. "It is. I'm early. I don't know

how I'm early."

No, Russell definitely wasn't a morning person. He'd cut himself shaving by the looks of things, and his flies were undone. Should I say something? This was always so awkward. If I mentioned it, he'd know I'd been looking, but if I didn't... Ugh.

The rattle of an approaching vehicle saved me from making a decision for a moment, and an ancient jeep appeared around the corner. Was this for us? I mean, how was it still running? The thing dated back at least three decades and seemed to be held together with rust and stickers advertising every store in town. A radio in the front footwell blasted out a call to prayer as the driver stopped in a cloud of dust, hopped out, and turned off the engine. Wow. He'd even brought his own prayer mat, which was far more organised than I would have been at that hour.

"Good morning. I'm Aqueel." He gave us a wave before dropping to his knees. "Please excuse me."

Tegan hopped into the front passenger seat while he prayed, leaving the back for Russell and me. Which was lovely as long as he didn't think it was premeditated.

"Is it far?" he asked when Aqueel climbed back in. I understood what he really meant: will the jeep make it that far?

"One hour, inshallah. Or two hours. Please, you need to help with holding the roof on for the fast parts."

Holding the roof on? I glanced up at the canvas flapping on the metal frame. Good grief.

Could this get any worse?

Yes, it turned out it could. Aqueel twisted the key in the ignition once, twice, three times, and on each attempt, the engine sputtered and died. Then the cherry on top—Ren jogged along the street, all muscles and sweat and cocky grin, looking far perkier than should have been legal at that time of day.

"Got a problem, guys?"

Aqueel shrugged, hit the dashboard, and tried again. Nothing. "This has never happened before," he muttered.

Now *that* I found hard to believe.

"We're supposed to be going to visit an archaeological dig," Tegan told Ren, disappointment clouding her voice. "Except it seems like we'll be going back to bed instead."

He peered in through the back window. "Some people look as if they'd be happy about that."

Oh, hell. It was too early to deal with Ren. I scrambled out of the car, gritting my teeth.

"We'll be fine, so if you just want to go inside—"

"Do you smell that?"

"Smell what?"

"Petrol." I followed his gaze to the back of the vehicle, where a dark stain was spreading across the dusty road. "I'm not a mechanic, but I'd say you've got a problem with the fuel system."

So that meant we were basically sitting on a giant bomb. Brilliant. Thursday was officially the new Monday. I'd dragged everyone out of bed at stupid o'clock, and now we couldn't even go anywhere.

"How about we take a cab?" Russell suggested, joining me outside the car. Funnily enough, the others soon followed.

Aqueel shook his head. "Need jeep. Too rocky."

"Want me to give you a ride?" Ren asked.

I couldn't help rolling my eyes. "In what?"

"My SUV."

"You've only been here for four days. Where did you get an SUV from?"

"Rented it. I like having wheels." He glanced down at Russell. "Zipper, buddy. You're Tai's friend?"

Russell turned red and scrambled for his flies. "That's right." Once he was decent, he offered a hand, polite as always. "Russell Weisz."

"Renato Fontana. Ren. I live with Tai and Tegan."

"He rents an apartment next door," I hurried to clarify, just to emphasise the fact that I was in no way associated with our unwanted guest.

"She's mentioned you, yes."

"Oh?" For the first time ever, Ren looked uncertain. Did he realise what a dick he could be?

"Only in passing." Russell sidestepped the implied question neatly. "Tai, what's it to be? Do you want to go with Ren?"

An excellent question. Did I? Saying no would mean we'd all woken up pointlessly, plus we'd be letting down Miles who'd most likely cleared a spot in his schedule for us. Not to mention the fact that I'd been looking forward to seeing a real archaeological dig, and Tegan seemed keen too. Russell would probably want to go back to his hotel and work.

But accepting Ren's offer would mean I had to spend the day with him because we could hardly send him back and expect him to pick us up later. A big drawback.

I sighed, because although I knew I had to be gracious and say yes to the American Idiot, I wanted him to know I was doing it under duress.

"Thank you, Ren. It's very kind of you to take us."

CHAPTER 16 - TAI

"WHAT HAPPENED TO the jeep?" Miles asked when we arrived in—literally—the middle of nowhere.

He hadn't been kidding about the remoteness of the place. After we crossed the Nile and branched off the main road through some fields and up an old dried-up river bed, the only sign of life I'd seen until we arrived at the dig was a guy walking with two camels in the distance. We'd spent over an hour bouncing through ruts and swerving around rocks, and while I admit I'd wanted to get closer to Russell, being wedged between him and Tegan while Ren tested the off-road capabilities of his jeep wasn't quite what I'd had in mind. At least Ren had hired a decent vehicle. The Land Cruiser was well-dented on the outside, but it appeared to be mechanically sound, and almost as importantly, the AC worked.

"Jeep broken," Aqueel told Miles. "Sayid will fix it."

Aqueel had spent half the trip jabbering away on the phone, and it seemed Sayid did more than rent apartments and sell hash. He was a jack of all trades, and if he couldn't solve a problem himself, he knew somebody who could.

"Did he say how long?" Miles asked.

"Maybe a day. Maybe a week."

Miles just laughed as he turned to face me.

"Welcome to Egypt, where nothing is ever certain. I'm glad you made it."

"So are we. I hope it's okay that there's an extra person. Our neighbour offered to drive."

"Not a problem. So, who have we got?"

"This is Tegan and Russell, and the driver's Ren."

Cue handshakes all around. When Ren stretched his arms above his head, I noticed Miles taking a good look at his abs, but he quickly refocused on Ren's face before anyone else saw.

"Have we met before?" Miles asked him.

"I only arrived in Luxor on Sunday."

"Really? You look familiar."

"I've just got one of those faces."

One of those faces? The only place Ren wouldn't stick out was in a line-up between Christian Bale and Henry Cavill, so unless Miles made a habit of hanging out with superheroes...

"I've never been very good at remembering people. Too much time spent with my head in books."

"Unless it's the pharaohs all the way from the predynastic period to the Ptolemaic dynasty," a voice said, and I turned to see a petite brunette approaching. Sun glinted off her wire-framed glasses, and even at this early hour, the smudges of dirt on her clothing suggested she'd been working for a while. "Miles can name every single one in order, and their families too."

"Meet Caroline," Miles said. "My second in command. She's an expert on the nineteenth and twentieth dynasties."

"All the Ramesses. One through eleven. Although Ramesses VIII only ruled for a year, so he barely counts."

"Caroline comes from New York, she got her doctorate at Cambridge, and now she lectures at Harvard and Stanford in between fieldwork."

"Sometimes, I really miss having AC," she quipped. "But this is without a doubt the most interesting site I've ever worked on. Every day, we discover something new."

I took a moment to look around. We were standing in a dusty bowl surrounded by craggy cliffs, a natural amphitheatre if you like. The boulders strewn around reminded me of the surface of Mars, except a lighter colour. Stark. That was a good description.

"What have you found so far?" I asked.

Miles took over again. "First, I should tell you a bit about the site. As far as we can ascertain, it was a village for labourers working on the tombs in the Theban Necropolis—the valleys of the kings, queens, nobles, and workers, plus the various mortuary temples in the area. Probably the best known of those is the Temple of Hatshepsut. Have you had a chance to visit it yet?"

"Not so far."

"Then you're in for a treat. It's fascinating. Simply fascinating. Anyhow, most of the labourers in the eighteenth to twentieth dynasties, which is the time period we're concerned with here, lived closer to the action, so to speak, in Deir el-Medina, or Set-Maat as it was known back then. The place of truth."

"What was this place called?"

"Tu-ra al-Nahhasin, which means the caves of the copper workers. But we've shortened it to al-Nahas, which is slightly more manageable."

"Copper," Caroline translated.

"Did the ancient Egyptians use copper, then?" I asked.

"Tons of the stuff," Miles said. "Gold gets all the publicity, but copper was the staple. The workhorse of metals. They used it to make pots and pans for cooking, plus tools for agriculture and crafts. Egyptian copper was mined in the Sinai, and it contained relatively high traces of natural arsenic, which made it particularly hard."

"Didn't that poison them? I mean, if they were using it for cooking?"

"The fumes during the production process probably did more harm. But the Egyptians were most likely the first group to discover that alloying it with tin to make bronze had the same effect—a harder metal that could be more easily sharpened into a blade. Most of the tin was imported from Cyprus or Crete. They were prolific traders, and at one point, copper was used as currency as well. Not coins, but by weight. Come, come."

Miles beckoned us to follow him, and I fell into step beside Caroline as we passed a collection of drab huts made from wonky mud bricks baked hard in the sun. One had a washing line outside, and colourful garments fluttered in the breeze.

"Do you *live* here?" I asked her.

"You sound surprised."

"I guess I just figured you'd stay in a hotel and travel here each day like we did. I mean, it's so...so..."

"Isolated? Primitive? Hot?"

"Yes, all of that."

"Archaeology doesn't pay enough for us to stay in fancy hotels. We do this for the love, not the money. And sleeping here's the most practical option. Better for security, and we don't waste hours driving through the desert each day."

"Security? Do people steal stuff?"

"There's always been a thriving black market for antiquities. The first tomb raiders appeared right after the first pharaoh was buried. It's how we discovered this place, in fact. Exquisite old copper artifacts kept popping up in strange places, and when the staff at the Ministry of Antiquities investigated, it led back to a Bedouin who'd discovered a small cache of tools buried by that rock over there." Caroline waved her hand at the far side of the hollow. "One of his goats unearthed it, apparently."

"How did you get involved?"

"I did a couple of joint lectures with Miles at Stanford a while ago, and when the Minister for Antiquities wanted to know whether he'd consider heading up the dig, he asked if I'd be interested in joining him. Of course, I jumped at the chance. This is the opportunity of a lifetime." She touched my arm and veered towards one of the huts. "Here, take a look inside. It's not that bad."

When I watched Indiana Jones, the life of an archaeologist always seemed like one big adventure, but here was the reality. A narrow doorway I had to stoop to go through, and a one-room home with a cot to sleep on and a single chest of drawers. A large copper bowl on top beside a jug of water reminded me of an old Victorian wash set.

Caroline saw me looking. "We do have showers and proper flushing toilets, but they're in a trailer on the other side of the camp. Sometimes when I'm tired, it's easier to clean up quickly here. Plus we always need to conserve water. It gets trucked in once a week and stored in a tank. But we have a generator for electricity, and last year, a German student visited on a working vacation and rigged up a satellite dish so we can watch TV in the dining room."

Woven mats covered the floor, and a beanbag chair sat in one corner. The walls were covered in photos—Caroline with friends, old-looking trinkets, and various half-dug holes with objects sticking out of the dirt.

"I like to keep a record of everything," she said. "My ex-boyfriend always said I lived too much in the past, but the past shapes our future, don't you think?"

My past had certainly impacted mine, mostly for the worse, although I was determined to change that. "In some ways. What's with all the cushions?"

While the rest of the hut was stark, utilitarian, the cot had a silky pink cover and half a dozen tasselled throw-pillows. Caroline struck me as the practical type, and they didn't seem to match her style.

Her ski-jump nose crinkled as she giggled. "Oh, those are from Miles's boyfriend. He's always sending care packages. You should see Miles's room—it's basically a branch of Pottery Barn."

"That's really generous."

"Bradley's a real sweetheart, but he's not always practical. He tried to send us a Jacuzzi last year, and then there was all the melted chocolate..."

"Caroline?" Miles called from outside. "We're moving on to H27."

"On our way," she shouted back. "H27 is one of our outside trenches. They've each got a number."

"What does the H stand for?"

"Hot."

She wasn't kidding. The sun was rising, and even though someone had set up a canopy over the hole to give a bit of shade, the heat gathered underneath like a budget sauna. Sweat dripped down my back, and I wafted my T-shirt for some cool air before I realised that looked stupid and stopped myself. Russell didn't seem too comfortable in his chinos either, and Tegan swigged from her bottle of water like an alcoholic who'd just found gin. Only Ren appeared at home in the heat, with his board shorts and fancy wraparound sunglasses. At least he'd worn hiking boots in a nod to practicality.

"This is our current project," Miles said, pointing into the hole, which had to be twenty metres long. It varied in depth, but there was nothing haphazard about it. Each section had perfectly perpendicular sides and a level bottom, as if somebody had checked every measurement with a spirit level. Caroline hopped down a series of steps carved into the hard-packed dirt at one end, and as we watched, she picked up a small trowel and gently scraped away at a patch of sandy soil.

"We think that may be a pot of some sort," Miles said, crouching to take a better look. "See that dark patch? That's the handle."

"How old is it?" Russell asked. "The eighteenth dynasty started in 1550 BC, didn't it?"

"Indeed it did. You have an interest in archaeology?"

"Only what I've learned since I got here. I took a tour of Karnak temple then started reading up on the history of the area."

"And what a rich history it is. I've been studying the subject my whole life, and Luxor beats every other site hands down."

Tegan raised an eyebrow. "Even the pyramids?"

"As individual monuments, they're certainly spectacular, but Luxor's history covers a much longer period, and even though most of the tombs were ransacked years ago, there are still places like this that can tell us so much about daily life. Just think—over three thousand years ago, a woman stood where you are, preparing dinner for the men returning from their daily toil."

"What did they eat?"

"Bread and beer were their staples."

"Beer?" Ren said. "I was born in the wrong century."

"Yes, but it wasn't beer as you'd know it. This was thick, more like a milkshake, and it didn't have a very high alcohol content. Think of it as one of those meal-replacement shakes you get nowadays. Even back then, the water from the Nile wasn't clean, so they had to adapt to their environment and avoid drinking it."

"You mentioned caves earlier. As in 'the caves of the copper workers?' Did they sit in those to keep cool?"

"That's right. The caves are in those cliffs behind you, and they also used them for storage and accommodation. Some of them have paintings on the walls, although many of those have been ruined over the years by graffiti."

"Can we see inside them?"

"We'll save those for last—that way, everyone's grateful to get out of the heat."

Miles carried on around the rest of the site, stopping at a larger hut to show us a collection of the objects they'd dug up so far. Pottery, water vessels, dishes, a necklace inlaid with turquoise, a saw, amulets, a cracked bronze mirror, and small cylindrical stones with spheres on the top that were apparently part of an ancient Egyptian board game called Senet. Tegan in particular seemed riveted, sticking hot on his heels and hanging onto his every word.

He handed her a small figurine. "This is the pharaoh Ay. He ruled from 1324 to 1320 BC, so this little guy is older than much of the Bible."

"Wow."

"And here, Tai, we have the engraved cartouche of Ramesses IV." I turned the small black pot he passed me over in my hands, examining the symbols. "It was in his reign that Egyptian power started to decline. This canopic jar was most likely meant for one of his subjects."

"What's a canopic jar?"

"They used them to store the internal organs of the dead for their journey to the afterlife." I almost dropped the flipping thing, but thankfully, Miles quickly took it and set it back on the shelf. "We don't believe this one was used."

"What do you think?" I whispered to Russell as we headed for the caves. "I had no idea how they lived until now."

"It's intriguing. And humbling. As a man who suffers from palpitations if I don't have a phone signal, it's intriguing how they managed to do so much with so little." He glanced back at the camp. "How they still do. It makes me feel guilty for staying in the Winter Palace."

"I guess when you're passionate about something, you'll do anything in pursuit of your goal."

"Do you have a goal, Tai?"

I'd never thought about it in such black-and-white terms before. No, I didn't have a goal, not since I'd escaped from Garrett-Hart. Perhaps that was why my life felt so aimless?

"I do now. My goal is to set a goal."

Russell laughed as we walked into the first cave, and Miles was right. The cool shadows were a welcome respite to the fast-growing heat outside. And it was bigger than I thought. The space opened up into a large cavern beyond the entrance, a strange cross between nature's hand and the efforts of man. A flat floor covered in soft sand, sides decorated with hieroglyphics, and a ceiling too smooth to be natural. Lights had been set up, strung along both sides on metal stands, and I couldn't see all the way to the back.

"Quite something, isn't it?" Miles said. "It looks as though they exploited a natural fissure in the rock and enlarged it into what we see today. The entrance was entirely blocked by boulders when we first arrived."

I stopped to study a piece of artwork on the wall, a collection of perfectly preserved hieroglyphics and figures clustered around a set of scales held by Anubis, the dog-headed god. My fingers itched to touch it, but that would have felt somehow sacrilegious.

"It's a spell," Caroline said. "The first known depiction of the 'weighing of the heart.' The gods judged the actions of the deceased while they were alive against the ideals under the Maat—the ancient Egyptian concepts of truth, balance, order, harmony, law, morality, and justice. If they were considered worthy, their soul was released to the afterlife."

I stepped back, and too late, I realised Ren was

right behind me. First, I trod on his foot, then I tripped in my haste to get away from him. His hands seared into my hips as he steadied me.

"Easy, babe. It's not that scary." He turned to Caroline. "What happened if they failed the test? They went to hell?"

"Worse. They ceased to exist at all. For the Egyptians and their obsession with life after death, that was a far worse fate." Caroline grinned. "And they also weighed the heart literally then put it back."

Ick. That was actually worse than the canopic jars. The ancient Egyptians sure did have some strange ideas, although I suppose they seemed totally rational back in those days.

"Hey, what's down there?" Ren asked, pausing to peer along a side passage as we hurried to catch up with the others.

Caroline didn't stop. "Uh, nothing. A dead end. These caves are full of them. Do you both have enough water? It's important not to get dehydrated."

Mum had always lectured me on the importance of drinking enough, so I had plenty. "Still got half a bottle left."

"Good, good. Ah, here's Miles with one of our favourite finds—a fully intact oil lamp."

Miles held it out for me to see. "It's tempting to light it, but we can't risk causing any damage. Our goal is to one day open this place up as an open-air museum with a focus on daily life. Tourism in Luxor's been declining with all the trouble in the Middle East, and another visitor attraction may help the town to pull in some much-needed revenue."

"Do you have much digging left to do?" Tegan

asked.

"Oh, a few years yet. Why? Would you be interested in volunteering?"

"Is that allowed?"

"New blood's always welcome, although we do ask for a small donation towards the running costs of the site."

"When can I start? Guys, do you want to come as well? Tai?"

"I'll do a day," Russell said. "And I'm happy to make an extra donation. But how will we get here?"

Tegan sidled up to Ren. "Pleeeeease will you come? You know you want to."

Surprisingly, he agreed. "I'm free tomorrow. Does that work?"

Miles nodded. "Yes, we've got enough staff to assist. Caroline can train you in the basics—planning, excavation, levelling, section drawing, and photography."

Great—now I was the only holdout, and I had to weigh up spending a day with Russell against spending a day with Ren. The American Idiot. AI. Normally, that stood for Artificial Intelligence, but I wasn't sure Ren had room for a brain in his skull as well as his ego. And worse, I could still feel the imprints of his hands on my hips as if he'd branded me. I hated the way my heart raced whenever he came near even as common sense told me he was bad in ways I couldn't imagine.

"Tai?" Tegan asked again. "What's it to be? Are you coming with us?"

CHAPTER 17 - TAI

"WHAT'S UP WITH you?" Ren lowered his voice. "Is it that time of the month?"

No, it flipping wasn't, but I wasn't going to dignify Ren's question with an answer. Against my better judgement, I'd agreed to go to the dig today, which meant another hideously early morning and another day of pretending Ren didn't affect my stupid libido in the horrible way that he did.

Okay, there, I said it. Ren turned me on, and I absolutely hated that. Hated his smug words. Hated his effortless confidence. Hated the way he made my blood boil then burn. Really, really hated that I'd dreamed about him again last night. *Detested* myself because I should have been imagining Russell doing all those things to me with his tongue instead.

Although when the ping of my phone woke me at five o'clock and it was a message from Russell, I forgave myself just a tiny bit.

Tai,

Sincere apologies, but there's a problem at work and I need to stay here to solve it this morning. Can we do dinner this evening instead?

Russell

P.S. I've emailed you some interesting articles on

the Theban Necropolis.

For half an hour, I agonised over whether to throw a sickie. A headache, a funny tummy, heatstroke... They'd all have been plausible. But Miles and Caroline were expecting us, and it was bad enough that one person had let them down without a second backing out. No, I'd go, but I didn't have to enjoy it.

And Russell? Well, logically I understood that his work had to come first, but I still felt a tiny bit annoyed, even if he was trying to make it up to me. I'd go for dinner, but he could blooming well wait for my answer.

While I was in the shower, I gave in and downloaded the email app onto my phone again because then at least I could read about ancient Luxor on the way to al-Nahas. Was tempting me with historical titbits Russell's way of getting me to embrace technology again? I'd warned him the other day when he asked for my email address that I rarely checked it, and he'd just given me an irritating shrug he could have learned from Ren and said, "We'll see."

Ren's lips quirked up as he watched me throw my bag into the back of the Land Cruiser. Sunscreen, snacks, gallons of water, a floppy hat and pashmina I'd bought in the souk with Tegan, lip balm, hair bands, a phone charger, paper and pens—I'd stuffed in everything I could need for a day at a remote archaeological site. Tegan came running out a minute later with a bag as full as mine plus a folding chair.

"Where's Russell? Are we picking him up on the way?"

"He's not coming. Work."

"Aww, sad. Maybe he'll join us another time." She

went to put her bag in the passenger side then paused. "Do you want to ride in the front today?"

Certainly not. "No, you go ahead."

Without Aqueel in the car, Ren turned on the satnav for guidance then drowned it out with the radio —some Arabic station that played an odd mix of traditional Egyptian music and American pop. Tegan sang along with the English songs while I did my best to pretend I was alone.

What had Russell sent me?

A brief history of the pharaohs, a map of Thebes and the surrounding areas that he'd annotated with the location of al-Nahas, and a gifted eBook on the uses for copper in ancient times. Of course, I checked the price right away because every girl did that. £19.99. Ooh, that was generous. And what was that fourth attachment? A gift voucher for a massage in the spa at the Hilton Hotel. Oh, that was too sweet. I quickly fired off an email thanking him and saying I'd meet him at seven for dinner, and then felt guilty for being so easily bought.

"Good, you're smiling," Ren said, and I looked up to find him watching me in the rear-view mirror. "Feeling better?"

"You should watch the road."

"We're in the middle of nowhere, babe."

"I'm not your babe."

"True. You're more of a cactus. In the desert and kinda prickly."

It would have been so easy to lean forward, put my hands around Ren's throat, and squeeze. But that could have got awkward on account of I didn't bring a shovel to bury the body and there was also a witness giggling in the passenger seat.

Stay calm, Tai.

Slowly, deliberately, I scrolled through my unread emails. And scrolled, and scrolled, and scrolled, all the way back to the beginning. If I was deleting spam, I couldn't be committing murder, could I?

At least I had plenty to keep me occupied for the rest of the journey. A miracle cure for toenail fungus, a way to lower my electricity bills, magic pills to help with my erectile dysfunction, and—be still my beating heart—yet another email from an African prince offering riches beyond my wildest dreams if I'd only send him my bank details.

Then we got to the good stuff.

From: Matthew Smart

Subject: Where the hell are you?

Tai,

Have you had some sort of breakdown? When I received your first message, I assumed your phone had been hacked, but this has gone beyond a joke now.

Failing to turn up for work without producing a valid doctor's certificate is a disciplinary matter under clause 13.7 in the company handbook.

Matt

From: S Cheeseman

Subject: Your text message to Matthew

Tai,

Matthew is concerned your phone may have been hacked. Please could you call me?

Sarah Cheeseman

Human Resources Executive

Garrett-Hart

From: Mum
    Subject: Where are you?
    Tai,
    That nice young man you work with keeps calling. Why haven't you gone to the office? Are you okay?
    Mum

From: Matthew Smart
    Subject: Unacceptable
    Tai,
    Should you wish to resign, your notice period is ONE MONTH. I insist you return to work because I don't have time to finish compiling the manual for the HandyPurge 3000.
    CALL ME.
    Matthew

From: Mum
    Subject: Where are you?
    Tai,
    Matthew phoned again—he's concerned for your welfare, and also he wants to know how to make the photocopier do double-sided. Apparently it's urgent.
    Mum

To be honest, I'd be surprised if he'd managed to copy anything single-sided. Every time the machine jammed, he called me, even if I was on the beach in Marbella.

From: Mum

Subject: FW: Where are you?
See my previous emails below. Why aren't you answering?

From: Peony
Subject: Are you dead?
T,
Mum's doing her nut! She sent the police round to your flat and your landlord said you'd moved out. I told her you're probably just going through an early mid-life crisis, but she's convinced you've been kidnapped. You should call her.
P

From: Matthew Smart
Subject: Call Victor Andrews NOW!
Last chance, Tai. If you don't call within one hour, you're fired. And I'm not writing you a reference either.

From: Mum
Subject: This isn't funny anymore
Taisiya,
This is no laughing matter. The police are involved now, and you're wasting taxpayers' funds. If you're having a breakdown, your father's agreed to pay for a consultation with a psychiatrist.
Mum

From: S Cheeseman
Subject: Employment status
Taisiya,
Due to your persistent absence and lack of

communication, I'm afraid we're terminating your employment with Garrett-Hart. Any personal items from your desk will be kept for a period of one month and can be collected from the HR office.

Sarah Cheeseman
Human Resources Executive
Garrett-Hart

Phew. It was over. The only personal items I'd left in my desk were my emergency cookies and a stash of hairbands because I was always losing them. Sarah was welcome to the cookies. She'd probably need them seeing as she still had to work in the same building as Matthew Smart.

I checked the dates on the messages and saw that I'd sent my "I'm absolutely fine" email to Mum right after that. Which should have been the end of it, right? I was on holiday, not locked in a basement dungeon being tortured with poorly prepared PowerPoint documents.

Except the emails carried on...

From: V Andrews
Subject: Payroll irregularities
Taisiya,
The accounting department has just informed me of payroll irregularities dating back a year, which appear to have originated from your computer. Coupled with the timing of your recent departure, I'm sure you'll agree this looks suspicious.
As a courtesy, I'm allowing you twenty-four hours to get in touch with an explanation, but if I don't hear from you, I'll have no choice but to inform the

authorities.
    Victor Andrews

Uh, what? Payroll irregularities? Dating back a year? But I didn't have anything to do with accounting. I was just a glorified lackey with a knack for unjamming the photocopier, and until two weeks ago, a willingness to overlook Mathew Smart's incompetence and the rampant misogyny that pervaded the company.

When was that email sent? Monday afternoon. Almost five days ago. Oh, heck.

And yes, of course it got worse.

From: Mum
    Subject: This isn't what I expect from a daughter I brought up
    Taisiya,
    The police have just been at the door, wanting to question you on suspicion of embezzling sixty thousand pounds from your former employer. Do you have any idea how embarrassing it was trying to explain that I don't know where you are? I'm sure they didn't believe me, and the neighbours are bound to start asking questions. If you've got any consideration for your family, you'll come home and sort this mess out RIGHT NOW.
    Mum

From: Peony
    Subject: ????
    Holy shit, sis. What did you do?

Holy shit indeed. Between the words floating about on

the screen in front of me and the rocking of the car as Ren bounced over bumps, I felt utterly sick. My hand trembled as I reached over to open the window. Air. I needed air.

"Tai?" Tegan asked. "What are you doing? You're letting all the cold out."

"I... I don't feel very well."

Ren sucked in a breath. "If you're gonna puke, do me a favour and chuck up outside. Want me to stop?"

Breathe, Tai. Just breathe.

The r-r-ratchet of handcuffs grated through me. I'd only heard it in person once before—the night the police took Paul away, and he'd gone to prison. What if it was my turn next? Just last month, the local paper had reported how a man spent five years in jail for fraud, only to be exonerated when the real culprit got drunk and confessed.

Hold on, hold on... As Ren had pointed out, Egypt didn't have an extradition treaty with Australia. Did it have one with the UK? A quick search on my phone revealed that no, it didn't. I was safe for now, but what should I do next? Stay in hiding? Call Victor Andrews and try to clear my name? Do the honourable thing and return to England? Despite the building heat, a chill washed over me. I'd never been on the wrong side of the law before, and I hated the thought of being branded a criminal. What should I do?

CHAPTER 18 - TAI

THREE HOURS LATER, sweat dripped down my back as I oh-so-carefully scraped away the soil from around a piece of pottery. Each step had to be carefully documented, and right now, we didn't know whether it was a broken shard or something bigger. Ren and Tegan had their own mystery objects a few feet away, and Caroline flitted between the three of us, making sure we didn't mess things up. Although I noticed she spent more time watching the way Ren's muscles rippled under his T-shirt than anything else. Seriously, had the man never heard of loose-fit?

For now, I'd decided to keep my head down until I figured out what to do about the situation at Garrett-Hart. The thought of flying back to England terrified me. What if they arrested me at the airport in front of everyone? And I didn't know what to say to Victor Andrews either. I'd only spoken to the man a handful of times since I started at the company, and half of those occasions were just him asking me to bring tea—two sugars, demerara not white, milky but not *too* milky, and don't put the milk in first. I could tell from the way he shook his head that I got the colour wrong every single time.

As I dug, I found myself wondering whether Ren's suspicions about Tegan were right. I'd shoved them to the back of my mind, but wouldn't it be ironic if we were both felons on the run?

Thankfully, Miles chose that moment to pop his head over the edge of the trench, smiling as always. A welcome distraction. He'd been in the caves all morning, so we hadn't seen much of him.

"How's everything going?"

Tegan beamed in his direction. She'd been asking questions constantly, which I was grateful for since it meant my relative silence went unnoticed.

"Caroline thinks this one's a water vessel, and it might even be whole. I've got a good feeling."

"I'll keep my fingers crossed. Did you know that the fast potter's wheel was introduced during the eighteenth dynasty? It was then that the pots got smoother, and they were able to speed up production." He peered down at my treasure. "That one looks a little broken, Tai. But no matter, because then we can study the internal properties of the clay, which will help us to identify its origins."

Fantastic. A broken pot. If that wasn't a metaphor for my life, then what was?

"Super."

"What do you have, Ren?" Miles's gaze strayed over Ren's body too. Good grief—yet another person who felt compelled to admire his physique. "A bigger pot?"

"Sure looks that way."

"Out of interest, whereabouts in the US are you from?"

"Born and raised in North Carolina."

"Do you still live there?"

"I've travelled around."

"Join the club. Does anyone want a drink? I'm just

going to make a cup of tea."

"In this heat?" Ren asked.

"I'm British."

Caroline stretched her arms above her head, working her spine backwards and forwards. "I'll come with you. I could do with a walk."

Tegan stood up too. "Same here. I've got pins and needles in my legs."

I didn't particularly want to stay with Ren, but nor did I fancy getting stuck in a conversation in the dining room when I couldn't even think straight. Earlier, Caroline had told us how ancient Egyptian embalmers removed a person's brain through their nose with a metal hook, and that was pretty much how I felt at that moment.

"Would you be able to refill my water bottle?" I held up the empty one I'd just finished.

"Sure."

Ten minutes later, with the *scrape-scrape-scrape* of Ren's trowel grating on my last jagged nerve, I wished I'd braved the sun and gone to stretch my legs. If I gritted my teeth any harder, I'd need to find a dentist. Between the heat, the buzzing mosquito that avoided my slaps like a politician dodging questions, and the grit that'd worked its way into my trainers even though I'd laced them up really tightly, I was ready to snap.

Then the noise stopped, which was possibly worse.

"You okay?"

I channelled Peony with a fake-but-perky smile. "Why wouldn't I be?"

"You've been quiet all morning. Is it because that dude stood you up?"

"He did *not* stand me up. He had to work."

"So he said."

"He did!"

"What does he do?"

"I don't know. Something with computers. Testing software, he said. Why do you always ask so many questions?"

"Just naturally curious, I guess."

"Nosy, more like."

"Don't you ever ask questions?"

"Questions about what? We're in a giant sandpit miles from anywhere, and it's not exactly a hive of activity in case you hadn't noticed."

"Don't you want to know more about the caves? Like what's at the other end of that passage Caroline told us was a dead end?"

"Uh, probably nothing?"

"For nothing, there sure were a lot of footprints leading that way."

Really? Ren was too observant for his own good. On any other day, I might have been interested, but that morning, I just wanted to dig up my piece of pot and go home so I could panic properly.

"They're probably using it for storage or something."

"Mmm."

"What's 'mmm' supposed to mean?"

"You're even more tetchy than usual, cactus. Sure you're okay?"

"Stop calling me cactus. I think I preferred babe."

Now I got a proper, full-beam grin. "Suit yourself, babe."

Saved by Caroline. She came down the steps,

placing her feet carefully and precisely, and passed me my water.

"Tegan's gone to the bathroom, but she's gonna pick up snacks on her way back. How's that pot going?"

"Slowly."

"Welcome to the world of archaeology. Actually, it looks similar to a piece I found last year, although mine was possibly more intact. I'll get one of the guys to bring it over so you can have a look." She climbed up the steps again. "Ya, Mustafa!"

No answer.

"Where is he? If he's sitting in the caves playing on his phone again—"

A crack sounded, short and sharp, and suddenly, Caroline wasn't standing above me anymore. She hit the ground at my feet with all the grace of a sack of potatoes.

"What the—"

I must have heard the phrase *time stood still* a thousand times in my life, but until that moment, I'd never truly experienced it. I tremored with each individual *thump* of my heart against my ribcage, felt each bead of sweat pop out on the back of my neck. The only thing that moved was Ren, and when he rolled Caroline over, a bloom of red was fast blossoming across her pale-pink T-shirt.

"Get down."

He shoved me towards the wall, forcing me into a crouch. Grit dug into my skin, and the sharp pain told me the stones had drawn blood.

"What happened? I don't understand."

"There's somebody up there with a gun, and we're sitting fucking ducks."

"A gun? But... But... She's *dead*?"

A scream punched its way out of my chest, but Ren clamped his hand over my mouth before it could escape.

"Shh."

All morning, I'd been trying not to vomit, but now I wrenched myself to the side and threw up. Caroline was dead, and now I saw the neat round hole over her heart where a bullet had torn through her.

"Oh, hell! What do we do? What do we do?"

Ren squashed me against the wall, making a cutting motion across his throat. Now panic turned into icy fear as the *crunch, crunch, crunch* of footsteps came towards us. Friend or enemy? If one of us dared to look and it turned out to be the latter, we'd probably get our brains blown out.

A shadow fell over the pit, a pit that felt more like a grave with Caroline's still-twitching body at my feet. Could the person up there hear the blood rushing through my veins? I glanced skywards, then wished I hadn't as the black barrel of a rifle inched forward over my head.

I was dead.

And do you know what my last thought was? That at least I could avoid an awkward conversation with my mother.

Strangely, Ren didn't seem to share my abject terror. No, he seemed calm, almost Zen-like as he waited to meet his maker. Ponderative.

Then he sprang.

Before I fully processed what was happening, our attacker was on the ground next to Caroline, and his gun—an ugly-looking black thing with a canvas strap hanging from it—was in Ren's hand. And before I could beg him to stop, Ren had shot the man in the head.

"Oh my—"

Ren's hand came back to my mouth, and this time it was blood-spattered. "Shut the fuck up or we're dead."

I managed to nod, then more gunfire chattered overhead and I almost joined Caroline and the guy with half a face as my knees gave way. Ren's free arm fastened around my waist like a steel band as he held the gun steady, focused on the rim of our burial pit.

"We've got to get out of here."

"Are you crazy?" I hissed. "There are people shooting up there."

"And they'll be shooting down here if we stick around. That trick I pulled'll only work once."

"So what do we do?" I ended on a screech-whisper, if there was such a thing.

"We need to get to those rocks by the cliff. They'll provide cover. Stay low until we reach the top of the steps, and when I pat you on the back, you run, okay?"

I wasn't sure my legs would work, but what could I do but nod?

"Keep your head down and don't look back, got it?"

"Yes."

The pot I'd spent so many hours excavating crunched underfoot as Ren half carried me across the pit. Bullets whizzed over us, and somebody screamed. Where was Tegan?

I had no time to think as we reached the top of the steps.

"Go!"

That wasn't my back he patted, that was my freaking ass. But I stumbled across the open ground towards the safety of the boulders bordering the amphitheatre, praying the footsteps behind me didn't stop because that would mean Ren was dead and I was on my own.

The boulders were within reach when I tripped, and Ren picked me up and threw me the rest of the way. I sprawled in the dirt as he crouched beside me, gun at the ready.

"You okay?"

"No, I'm not bloody okay."

He flashed me a grin. "Haven't lost your charm, cactus."

Then he began shooting. One, two, three, four men fell as bullets rained down around us. A flying chip of stone caught Ren on the leg, but he ignored the pain and carried on while I scanned left and right for any sign of Tegan. And Miles. Ohmigosh—where was Miles?

"Up there!" I tugged at Ren's shirt. "On the hill."

A silhouette had detached itself from the mosaic of a rocky outcrop, and I saw a gun in his hand. Ren aimed and fired, and the man tumbled all the way to the valley floor, landing with a muffled *thump*.

A moment of silence, and I heard a cry from the other side of the hollow. Who was that?

"Someone's in trouble."

"We're all in fucking trouble, babe." A sigh. "We need to move around the edge. Stay behind me. If you stick your pretty little head out, you'll lose it."

All around, the desert floor was littered with the dead or the dying. Our people, the enemy—I couldn't tell who was who anymore. I could only tippy-toe behind Ren as he moved silently between clusters of rocks, careful to keep us hidden and protected from stray bullets. Little made sense right now, but the one thing I did know for sure was that the safest place was right on his heels.

"Who's doing this?" I whispered. "Why?"

"Those are questions for later."

Ren froze as a shadow crossed between two of the huts up ahead. More attackers? I'd never seen a dead body before today, and now I'd been up-close and personal with enough to last a lifetime.

"Friend or foe?" he called, first in English, and then in a language I didn't understand. Was that Arabic?

"Ren?"

Tegan peeped around the corner of the building, and I almost wept with relief. Then my jaw dropped when I saw what was in her hand. Was I the only person here who didn't know how to use a gun?

"You intact?"

"Yeah, and Miles is with me. Can you cover us?"

"Hurry up."

Seconds later, Tegan ran across to us with Miles in tow and hunkered down behind the boulder. He looked as sick as I felt, and I wasn't at all surprised when he slumped onto a rock and retched. Why were people shooting at us? Was this a terrorist attack? One thing was for sure—we were on our own because nobody would hear the gunfire out there.

Ren hadn't stopped scanning the area, but now he spoke again.

"One question. What the fuck?"

It was Tegan who answered. "Miles and his friends were holding back on us. It seems there's more here than broken tools and old pottery."

"Such as?"

Miles groaned. "Eight mummies, and enough treasure to make Tutankhamun's tomb look like small change. Every piece is significant, but two are priceless —the burial mask of Ay and a cartouche belonging to Ramesses VII. Both solid gold."

"And where exactly were these being kept?"

"In the caves. There's a small passage off to the left-hand side."

Ren had been right all along. About the cave, and most likely about Tegan too seeing as she'd morphed from a yoga-loving digital artist into a freaking commando. But he still had a lot of explaining to do, because *who the hell was he*? How many property relocation executives or whatever it was he claimed to be could shoot I-don't-know-how-many men without breaking a sweat?

Tempting though it was to demand answers, that would have to wait because Ren sucked in a breath and turned to Tegan.

"If I go over there, are you capable of protecting these two?"

She hesitated a second, but then she nodded as she reached into her back pocket then held out a spare gun magazine to Ren. "Take this. You might need it."

I finally found my tongue. "Wait! Are you insane?"

Another grin from Ren. "It's been suggested a time or two."

Then he was gone, a wraith moving through the shadows at the edge of the...the killing field. Because that was what it was. In the blink of an eye, a peaceful place of camaraderie and history had turned into a battleground for a war I didn't understand.

Al-Nahas had become hell on earth. Yes, it was even worse than working at Garrett-Hart.

CHAPTER 19 - TAI

TEGAN PEERED AROUND the edge of the boulder, scanning left and right, the gun raised in front of her. Her mouth was set in a hard line, but I saw a tremble in her hands. Was she okay?

"Guys, watch our backs. Tai, you look south. Miles, take the north."

"Which way's south?"

"To your left. Crouch down to make yourself as small as possible, but stay on your feet. I need you ready to run if necessary."

"Who are you? Where did you learn to shoot a gun?"

"In a past life, I was a cop."

"She's okay," Miles whispered. "She saved my life."

I realised he was trembling almost as much as me, so I squeezed his hand. His tanned skin was practically white, bleached out by the horrors in front of us. Little snippets from my high school first aid course filtered back. Was he going into shock? It seemed like a definite possibility, but I couldn't remember what to do.

A cry from somewhere beyond the buildings sent a fresh wave of fear through me. "People are hurt," I whispered. "Shouldn't we be trying to help them?"

"Not until it's safe. I'm not sure who's even on our side."

"What do you mean?"

"Aqueel tried to shoot us," Miles said, incredulity evident in his voice. "If Tegan hadn't grabbed the gun..."

"*Aqueel*? Our driver?"

Tegan nodded. "Traitorous little snake. And I've seen at least two more people who worked here siding with whoever these guys are."

"I can't believe it," Miles muttered. "I just can't believe it. All of these people were vetted."

"Not well enough."

Fresh gunfire put an end to the conversation. Never in my life had I felt so scared, even when I was stuck in the pit. Fear combined with helplessness to make a whole new beast, one that clawed at my guts from the inside out.

"Where's Ren? Can anybody see Ren?"

"Someone's coming," Miles hissed. "From the huts. Oh, it's Kamal. He's our handyman. Over here, Kamal."

I recognised him too. He'd carried our tray of drinks over to the trench that morning, the strong, sweet coffee so desperately needed to focus my thoughts. Now, he looked terrified, his white clothes splashed with blood. Then his fright morphed into determination, and a gun appeared from between the folds of his robe, the muzzle rising towards us with deadly intent. You know how they say your life flashes before your eyes? Well, all I saw was the glint of sunlight on the metal barrel followed by a red haze as his head disintegrated.

Oh hell, oh hell, oh hell. My ears rang from the shot, so loud I could barely hear Tegan speak.

"Fuck knows what they've loaded this with. It's

vicious."

Miles pressed the heels of his hands against his ears and screwed his eyes shut. Hear no evil, see no evil. "Why are they doing this?"

"In this region?" Tegan said. "At a guess, I'd say greed with an outside chance of religion."

Another minute passed. Perhaps two or five or ten. Every second felt like an hour and time didn't make sense anymore. Nothing made sense. Yesterday, I'd been content—I'd even go so far as to say happy—and my biggest problem had been a neighbour who made inappropriate comments and stole my books. Now? The rug had been pulled out from under my whole life.

"Coming back." A voice sounded from nearby. *Ren.* I sagged against the rock in relief. "For fuck's sake don't shoot."

Blood ran down his left arm, dark and sticky, and he wasn't walking right either. What was in the bag he was carrying? It looked heavy.

"What happened?" I gasped. "Are you hurt?"

"Just got winged by flying shrapnel, that's all. And twisted my ankle." He passed the bag to Miles. "They escaped on camels, but I got that off the last guy. Feels like metal."

"Is there a first aid kit anywhere?" Tegan asked.

Miles nodded. "In the dining room. What's left of it." It took him a few goes to get the buckles on the bag undone, then he drew out the prize within. Holy hell. Gold glinted in the sun, and yes, it was only metal, but at the same time, it wasn't.

I'd never understood how somebody could take a life in cold blood, but if anything was worth fighting over, it was the piece in front of me. Exquisite. There was no other way to describe it. Ten inches of gleaming brilliance, decorated with hieroglyphics and inlaid with gemstones, as beautiful now as the day it was created thousands of years ago.

"It's the Ramesses cartouche. The words are a spell to help guide him through the afterlife."

"Nearly worked on me," Ren muttered.

Ramesses cartouche... *Ramesses cartouche*. The words sparked off a memory buried deep in my brain. I'd heard somebody mention it recently, but where?

"You didn't see the mask, did you?" Miles asked.

"Sorry. Either it's still in the cave or they got away with it."

"I'll go with Miles to get the first aid kit," Tegan said.

Ren drew a phone out of his pocket. I'd always pictured him as an iPhone guy, but the chunky black thing looked too utilitarian to be trendy.

"And I need to make some calls. This requires damage control."

Tegan froze. "Calls? Who to? The police?"

Ren barked out a laugh. "Here? They're probably involved. Miles, you'll want to call your people too."

"At the Ministry of Antiquities? What in heaven's name am I meant to say? They employed half of these people. They were supposed to have done background checks. How do I know who to trust?"

"Actually, I was thinking more of Blackwood."

Blackwood? What the heck was Blackwood? Why did I get the feeling I'd stepped into a parallel universe?

Miles's eyes widened in shock. "How do you know about Blackwood?" Then the shock slowly changed into something else. Recognition. "Now I know where I've seen you before. At Riverley. Why didn't you say anything before?"

Riverley? They were speaking in code.

"I prefer to keep a low profile."

"I can't call Bradley. He'll lose his mind if I tell him I got shot at."

"Then phone Emmy."

That was it! I'd had enough of being kept in the dark. "Will someone tell me what the bloody hell is going on?"

"Tegan, go and fetch the first aid kit while I explain this, would ya?"

"But—" she started.

"Please?"

Once Tegan and Miles had jogged out of earshot, an eerie silence descended on the whole place. The eight mummies had been joined by fresh souls, and I felt as if they were watching us. Waiting. Judging.

Ren pushed gently on my shoulder until I sat on a rock, its surface worn smooth by years of exposure to the elements. An ancient resting place. We'd come here to study history, and now we were making it ourselves in the worst possible way.

"How are you feeling? I don't like your colour."

"Just tell me what's going on. The truth, because everybody seems to have been spouting lies right, left, and centre so far, and I'm sick of it. Who are you? Jason Bourne's scruffier brother?"

"I may possibly work for an unnamed employer doing things I can't talk about without security clearances being involved."

"As in, you could tell me but then you'd have to kill me? You *are* a spy?"

"I'm just a guy on vacation."

"Bullshit."

"I'm serious. I'm supposed to be lying on a beach right now."

"Then why are you here?"

"Because I have a weakness for pretty girls."

"Tegan?"

Ren sighed. "I need to make these calls. This whole situation's gonna spiral out of control if we don't get a lid on it."

"What's Blackwood?"

"Blackwood's a security company. One of the largest in the world, and the owners have plenty of clout. Miles's boyfriend works for them."

"He also shoots people?"

"Fuck no. Bradley decorates. Last I heard, he had a single pink handgun he refused to fire because he didn't like the noise."

"And how do you know them?"

"Friend of a friend. My boss goes way back with the head honcho's wife, and sometimes we hang out at her place." Ren scrubbed a hand through his hair, which was the first time I'd seen him look stressed. "Fuck, this is a mess. Luxor isn't one of my stomping grounds, and I don't know who's on our side. Right now, there are only two people I trust."

"Who?"

"Miles, because of his connections, and you."

"That's flattering, but you hardly know me."

"No offence, cactus, but you're not capable of getting involved in this shit."

"You're saying I'm incompetent?"

Even in the middle of a horror show, he just

couldn't resist digging the knife in, could he?

"Incompetent's the wrong word."

"Is it because I'm a girl? Because Tegan's a girl."

"You don't have the same hard edges Tegan does."

"And what about her? Don't you trust her?"

"The jury's still out on that. I know her name isn't Tegan Wallace, to begin with."

"Then what is it?"

"Who knows? I only got a buddy to do a preliminary background check, and it turned out she didn't exist. But she seemed relatively harmless, so I left it at that and just kept an eye on her."

Little blocks of information slotted into place. The way Ren knew about things that I didn't—like Sayid's hash dealing, for example, and Australia's extradition treaties. And my full freaking name.

"Wait. Did you background-check *me*?"

"Just the basics." That lopsided smile made me want to slap him. Hard. "Sorry, bad habit."

"You're a massive dick."

"I'm not gonna deny that."

"I said *are*, not *have*."

He pressed the phone to his ear. "Shh. It's ringing."

Good thing I was sitting on the rock, because my legs wouldn't have held me up. In fact, I was shaking all over. Tegan and Miles came back while Ren was talking, and Tegan looked more scared than ever as Ren gave whoever he was talking to a brief precis of what had happened then whispered about body counts and investigations and robbery and betrayal. What had she done to end up here? From the way she shifted from foot to foot, I wouldn't have been surprised if she'd taken off running before Ren finished his call. I couldn't hear what was being said on the other end, but from his tense expression, the road forward wasn't going to be smooth.

"We need to check for survivors," he said after he hung up. "Help's on its way, but since this is now a diplomatic crisis as well as mass murder, there's a lot of red tape to deal with. Did you see anyone else on your way to the dining room?"

"Nobody still breathing." Tegan had gone whiter than Miles, and a tear rolled down her cheek. "I can't be here. I'm sorry, and I want to help, but I just can't."

"What are you running from, Tegan? Why did you pick the name Tegan, by the way? Does it mean something? Or did you just take whatever passport you could get?"

So it wasn't just me he was snide with.

"Don't be so horrible," I said. "Can't you see she's upset?"

"I'm just sick of being lied to, that's all."

"Hello, pot. Have you met kettle?" And the skeletons in Tegan's cupboard were no excuse for being mean. I wrapped an arm around her shoulders because she looked as though she needed a hug. "Is it something to do with your time in the police force?" I asked her.

Now it was Ren's turn to raise an eyebrow. "Police force?"

"Yeah, I was a cop, okay? For five years. Catch the bad guys, protect and serve, get framed by your treasonous colleagues for murder, that sort of thing. There. That's my secret. Now are you happy?"

"If you were framed, why run? Why not stay and clear your name?"

She gave a hollow laugh, even though there was nothing remotely funny about the situation. "You didn't see the evidence. Credit where credit's due—they did an excellent job of fabricating it."

"So you took off?"

"I found a key piece of evidence planted in my home and realised I was about to be arrested. How long do you think I'd have lasted in a jail where I'd put a significant number of the inmates behind bars?"

"What now? You're gonna run again?"

"You think I want to end up in an Egyptian prison instead of an Australian one? Maybe you've got friends in high places, but I don't. I just shot five people, Ren."

He rubbed his temples. "Shit. We need to get this story straight. I took out seven, so with your five, that makes twelve. If we tell the authorities I shot them all, I'll look like the Terminator."

"You'd cover for me?"

"Right now, I haven't made up my mind. At a guess, we've got forty-five minutes before anyone gets here, and our first task is to check this site. The bad guys've bugged out, but we need to check the status of everyone left."

One person. We found one other person who'd survived—the cook's wife, who sometimes came to help with meal preparation, according to Miles. She didn't speak a word of English, but Ren jabbered away in Arabic and found out she'd hidden behind the water tank when the shooting started. And it seemed the thieves had known precisely what they were targeting. Apart from the cartouche, the only thing they'd touched was the mask of Ay, hidden deep within the caves.

Two priceless objects, and they'd left everything

else behind. Mummies, amulets, giant sarcophagi, perfectly intact pottery decorated with glass and precious stones. A real Aladdin's cave.

Ren gave a low whistle. "If news of this treasure gets out, the media's gonna go mental," he whispered, quiet enough that the others couldn't hear.

I was no expert, but I imagined the eyes of the world would be on this tiny patch of sand and rocks in the middle of the Sahara desert, which wasn't ideal considering what had just happened there.

"*Will* it get out?"

"Not if we can help it."

"What are you going to do about Tegan? Do you believe her?"

"If I can get her real name, I'll check out her story." He leaned in closer, his face shadowed in the gloom of the cave. "Will you help me? She responds better to you."

"I can't think why." Could I be underhanded like that? Probe Tegan for her secrets then give them away? "What will you do if it's true?"

"If she's innocent, I don't want to see her go to prison." He blew out a short breath, as if to say *why me*? "Sorting out this problem'll be tricky enough without adding a fugitive into the mix."

At the mention of the F-word, the bomb I'd found lurking in my inbox that morning ticked louder, eclipsing the remnants of the ringing in my ears. I didn't want to add to the burden or admit to my own failings, but Ren said he hated being lied to, and if he found out later on that I'd withheld important facts, he'd undoubtedly be upset. And I couldn't blame him for that.

No, I had to tell him. He might have been an asshole, but he'd saved my life today, and I couldn't see myself getting through this nightmare without his help.

"Uh, that may actually be two fugitives."

"Huh?"

"I might be having a small legal issue too."

"You? Are you serious? What did you do? Forget to polish your damn halo?"

"I didn't *do* anything. I swear. And I only found out this morning. Somebody stole some money from the company I used to work for, and the managing director thinks it was me."

"For the love of fuck." He raised his eyes to the sky. "I still keep hoping this is an elaborate drill the Agency's set up to test me. That any moment, my boss is gonna walk out from behind one of those boulders with a couple of cold beers and a ticket back to Langley."

"Sorry."

Totally inadequate, but what else could I say?

"I should've stayed in Dahab." Another sigh. "Except then you'd be dead, and I'd probably be sunburned."

"What do we do now?" I asked in a small voice.

Ren took a step forward, and he kept coming until he'd backed me into one of the ornately decorated cave walls. I almost protested about him desecrating ancient art, but his dark expression made me bite my tongue. Heat flared in my belly as he caged me in with his arms.

"Do you trust me, Taisiya?"

A big question. Did I? I'd literally put my life in his hands this afternoon, and I was still there to tell the tale. Yes, Ren was intrusive and sometimes evasive, but apart from fibbing about his occupation initially, I didn't think he'd lied to me. And while he was irritating as hell, there was a difference between disliking somebody's personality and distrusting their character.

"Yes, I trust you. But I still think you're a dick."

He pushed back, giving me space to breathe again. "That I can live with. I promise I'll do my best to fix this. It might get rocky along the way, but if you go with my decisions, I'll get you through to the other side. Okay?"

I met Ren's gaze, his eyes glittering gold among all the treasures, and made my deal with the devil.

"Okay."

CHAPTER 20 - TAI

"DID YOU CALL Emmy?" Ren asked Miles.

"Not yet."

"Why not?"

Miles sank to his knees beside one of the sarcophagi, fishing around in the sand until he came up with a stone amulet. A tiny beetle. I'd seen them in the souvenir shops in the souk, but this was the real thing.

"Did you know the scarab was the symbol of rebirth?"

Yes, Miles was definitely in some kind of shock. Denial. Rather than facing up to the carnage outside, he'd retreated to his sanctuary and what he knew. I didn't need to be a psychologist to work that out, because I felt like crawling into bed with half a dozen Crunchie bars and a pint of Ben and Jerry's myself.

"Miles, you need to call her," Ren said.

"And what am I supposed to say? How can I explain this?"

"Ten bucks says she already knows, and she's dealt with a lot worse. Remember the time her house got invaded by a team of commandos?"

A what? "I'm sorry? Commandos? Uh, are you really sure getting this person involved is a good idea?"

"Yes. Call her, Miles. The clock's ticking, and Tai and Tegan need to get out of here. Is there another route back to Luxor besides the one we took?"

Tegan looked across sharply from her perch on the largest sarcophagus. The cook's wife sat next to her, sobbing quietly. "You're letting us go?"

"Temporarily. I'll meet you back in town. Miles? Is there another route?"

"Yes. Yes, there is, but it's twice as long."

"Perfect. Let's head over to the car. Who knows we're staying at Sayid's? Just the driver, or did you tell anyone else?"

"Only Aqueel."

"And he's dead. Good. Come on, I can program the satnav while you make your call."

Miles was in a daze as he ambled along, and I took his elbow to guide him. We had to pass a body on the way, a slight man wearing jeans and a button-down shirt. If I'd seen him on the street, I wouldn't have given him a second glance, but the rifle by his side told me everything his face never would. Flies were already crawling over the messy wound in his chest. I gagged and willed myself not to throw up in front of Ren.

"It's okay, just keep going," I said, ostensibly to Miles but mostly trying to convince myself.

At the car, he collapsed into the front seat then fumbled awkwardly in the pocket of his cargo pants for his phone as Tegan helped the cook's wife to sit on a nearby rock. Five or six attempts later, he managed to dial the right number and prop it up on the dash.

One ring, two, and someone picked up.

"Miles?"

"Emmy? I... I..."

"I was expecting you to call." She was British? "An actual massacre? Wow. This makes the time I went to a health farm and got embroiled in a kidnapping plot look positively boring. Is Ren there with you?"

"I'm here."

"I've had a summary of what happened from Jed. What else do I need to know?"

"There's one survivor besides us. A civilian who doesn't speak any English. Twelve dead tangos plus eleven of ours. Looks as if half a dozen men defected."

"Motive? Jed erred on the side of robbery rather than terrorism."

"Agreed. They went for two pieces and got away with one. A gold mask. I never saw it, but I'm guessing something like Tutankhamun's."

"Better," Miles muttered. "Ay's was slightly smaller, but the craftsmanship was unsurpassed."

"So half a million bucks on gold value alone. What's that, thirty-five thousand a hit? Life's cheap out there."

"They can't melt it down," Miles said, his voice barely audible. "Its value's unfathomable. And the historical significance…"

"We'll get it back. I'm otherwise indisposed until the middle of next week, unfortunately, but Jed's flying out this afternoon with Logan. Evening your time. What else do you need?"

"Interference, mainly. Two of the witnesses have reasons for wanting to avoid the cops, and I don't need any hassle either."

"I'll fix it. The tourism minister's trying to convince us to invest in a new hotel right now, so if they want us to fork out the cash, they'll tread carefully. Plus nobody wants a massacre splashed all over the news, and like I said, life's cheap."

How could she be so matter-of-fact? So cold?

"Miles is concerned about Bradley's reaction."

"Him and me both. I haven't told him yet."

"Perhaps we could keep it quiet for a day or two?" Miles suggested. "I don't want to worry him."

"Hmm. That might not actually be a bad idea."

CHAPTER 21 - TAI

"ARE WE EVER going to reach civilisation?" I asked.

Was it possible to get seasick on dry land? We'd been bumping through the desert for an hour so far, Tegan at the wheel of Ren's Land Cruiser and me in the passenger seat. Miles hadn't been kidding when he said the drive would take twice as long. We hadn't got out of second gear the whole way, and all the satnav showed was miles and miles of sand without a road in sight.

And not even the pretty sand you saw in the movies. No flat plains, no rolling sand dunes. No, this was rocky with dips and hillocks with the odd scrubby tree for variety.

"We'd bloody better," Tegan said. "Although the longer we keep driving, the longer I can pretend none of this is happening." She thumped the steering wheel with her fist, then held her hand out flat in front of her. "Look at me—I'm shaking. I hate running. I *hate* it."

"You're planning to leave again?"

"What choice do I have? If I can get to the airport before the police tighten the security, I might stand a chance." Another tear rolled down her cheek, just one, and I admired her self-control. If I let a tear out, I'd end up bawling. "Dammit, I really liked it here. Nice weather, nice food, nice people. Until they tried to kill us, anyway."

"Nobody else knows we were there. What if Ren can sort everything out the way he said?"

With the arrival of the cavalry imminent, he'd stayed at the dig site with Miles and the Egyptian lady to face the music. The idea of him undergoing an interrogation worried me, but he'd confessed to having a diplomatic passport and said he'd been through worse before.

I dreaded to think.

"You truly trust him?" Tegan asked.

"Yes, I do. I don't like him, but I trust him."

"For me, it's the other way around. I like him, but I don't trust him. Men are fun to play with for a few hours, but they always screw you over, Tai."

"It was men who set you up?"

"Yup. Including my so-called boyfriend, the scumbag. My only regret about leaving Australia so fast is that I didn't get a chance to put his dick in a blender first."

"What happened? Or don't you want to talk about it?"

"I don't even want to think about it."

Rats. Now what? I totally wasn't cut out for this espionage stuff.

"And do you know the shame of it?" Tegan continued. "I actually thought this might be it for me. Staying in Luxor, I mean. That I could rent a place long term. Maybe volunteer at the dig for a while and meet more of the locals. Serves me right for being optimistic for once, huh? Now I wish I'd skipped visiting this country completely."

"Don't say that."

"It's true. I should have stayed in Russia. I may

have gotten groped by men tanked up on vodka the whole time, but at least they didn't shoot at me."

"Well, I don't regret it, and my situation isn't all that different to yours. We had fun, didn't we? Trekking around the souk, buying those awful gold pants, the Fellah's Tent."

"Apart from Dale."

Oh, who could forget Dale and his inability to shut up? "Did I tell you I ended up hiding from him in a storeroom?" Wait. *Wait.* "That's it!"

"What's what? Reckon I should go around this hill or try driving over it?"

"Uh, go around." Better to be safe than sorry. The last thing we wanted to do was drive off a cliff, Thelma and Louise-style. "I knew I'd heard someone talking about Ay's mask and the Ramesses cartouche before, and I couldn't remember where. But I overheard a conversation while I was hiding from Dale."

Tegan stared at me, which meant she took her eyes off where we were going, and we hit a rock with an almighty jolt.

"Dammit! Sorry. What did they say?"

"Not much," I admitted. "Just that they had a buyer for both and now they had to deliver them. One of them mentioned a contact and a boss who was pleased with progress, so I guess that's who was handling the job."

"Holy shit. You overheard them planning the crime? Why didn't you tell anyone?"

"Why would I? I thought they were discussing trinkets from the souk or something. I'd never even heard of Ay or a cartouche before that."

"Did you see who was speaking?"

"No, they stayed on the other side of the door. The

guy liaising with the buyer sounded American—from Minnesota, he said—and the one doing the delivering was definitely British. A London accent, I think? Or maybe Home Counties. Something from the south, anyway. And he lisped some of his *S*'s. That's all I remember."

"Hey, that's better than nothing. At least now we know for more-or-less certain that we're dealing with antiquities smuggling rather than a random terrorist attack."

"You say that like it's a good thing."

"It is. Think about it—the thieves knew what they were stealing, and the raid was well-planned. They'll have left a trail, no matter how carefully they've tried to hide it. And their thought process is likely to be logical. Rational. If it was a bunch of extremists who just wanted to kill people to make a political point, then we'd be dealing with crazies. Totally unstable and harder to predict their actions."

"We?"

"Huh?"

"You said '*we'd* be dealing with crazies.' Are you going to stay now?"

"Uh, no. No way, I can't."

"So what will you do? Go to another country? Oman or China like you mentioned before?"

"I'll head for the first non-extradition place I can get a flight to. It's kind of awkward because I can't transit through most countries either."

"Will you change your name again?"

"I've only got one fake passport. If that gets compromised, I'm screwed. Even if the country doesn't have an extradition treaty, there's always a risk from using my real name. Not all government agencies play by the rules."

"What is your real name?"

A quick glance, followed by a sheepish smile. "Kylie."

"Like the singer?"

"If I had a dollar for every time someone's said that to me... My mum's a big fan."

"Do you miss her?"

"My mum? Every hour of every day, and my dad. The police... I guess they were my family too, except we had a really, really messy divorce."

"Do you regret joining? Apart from the obvious, I mean."

"It was hard at times, but the camaraderie and the satisfaction of putting criminals in jail where they belonged beat everything. Although I have to keep reminding myself that I wasn't much of a detective if I couldn't see the double-crossing that was going on under my own nose."

"Don't belittle yourself. I couldn't have done what you did today. I just froze."

"Would you believe that until this morning, I'd only ever shot one person?"

"I ran over a squirrel once and cried."

We looked at each other, and what could we do but laugh? This whole situation was so horrible it was either that or curl into a ball and rock. When I abandoned my car at the side of the road near Heathrow, this wasn't quite the adventure I'd had in mind—almost dying only to find out that the man who'd been driving me insane for the last week was some sort of secret agent. He'd mentioned Langley...

Wasn't the Pentagon in Langley?

Tegan wiped her face as we both cried tears of laughter, tears of shock, tears, tears, more tears. The car rumbled slowly on, and every few minutes, one of us would burst into giggles again because we'd lost the freaking plot. I mean, this was insane. If I ever told the story to Peony, she'd put on that condescending expression she'd perfected as a child and tell me lying was a sin.

Fifteen minutes passed, maybe twenty, and I finally began to sober up, so to speak. *Behold, a reformed lunatic.* Then out of the corner of my eye, I caught a flashing light on the dashboard. A red light. That was never a good thing, right?

"Uh, what does that mean?"

"Aw, shit. I think it's the temperature warning light."

"You *think*?"

"I'm, like, ninety-nine percent sure. The one percent is more clutching at straws. Is there an owner's manual in the glove compartment?"

Yes, along with a map of Luxor, a packet of crisps, chewing gum, and a giant bag of candy. Ren had some nerve buying all that considering he'd insisted on baked potatoes rather than fries on Sunday evening. *It's important to stay healthy*, he'd said. Well, right now, I was more concerned with staying alive. At least we wouldn't starve, but the manual was of no use whatsoever.

"It's in Arabic."

"Doesn't matter anymore." Tegan pointed at the temperature gauge where the needle was creeping towards disaster. "The radiator must have gotten damaged when we scraped that rock."

"Now what?" I'd gone shrill again, but I couldn't help it. What if the engine blew up and we got stuck out there in the baking sun? Not so long ago, we'd passed the sun-bleached bones of an animal unfortunate enough to die in this place—a camel or perhaps a horse —and if we didn't find a solution, that would be us. "What do we do?"

"Have you got a phone signal?"

"Not for the past half hour."

"What we need is Ren's fancy satellite phone."

"That's what he has?"

"And Miles too. They're really good ones—lighter than any I've ever seen. I did kind of wonder where they got them from, but now that we know their backgrounds, it makes perfect sense."

Which was all very interesting but also utterly useless since Ren and Miles and their phones were still in al-Nahas.

"How many miles do we have left?"

"Twenty-one according to the satnav."

"Can't we keep going? How long will it last like this?"

Tegan pointed to the first wisps of steam curling out from under the bonnet. "Not long enough, I don't think. We need to stop."

She steered the vehicle to a shuddering halt in the shade of a rocky overhang. Okay, on a scale of one to the massacre at al-Nahas, this only rated as a five or so, but we were still stuck in the middle of the freaking wilderness.

"What if we tried to walk?" I suggested. "How long would it take? We've got..." I twisted to check in the back seat. "Four bottles of water and an entire sweet shop."

"Too long, even if we didn't get lost. Dammit to hell!" Now Tegan's hysterical tears turned to woe. "I needed to get to the airport an hour ago. If the authorities have got half a brain between them, they'll close it, and then I'll be stuck here."

"Somebody might go past and give us a lift."

"Really? Out here? How many cars have you seen today?"

"I'm only trying to stay positive."

"Don't bother."

Tegan climbed out of the car and slammed the door behind her. I understood why she was upset, but I still hated the way she took her anger out on me. If I could have done something to help, I would have.

Okay, Tai, just breathe. Think logically. When we didn't turn up at Sayid's, Ren would send out a search party, right? All we had to do was sit tight and try to avoid heatstroke or dehydration. Or getting bitten by a snake. Or a scorpion. Or running into a stray bandit.

Shit. Tegan was right—we had to get out of there. After a minute of searching, I found the catch to open the bonnet and followed Tegan into the early afternoon heat.

"What? Are you a mechanic now?" she asked.

"I thought I'd take a look and see how much damage there is. If the hole's small, we might be able to refill the radiator and make it back."

"We won't. We lost enough water to make the engine overheat in only twenty minutes."

True, and I should have known that. I'd spent three years studying engineering, for crying out loud, but my brain had turned to mush today. *Think, Tai. Think.*

Okay, if there was a hole in the radiator, we needed to fix it somehow. Did this vehicle come with a toolkit? Ren struck me as the type of man who'd be prepared, and I hit the jackpot when I found a torch in the boot. The hot sand scraped against my shoulders as I wriggled underneath the engine, and sure enough, there were scrapes crisscrossing the bottom of the radiator. But only a couple of spots where water was drip-drip-dripping out. Phew. If it had been totally mangled, I'd have joined Tegan with my legs outstretched at the bottom of the rocks.

But with two holes and the perfect thing to block them up with, I had hope as I scrambled back to my feet.

"We need to wait for the leaking to stop and the engine to cool down, then dry the area around the holes. After that, we should be able to seal them with gum well enough to get back. Are you ready to start chewing?"

"You really believe that'll work?"

"As long as we leave the radiator cap off, the pressure shouldn't build up enough to blow the holes open again. If I fasten an empty crisp packet over the top with my hairband and pierce it, that'll stop most of the water from slopping out."

"Ohmigosh. You're a genius!"

Not exactly, but that afternoon, I didn't feel like a total idiot, and that was something at least. Survival trumped getting my degree certificate.

But with a plan in place and the prospect of getting back to Luxor in one piece, I was left with a dilemma over Tegan. Back in al-Nahas, Ren had asked me to pass on any information I gleaned about her true identity, and although I had to be the most reluctant spy on the planet, not to mention the least competent, I'd managed to ferret out a few facts, such as her real first name, for instance, and the fact that both her parents were still alive. Although Tegan hadn't specifically said not to pass the information on to Ren, doing so would feel like a breach of confidence, and she'd already said she didn't trust him.

Did I risk betraying her? Or believe in Ren and hope he'd do the right thing? With Tegan's freedom hanging in the balance, it was one of the hardest decisions I'd ever had to make.

CHAPTER 22 - TAI

"WHERE THE HELL have you been?" Ren asked when we finally stumbled through the apartment gate. "I was about to send out a search party."

"There was a small problem with the Land Cruiser."

"How small?"

I held up my fingers and thumb half an inch apart.

"About this small."

"The radiator sprang a leak," Tegan explained, and I noticed her voice had developed a tremble that wasn't there before. Was the adrenaline wearing off? I was quaking inside myself. "It got scraped when I hit a rock, but Tai blocked it up with chewing gum."

"Nice move, cactus."

Miles stood next to him, still pale, although he'd washed the blood and dirt off himself now. It seemed Ren had lent him some clothes because I'd bet the contents of my suitcase that those green-and-blue board shorts didn't belong to the archaeologist. Not only were they brighter than anything else I'd seen him wear, but they also had to be at least four sizes too big. Ren himself looked as though he'd just got back from a day at the beach apart from the fresh bandage on his arm.

"I'll get Bradley to arrange a new car," Miles said. "He's good at things like that." Ren just stared at him, and he took a step backwards. "Oh. Yes. Right. I wasn't thinking. Perhaps we could hire a vehicle?"

"Forget the car—Uncle Sam'll send us a replacement. Did you find the matches? The barbecue won't light itself."

The barbecue? *What?* "I'm sorry? How can you even contemplate eating?"

"Because I missed lunch?"

My stomach churned from the mere thought of food. "Don't you feel sick?"

Ren settled an arm over my shoulders. "Today wasn't the first time I've seen a dead body, or the first time I've been responsible for one. But I get that it's difficult. Go ahead and puke if you need to, then come back out here and eat something. It's important to keep your strength up."

I swallowed down the bile rising in my throat, but Miles turned kind of green and ran into Ren's apartment. The sound of retching followed moments later.

"Is he okay?" I asked Ren.

"He's in shock. I tried to make him lie down, but that didn't work out so well. How are you feeling?"

Honestly? I wasn't sure. I kept trying to block everything out, but if I let my thoughts wander for too long, I saw Caroline's body falling again. Heard that sickening thud. Smelled that distinctive metallic tang as blood trickled from her chest.

"I'm trying not to think about the worst of it. What happened at al-Nahas after we left? I mean, there were bodies everywhere."

"We'll talk about that later."

"What did the police say?"

"I'll tell you over dinner."

Dinner... Dinner... I clapped a hand over my mouth. "Oh, crap! I'm supposed to be having dinner with Russell tonight. What time is it?"

"Cancel."

"What should I say? What am I supposed to tell Russell? Or should I say I left before the shooting started?"

"Don't mention the shooting at all. We're keeping that quiet for the moment."

"How? How can you possibly keep something like that quiet? Twenty-three people freaking died!"

"The roof in one of the caves collapsed. The whole site's been blocked off. Dangerous."

"They're covering this up? And you're helping them?"

Rather than answering, Ren steered me over to a chair. "Sit down. You too, Aussie. Are you gonna tell us your real name yet?"

Tegan slumped onto a seat beside me. After we'd resurrected the radiator, she'd barely spoken on the trip back, just focused on driving, gripping the wheel so hard her knuckles turned white. I'd half expected her to throw a few clothes into a suitcase and take off for the airport, but the police were already putting roadblocks in. We'd beaten them by half a minute. I'd watched in the wing mirror as the vehicle two cars behind ours got stopped. Trying to leave by air on a fake passport probably wasn't a sensible idea at that particular moment.

"So, here's where we are." Ren ticked off the points on his fingers. "Six men from today's dig team—all Egyptian—were in league with the robbers, and they died in the shootout. Two more Egyptians and one American weren't there today, and we haven't located them yet. Of those, only the American knew about the mask of Ay and the Ramesses cartouche."

"He was the traitor? One of the men I overheard talking about the mask and the cartouche was American."

"Men? What men?"

I recounted the story about escaping from Dale the tour guide and hiding in the storeroom. "So you see, until today, I didn't realise the conversation might be important. Do you reckon it was the same person?"

"Possibly. When Miles and Caroline discovered the treasure two months ago, they immediately put a lid on it. Miles only told four people besides the American. Three of them are dead, and the fourth was the Minister of Antiquities."

"What if the minister talked to others?"

"That's one question we have to answer. Ironically, the reason they decided to leave the mask and cartouche in situ was that they were worried about theft."

"Several pieces have gone missing from museums in the last two years," Miles said, still looking green as he rejoined us. "Inside jobs. My contacts at the ministry suspect it's an organised network stealing them to order, but nobody's been able to catch the thieves yet. We thought the best option was to keep the discovery quiet until proper security could be arranged, but that was a mistake. A fatal mistake. All of those people dead... What can I tell Caroline's family?"

"Easy, buddy. Don't think about that right now."

"When *am* I meant to think about it? Her mother...

Her sister... And Vernon's due back from his vacation in three days. He'll walk into a war zone if we don't warn him first."

Was Vernon the American Ren had mentioned?

"We've got a cover story, remember?"

"Right. They died in a cave collapse." Miles didn't sound convinced. "Do you really think people will believe that?"

"Sure. Shit gets covered up all the time. Move the remaining artifacts somewhere safe, put the bodies inside, add a couple of properly placed charges, and boom. Nobody out here investigates anything properly. That's why we decided on our plan, wasn't it?"

"You can't blow up one of the caves! They're of great historical significance."

"Sometimes sacrifices need to be made. And keep your voice down out here. You never know who's listening."

"You're not destroying my site! I'll call the antiquities minister... Or the newspapers... Those people can't get away with murder."

"And they won't, but losing your head won't help."

Surprisingly, it was Tegan who stepped forward. "Ren's right. Getting upset won't help any of us. And involving the authorities more than they already are won't bring Caroline and the others back."

Ah. Perhaps not so surprising after all. Of course Tegan wouldn't want the police or the government sniffing around.

"Let's go inside and make tea," she continued. "Everyone could use a drink."

"Tea..." Miles said weakly. "Of course."

For the British, tea fixed all manner of ills. Tegan

steered Miles into her apartment, leaving me outside with Ren, who blew out a long breath.

"Fucking hell. He needs to keep it together or the rest of this plan won't work."

"What won't work? What plan?"

Ren held out a hand, and I shivered a little when I reached out and took it. The more I found out about him, the more nervous he made me.

"Let's discuss this inside. A cup of tea would do you some good too."

I settled for a can of cola because boy did I need the sugar rush. Plus Ren didn't have any milk, and I didn't want to disturb Tegan if Miles was finally calming down.

"Chip?" Ren offered, holding out a packet of crisps as he leaned against the kitchen counter.

"No, thanks. Just tell me what's happening, will you?"

"Okay, so I've had a bit of experience with governmental agencies in this part of the world, and they don't work the way they do in the UK or the US. Criminal investigators haven't got access to the same equipment, and training's rudimentary at best. Plus they're usually hobbled by the higher-ups who all have their own agendas. Today's massacre? The Egyptians don't want anyone to find out about it because of the dent it'll make in their tourism industry. When I suggested keeping it quiet, they agreed in two seconds flat."

"So they're not going to investigate?"

"They'll make some effort, but I doubt they'll get very far. And cops over here don't earn much. They're easy to bribe, and we don't know whose side they're on."

"Then what do we do? Just let these people get away with murdering everyone and stealing a priceless treasure?"

"Not quite. I've set a trap. More than likely, our gang found out about the gold from either Miles's buddy Vernon or via the Minister of Antiquities. We got one piece back, but that's not what we're telling people."

"I don't understand."

"When I went after the men, the group had split into two. The assholes at the front had the mask, and they didn't see me take the cartouche from the four at the rear. So it's simple—we let everyone think the second team still has it. The bad guys'll go crazy hunting for the missing piece, and that's when we'll find them."

That was...hmm... That was quite clever, actually. But would it work?

"What if they recognised you? You've been out in town."

"I grabbed a scarf off a dead guy and covered my face before I went after them."

Ick. I took half a pace back in case Ren had death cooties. How could he have had such presence of mind in the middle of a gunfight? I'd barely been able to keep breathing.

"Do you really believe they'll stick around? What if they decide to cut their losses?"

"They won't."

"How can you be so sure about that?"

He crunched up another crisp before answering. "Firstly, because the authorities'll keep the roadblocks in place until we tell them otherwise. Somebody owed my boss a favour. We told them we're looking for a group of forgers making fake artifacts. Secondly, because thieves are greedy. Why settle for a hundred million bucks when they could get two hundred million? From the conversation you overheard, they've got buyers waiting. Thirdly, because if there's one thing criminals hate, it's being double-crossed."

"And when you say '*we'll* find them...?' I'm not a detective, and they've got guns."

"I didn't mean you, cactus."

"Then who?"

"Me and a couple of buddies. Maybe Tegan. She seems to know her way around a gun. Did you find out anything else about her?"

After much deliberation, I'd decided to tell Ren what I knew. I couldn't help Tegan with her problems, but he might be able to.

"Her real name's Kylie. She didn't tell me her surname, only that her parents are still alive and she misses them. But how come she gets to help and I don't?"

"Two seconds ago, you were worried it was dangerous."

"Yes, but that doesn't mean I want to be left out completely."

Ren sucked in a breath and rolled his eyes.

"What's that supposed to mean? Why do you always have to insult me?"

Now I got a shrug followed by a long pause.

"That's not an answer."

"I guess... I guess because it's easier."

"Easier? Why on earth would it be easier? Easier

than what?"

"Because I can't offer what you need. That boring geek from London was buzzing around, and I figured he'd be a better long-term bet for you. You're not one-night-stand material."

Wait. What was he saying? My brain was already overloaded with confusion today, and I struggled to unravel Ren's words.

"Are you... Are you saying you want to have a one-night stand with me?"

"If you were that type of girl, but you're not."

"Then that means...that you fancy me?"

"Ten out of ten for perceptiveness, cactus."

Wow. That was some revelation. Ren was way out of my league in the hotness stakes, even if his personality left something to be desired.

"But I still don't understand. If you like me, why are you so rude?"

"Because if you hate me, there's less chance of me pushing you up against a wall and fucking the stick out of your ass."

"I... I..." My eyes narrowed all of their own accord. "What do you mean, *less* chance? No chance is more like it."

"I've seen you staring at my butt when you think I'm not looking."

Dammit, I thought I'd been discreet about that. "So? I bet you've checked out mine."

"Sure I have."

And I hadn't noticed once. How totally unfair. Ren was literally trained to do this stuff, whereas in England, I hadn't even been able to tiptoe past my pathologically dull ex-neighbour's flat without him popping out to show me the latest addition to his stamp collection.

My mind rewound through the rest of the conversation. A one-night stand? Ren would ruin me. And what the hell was all that about a boring geek?

"You want to screw me, but you think I should date Russell?"

"No."

"No to which part?"

"No, I don't think you should date Russell. At least, not anymore."

"Why? I mean, what changed your mind?"

Funny how just for a moment, I managed to forget the horrors of al-Nahas as all my blood rushed south. Which absolutely shouldn't have happened in Ren's presence, but it did. It was as though he exuded a strange avalanche of pheromones that overwhelmed my senses and sent me floating into somebody else's body.

"You really need to ask after what happened this morning? Who was the one person notable by his absence?"

Aaaaaand... Back to earth with a bump.

"You can't seriously believe Russell had something to do with the robbery?"

"Don't you think it was convenient the way he cancelled at the last minute?"

"He had to work."

"Work? He's supposed to be on vacation."

I almost blurted out the details of our "dating" arrangement, but I managed to stop myself at the last second. No point in looking like even more of a loser in front of Ren—Tai Beaulieu: will pretend to be your girlfriend in exchange for room service food.

"It wasn't him, okay?"

"Tell me why you think that. You said there was an Englishman involved."

"Yes, but it definitely wasn't Russell. The man I overheard had a speech impediment. A lisp. Besides, I've spent more time with Russell than you have, and he isn't a monster."

"Well, if that's what you believe, then go out for dinner with him tonight. We should all carry on as normal so we don't arouse any suspicions."

Ren kept on eating crisps as if nothing was wrong. Chilli and lime flavour. Ick. If anyone was the monster here, it was him because those tasted disgusting. Last week, I'd tried one by accident because I couldn't read the writing on the packet and the picture looked more like a spring onion.

"What if a bad guy spots me? I could get kidnapped and tortured until I tell them where the cartouche is. Where *is* it, by the way?"

"Somewhere safe. Hardly anybody knew you were at the dig site today, and those that did are either dead or on our side. Unless an escaping robber happened to catch a glimpse and recognises you, which is unlikely because they're not the kind of people who make a habit of dining at the Winter Palace, then you won't be in any danger from them tonight. The question is..." He quirked up one annoying eyebrow. "How much do you trust your instincts?"

The way Ren asked, it came out as an insult. Like I couldn't possibly guess better than an American James Bond who worked at an agency he wouldn't even name. Probably he was right about that most of the time, but he'd barely met Russell, and I'd spent several days in his company. Russell was passionate about his work and didn't seem to care about money beyond having a nice room at the hotel. And he wasn't exactly poor, anyway. Would he really throw everything away by getting involved with such a vile gang of criminals?

I just couldn't see it, but then again, Ren had been annoyingly right about everything so far. And he wasn't an amateur at this game, that was for sure. Should I follow his instincts or mine? Hide away in my apartment for weeks and risk losing one of the few friends I'd managed to make, a man I genuinely liked, or risk meeting Russell and see where things led?

CHAPTER 23 - TAI

"THE BEETROOT SALAD'S good," Russell said. "I had it last night."

Yes, I'd decided to meet with him. Ren was wrong. He *had* to be wrong. Or maybe I just didn't want to believe I was such a lousy judge of character.

Anyhow, I'd taken a calculated risk. I'd weighed up the strong likelihood of losing a friend against the slim chance Ren might be right about Russell's involvement in the robbery and taken a cab to the Winter Palace. Surely nobody would start a war on the terrace of a five-star hotel?

Even so, I couldn't help looking around at the other diners who were talking softly in the candlelight. A young couple who appeared to be very much in love. A quartet of grey-haired tourists comparing Luxor to the city of Aswan further up the Nile. A bespectacled Middle Eastern businessman obsessed with checking his phone. A family with a toddler laughing as he covered his face in ketchup. None of them gave off "we're here to kill you" vibes.

"Okay, I'll try the salad." I still wasn't hungry. Secretly, I'd also hoped that dinner with Russell might take my mind off the terrible events at al-Nahas, but it hadn't helped at all. "Any suggestions for the main course? Something light."

"How about fish? The grilled snapper's a small portion. I could eat two and still have room left for dessert."

"Sounds good. How was work this morning?"

Russell waved the waiter over and ordered for both of us before answering. Steak and scalloped potatoes for him with a side order of seasoned carrots, which was another point against his possible involvement in the massacre at al-Nahas—he certainly hadn't lost his appetite.

"Work was painful. One of our newer team members made a mistake, and having to fix it remotely then apologise to the client by Skype was a hundred times more difficult than it would've been in person."

"Does that mean you'll be leaving soon?"

"Now you sound like my brother." Russell paused to swallow half a glass of wine, which was odd for a man who usually sipped. "He turned up unexpectedly and found me with my laptop, and from his reaction, you'd think he'd caught the love of his life cheating."

"He was upset?"

"That's an understatement. He accused me of being ungrateful for everything he'd organised and said that if I planned to spend the whole day with my computer, I might as well do that in England and save the hotel bill. I think he was serious. He even offered to help me pack."

"And will you go?"

"This place is growing on me. Did you know it was below freezing in London today?" Russell reached across the table and squeezed my hand, smiling. "The company's better in Luxor too."

Oh, hell. Did that little touch mean what I thought

it meant?

It was all happening today, wasn't it? First the massacre, followed by Ren admitting he liked my ass, and then the first indication that Russell might see me as slightly more than a prop. On any normal evening, the man trouble alone would have been enough to leave my head spinning, but at that moment, I felt positively dizzy.

Luckily, the waiter provided a distraction by sliding a plate of salad in front of me, and I realised my first mistake. The deep-red colour of the beetroot reminded me of the remains of Kamal the cook's head back in al-Nahas, and I gagged.

"Are you okay?" Russell asked.

"Just got something stuck in my throat."

"Here, drink this." He pushed a glass of water towards me. "It's still, but I can order sparkling if you'd prefer."

"Still's perfect, thank you. Tell me more about your work project. Do you have anything left to do on it?"

"Perhaps an hour or two, but since I'm staying in Egypt, I need to make the effort to get out more. I tried working at the table on the balcony earlier, but my laptop threatened to overheat so I had to go back inside."

"What would you do if it broke?"

"I've got three spares with me. And if they all malfunctioned, I guess I'd have my company courier over another one."

Wow. Russell's people would fly laptops to Egypt, whereas Garrett-Hart had refused to replace my keyboard for almost two months after my F key broke. Only after I submitted a report detailing a competitor's "radical shit in an unexpected direction" did they order me a new one.

I suppose that was one plus point at least—since the shooting, I'd barely thought about the mess waiting for me back in England. Although getting distracted from a crisis by an even bigger crisis wasn't anything to get excited over.

"Will you stay in the Winter Palace long-term?"

"I'm not sure. The luxury's nice, but weirdly, I miss the small things like making my own dinner. Sometimes, I get a strange craving for beans on toast."

"I can make you toast if you want."

Russell's eyes lit up. "You have a toaster?"

"Plus a hotplate and a microwave, but I don't have any beans. The supermarket might sell them—I've never looked."

"Maybe we could go to the market together? What are you doing tomorrow?"

"I'm not sure yet."

"You're not heading back to that archaeological site? How did today's trip there go, by the way?"

The one question I'd been hoping to avoid, and Russell had gone and asked it. "I, uh... Arrrgh! Something just ran over my foot!" I shoved my chair back in time to see a small, dark creature scuttle under the tablecloth. "Holy crap! Was that a scorpion?"

Saved by a deadly arthropod. Who'd have thought it?

Russell leapt up too, his cutlery clattering to the ground. "Where?"

"I didn't see where it went."

Great. Now everyone was staring at us except the young couple, who were checking under their table for any wayward creepy-crawlies. One of the older group climbed on a chair, and the toddler started crying. Only the businessman seemed unperturbed. Finally, a waiter ran outside with a broom and began swishing it under the tables with practised efficiency.

No scorpion.

"It ran away," he announced, smiling. "Is safe now."

We had very different ideas of safe. What if it was lurking in the bushes, biding its time until my toes made a reappearance?

"Russell, do you think we could move inside?"

"Of course."

He shepherded me into the dining room with one hand on the small of my back, as was his custom, and even pulled out my chair. An old-school gentleman, one who knew how to treat a lady well on a regular date and not just in the middle of a gunfight. Because this was a date, wasn't it? Russell hadn't so much as glanced at his emails all evening.

We got seated at our new table seconds before the chef swept in with a dome-covered plate and presented Russell with his steak.

"Rare, sir, exactly the way you like it."

Aw, hell. Blood oozed out as Russell cut into it, and I nearly vomited. Dammit, I should've stayed at home with milk-less tea and whatever Ren slung on the barbecue. At least he preferred his meat well-done.

"Do you need more water?" Russell asked.

"I think I actually need to visit the bathroom. Won't be a minute."

"Of course." Russell stood out of politeness. "Turn left out of the dining room, and it's along the hallway on the... Oh, hell."

I followed Russell's gaze to the man standing in the doorway. "Who's that?"

"Finn. My brother."

Brilliant. Could the evening get any more awkward? "Should I leave?"

"Please don't. You'll have to meet him sooner or later."

Not if I hid in my wardrobe for the next week, then flew to another non-extradition country. Tegan had a list. I could ask her for advice. Perhaps she'd even need a travelling companion? I longed to run out of the back door and escape across the gardens, scorpions be damned, but Finn was already walking towards us and I didn't want to look like a nutcase.

"Just smile, and I'll get rid of him as fast as I can," Russell muttered under his breath.

Smile. He said that like it was easy. I managed something more akin to a grimace, which matched Russell's own expression.

"Russ, who's this?" Finn asked, scowling.

"Tai. My girlfriend. You remember I told you about her? And my name's Russell, not Russ."

"Oh, right." Finn's scowl twisted into something resembling friendliness as he stuck out a hand. "Pleathed to meet you."

Pleathed? *Pleathed*?

Freaking...well, fuck wasn't too strong a word for it. A lisp. Finn had a freaking lisp. My heart rate went from a steady canter to a flat-out gallop in an instant as I searched for an escape route. I'd ended up seated in a corner, and Finn was blocking my way to the door.

Stay calm, Tai. Finn didn't know I'd been in al-Nahas. All I had to do was keep breathing until I could leave and get a cab back to the apartment. Ren would know what to do.

Ren always knew what to do.

He'd been right again, hadn't he? Russell was wrapped up in the theft, and my instincts were on a par with those of a suicidal lemming.

"It's n-n-nice to meet you too. S-s-sorry—I get nervous around new people."

"Did you want something?" Russell asked his brother.

"Thort of. I figured I should apologithe for earlier."

"Apology accepted. Can we finish our dinner now?"

"I need to talk to you. About *things*."

"Well, it'll have to wait." Russell cut his gaze in my direction, teeth gritted. "I'm on a date right now."

"But I have a favour to athk. When you fly home, I need you to take a box of trinkets for Mother. She's looking forward to retheiving them."

"For goodness' sake. Can't you just send them by mail?"

"They're fragile."

"How big a box?"

Finn demonstrated with his arms. About four feet square, it seemed. Boy, that was a lot of trinkets. Or possibly... Hmm... Possibly one big piece of gold? Could *I* have been right for once? Perhaps Russell wasn't involved, and this was Finn's ham-fisted attempt to enlist Russell in his smuggling operation?

"Fine. But you'll have to reimburse me for the excess baggage charges," Russell said.

"Excess baggage? Won't Terrence pick you up in his plane?"

"I doubt it."

"But he flew you here, didn't he?"

"Yes, but only because he was on his way to Saudi Arabia to meet with a client. He's not a taxi service. Terrence is one of my business partners, and he flies for a hobby," Russell explained for my benefit, then turned back to Russell. "Besides, I'm not going back to England yet. There's still so much I haven't seen in Luxor."

"You already went to both temples, right? And rode on a felucca?"

"And a camel too. But I didn't go to the temples or ride on a felucca with Tai, and what's more, I'm finding there's lots to do off the beaten track."

"Like what?"

Finn was the tour guide. Surely he should freaking know?

"Like exploring the far reaches of the souk. Watching sunsets over the Nile. And yesterday, we visited an archaeological dig. Tai went again this morning, didn't you, darling?"

Oh, double fuck. Now Finn focused on me with laser intensity.

"Really? An archaeological dig? Whereabouts?"

"I forgot the name. Somewhere out in the desert."

"Tu-ra al-Nahhasin," Russell added helpfully. "It translates as 'the caves of the copper workers.'"

Shit, shit, shit. "I didn't stay for long today. Tegan wasn't feeling well, so we were only there for half an hour, max, and then the driver brought us back."

"We must visit again another day. I was supposed to join them earlier," Russell told Finn. "But work got in the way, then you arrived in the afternoon and started shouting at me."

Now Finn paled. "You were thupposed to go? But you hate manual labour."

"Didn't you always tell me I should expand my horizons?"

"Yes, but—"

"Look, can we finish this conversation another time? Our food's getting cold. And I don't understand why you're acting like this—first you wanted me to stay in Luxor, and now you want me to go home. What's Mother been saying to you?"

Before Finn could answer, something cold splashed over me, and a red stain spread out on my cream shirt. My first thought was blood, and I screamed, but then I realised nothing hurt and Russell and Finn were both staring at me in confusion. Wine? No, it didn't smell like wine. What was it? Russell's eyes narrowed as he focused over my shoulder, and I turned to see the businessman from the terrace looking down at me with an almost-empty glass in his hand and an apologetic expression on his face.

"Sorry," he said, his accent thick and guttural. "I tripped."

On any other day, I'd have been mortified, but today, I could have kissed him.

"Accidents happen. I really need to rinse this off."

"Here." He tried to hand me a wedge of Egyptian fifty-pound notes. "I'll buy you new clothes."

"If I can wash this fast enough, I'm sure the stain'll come out."

"You are staying at the hotel?"

"No, I have an apartment nearby."

"Then let me call you a taxi so you can go home and change."

"There's no need—" Russell started, but I stopped him with a peck on the cheek.

"Thank you for dinner. I'll call you in the morning, okay?"

"Are you sure you'll be all right? If you want to come back for dessert...?"

"It's late, and I'm quite tired. Let's take a rain check."

"I suppose I can't blame you for wanting to do that." Russell glared at his brother. "Sorry this evening turned into such a farce."

"It's not your fault. We'll speak tomorrow."

I grabbed my handbag and practically ran into the lobby, heaving a sigh of relief when I spotted my saviour outside the front door speaking with the driver of the taxi he'd commandeered.

"Miss!" He waved me over. "This man will take you home. I've already paid him. Again, I am sorry."

And they said guardian angels didn't exist? I'd just met mine, and he came with a thick beard and an apologetic smile.

"It's okay, honestly. Thank you for the taxi."

Only once we'd rattled off into the night did I begin to breathe properly again. Finn was involved in the robbery, I was sure of it. But what about Russell? Did he suspect his brother was a criminal? I didn't think so, but after today, I realised that the investigation was best left to the professionals. I was way, way out of my depth there.

CHAPTER 24 - TAI

"WHAT HAPPENED?" REN asked the second I walked through the gate.

He'd been waiting in the shadows, and he nearly gave me a heart attack.

"Somebody spilled a drink on me. It's just karkade."

I'd worked it out in the taxi. Red, sticky, slightly sweet-smelling. A little taste confirmed my suspicions, then I realised the driver was watching me lick my shirt in the rear-view mirror and probably thought I was a fruitcake.

"No, I meant the rest of the stuff. Who was the guy who came up to your table?"

"Wait a minute. How do you know...?"

The gate opened behind me, and the businessman from the hotel walked through.

"Hey, buddy," he greeted Ren, except now he had an American accent.

"Oh."

"Taisiya, meet Logan. He's come to help."

Logan grinned, his eyes twinkling in the light spilling out from the apartments. "Lucky I was only in Beirut when the call came."

Every time I thought I understood what was going on, it turned out I was completely wrong. "You sent Logan to follow me this evening?"

"You didn't think I'd let you loose in town by yourself, did you?"

"I don't believe this. I was on a freaking date!"

"So? What was he gonna see? Cactus, you're not the type of girl who drags a guy into a dark corner and sucks his cock. How long do you wait before you get to the good parts? The fifth date? Tenth? Fifteenth?"

That... That asshole! "I hate you."

Red mist descended, but before I got tempted to kick Ren in the balls, I stormed into my apartment and slammed the door behind me. Only to find a blond-haired guy sitting at my dining table, staring at a laptop. If I'd been in a better mood, I might have paused to enjoy the view, but I wasn't, and I snapped before I could stop myself.

"Who the hell are you?"

"Jed Harker. You must be Tai? Ren said it'd be okay if I borrowed your living room."

"Oh he did, did he?"

Talk about emotional turbulence. I'd lost count of the number of times I'd gone from fear to anger today, and now I longed to lock myself in the bathroom and cry. When I came to Egypt, all I'd wanted was a holiday, and instead, I was living in a nightmare.

Back outside, I squared up to Ren. "How dare you let somebody use my apartment?"

"Because we're short of space, and we're supposed to be working as a team. Miles is asleep in my bed, which is the best thing for him right now, and Tegan's taking a shower. We can use her apartment afterwards, but her bathroom door doesn't shut properly." He leaned in close, and the hairs on the back of my neck prickled. "I'm sorry about the date comment. It was out of line. Just... Well, you know now why I say that shit. I can't help it."

"Try. For just one evening, try not to act like a total dick, okay?"

"Okay." Ren took a deep breath. Held it. Exhaled. Smiled. "What happened earlier? Logan said you suddenly looked scared, so he figured he'd better intervene."

I forced myself to un-ball my fists before I replied. Ren was the most frustrating man I'd ever met, and his ability to go from totally inappropriate to businesslike in the blink of an eye gave me whiplash.

"You were half right. I don't think Russell is involved, not knowingly anyway, but his brother is. That was who came over to our table, and he speaks with a lisp. I'm sure he's the man I overheard at the Fellah's Tent."

"You hated having to admit that, didn't you? That I was right?"

"*Half* right."

"Okay, half right."

"Yes, I hated it."

"I like that you're honest."

"I'm also terrified."

"Nothing'll happen to you, cactus. I promise. Let's talk inside."

While Russell had placed a soft hand on the small of my back, Ren wrapped his fingers around the nape of my neck, his skin hot against mine as he steered me back into my apartment. Jed looked up again, and this time, I managed a weak smile.

"What's Russell's brother's name?" Ren asked.

"Finn."

"Finn Weisz," he told Jed. "That's our guy with the lisp."

"Wait, I'm not a hundred percent sure..."

"Adult lisps are rare. I researched it." Ren gave the back of my neck a little squeeze. "The accent fits too, and in a town this size, I'd bet my motorbike he's our man. Nice work, babe."

Out of the thousand things I could have said, what I blurted was, "You have a motorbike?"

"Yeah, babe. Want a ride?"

Would he wear leather, because... *Stop it, Tai*! "No, I do not."

"Suit yourself." He turned businesslike again. "In that case, we need to find out everything there is to know about the second Mr. Weisz. Cactus, what did he say tonight?"

By some miracle, I managed to focus enough to explain how Finn had interrupted us with his request for Russell to play courier.

"Do you think that was his plan the whole time?" I asked. "Russell told me it was Finn who convinced him to come to Egypt in the first place."

"Perhaps," Jed said. "But he couldn't have relied on Russell playing along, and for good reason, it seems. I'd say it was more likely to be a backup, and his primary plan fell through because of the blocks we've put in place. Now he's desperate. How did Russell react to the request?"

"He seemed annoyed more than anything. Not upset like he'd just caused the deaths of a dozen people and lost a hundred million dollars."

"What about Finn? How was his demeanour?"

"Stressed. Edgy. Even after Russell told him they'd

talk later, he still brought up the box he wanted delivered. It must have been important."

"And Finn was sweating," Logan added, appearing at my elbow. Now he'd lost the glasses and undone his shirt, he looked like a clone of Ren except with extra muscles and more hair. They both had the same hard, confident aura about them. "Nervous sweat. I smelled it as he walked past me."

"Russell wasn't sweaty at all. I'd have noticed."

"Agreed." Logan perched on the edge of the table, and it creaked under his weight. "Either he's a sociopath and they're playing us, or he's innocent."

"Surely I'd have noticed if he was a sociopath?"

Ren shook his head. "Not necessarily. Many are good at hiding their true selves, especially if you haven't known them for long. Lying's a way of life. They'll manipulate others for their own benefit, and they won't care because they're just not wired up that way. Have you ever caught him in a fib?"

Russell had only ever been kind to me, and I wanted to think the best of him, but new, suspicious Tai couldn't overlook the fact that Russell had used me as his decoy girlfriend. Yes, the arrangement had suited me at the time, but how did that fit into the game? Had I been conned? Was Russell's deception an innocent cover story or something more?

And what should I tell Ren? Admitting to the truth was embarrassing.

"Russell isn't always honest with his brother."

"In what way?"

"Nothing huge, but sometimes he says he's busy doing something else when really he just doesn't want to go out with Finn."

"Hardly the crime of the century," Logan said.

But of course, Ren couldn't let it go. "Busy doing what?"

"Stuff."

"What stuff?"

"Me, okay? Originally, he asked me to pretend to be his girlfriend to keep Finn off his back. Russell only wanted to work in his hotel room in peace."

Ren laughed, and I itched to slap him.

"So tonight...?" he asked.

"No, that was a real date. Can we stick to the important things? Like the fact that Finn might very well be a mass murderer?"

"I guess we need to look on the bright side—if Russell is as innocent as you think he is, Finn probably doesn't know you were at al-Nahas."

"Uh, he actually does. Russell accidentally told him. But I said Tegan and I were only there for half an hour, so Finn doesn't realise I saw the shooting."

"And that's all you said?"

"Yes. Russell tried to ask me how the trip went earlier, but a scorpion ran over my foot before I could answer, and I might have got a bit upset."

Logan chuckled. "You shrieked loud enough to wake Tutankhamun. And it wasn't a scorpion, it was a cockroach."

"Really?"

"It went right past me. Scorpions usually avoid people and noise."

"Well, whatever it was, it had a lot of legs and a good sense of timing." As did Logan. He'd got me out of a tight spot at exactly the right moment, although that still left me in an awkward situation. "What if Russell asks more questions tomorrow? I promised to call him."

"I'm not sure that's a good idea," Logan said.

Now Ren smiled. Not his usual cheeky grin, but a new smile I hadn't seen before. A cunning smile.

"No, it's a great idea."

Huh? "I'm sorry?"

"Think about it. We've got a mole in their camp. If Tai hangs out with Russell, she might overhear something else that can help us."

Jed nodded his agreement while Logan looked dubious. "Are you sure that's wise? Tai isn't trained for this shit."

Understatement of the year there. I was barely capable of holding my own on a regular date, let alone pretending to enjoy dinner while doubling up as a low-budget spy. Then there was the small matter of the danger I'd be in.

"Are you crazy? There's a good chance Finn and his friends murdered eleven people today and tried to kill all of us too, and you want to send me out to have dinner with his brother again?"

"He doesn't know we're onto him," Ren said.

"But he knows I went to al-Nahas. What if he gets suspicious?"

"It's not as if you'll be on your own. We'll be following you."

"Oh, brilliant. Invasion of privacy as well as a risk of death. Tell me why I don't do this more often?"

"So you *will* do it?"

"I'm not sure..."

"It's not a difficult job as far as undercover work goes. Most of it, you've been doing already. Hang out with Russell, eat dinner, go back to his hotel room if he offers."

Had Ren lost his mind? "You honestly expect me to sleep with him after this?"

"No, I expect you to snoop. That comes naturally to women, right? Every girl I've ever dated has rifled through my drawers when they thought I wouldn't notice."

"Well, I don't do that sort of thing."

"You broke into my suitcase."

"That was an emergency! I needed to find your contact details."

"Cactus, you went through my wash bag."

"How the heck did you know that?"

That irritating grin came back, and I wanted to slap him.

"I didn't, but I do now."

"You're the most annoying man I've ever met."

"Nobody would disagree with that," Logan said. "But, Tai, we really need your help on this. You have something we don't."

"What?"

Ren just couldn't help himself. "Breasts."

Logan glared at him. "Not the time, asshole." At least I had an ally fighting in my corner now. "You have access and a history with one of the suspects. And we'll keep you safe. The three of us do this for a living, and when Ren keeps his mouth shut, he's good at his job."

That much I had to admit was true. If it wasn't for his quick thinking at al-Nahas, I'd be dead. And I desperately wanted to get justice for Caroline and all the other people who'd lost their lives in the desert. But I was scared. Even the mere thought of being in the same room as Finn again left sweat trickling down my spine.

Could I do it? Could I really sneak around like Lara Croft's incompetent cousin as we searched for priceless relics? I mean, since when did the Tomb Raider wear MC Hammer pants?

What should I do? If I agreed to Ren's plan, I'd probably screw up and make things even worse. Should I take a risk, or steer clear of Russell and his horrible brother?

CHAPTER 25 - TAI

WHY DID I agree to Ren's stupid plan? The instant the words "I'll do it" left my lips, I wanted to take them back again, but with the three men already hashing out their next moves, I hadn't dared. And now I had to invite myself to dinner with Russell tomorrow night. Well, tonight, since it was three o'clock in the morning. I'd been tossing and turning in bed for two long hours, exhausted but unable to sleep, and my sheets were drenched in sweat.

A drink. I needed a drink. Wine in the absence of something stronger, but when I got to the kitchen, I found the half-empty bottle of white missing from the fridge. Grrr. I couldn't imagine Tegan helping herself, which meant Ren or one of his friends had taken the only thing that stood between me and hysteria. And then I spotted the man himself sitting at the table on the patio with a glass in his hand.

Before I could think better of it, I marched outside.

"Nice pyjamas," he said, slowly looking me up and down.

If Ren didn't like Garfield, that was his problem. "Don't even start. Did you take my wine?"

"I gave it to Miles. He looked as if he was gonna have a nervous breakdown."

"What about me? What about *my* nervous

breakdown?"

Ren pushed his glass in my direction. "Here. Have my beer."

"Ugh. Beer's disgusting."

"Want me to go next door and get you a little gift from Sayid?"

Drugs? That was worse than beer. "No, I do not. Why are you up, anyway?"

"My turn to keep watch. Why are *you* awake? I thought you were tired?"

"I am." In fact, my legs would barely hold me up, and I slumped onto the seat opposite Ren. "But each time I close my eyes, I freak out."

"What about?"

"Everything. What I saw, what I did. What *you* did. What I still need to do. I just want to go home, but I can't do that either."

"It's PTSD, Cactus. Happens to the best of us."

"Have you had it?"

"It's always there, lurking at the back of my mind."

"How do you cope?"

"Various ways."

"Like what?"

"Distractions. Meditation. Work sent me to a shrink."

"Did that help?"

"Took my mind off things for a while, but then she moved to California. They tried sending me to a new guy, but that didn't work out."

"Why? What was wrong with him?"

"He was male."

"So?"

"And I'm straight."

It took a moment for Ren's words to sink in, and when they did, I raised my eyes to the sky. Lord, deliver me from this manwhore.

"You slept with your therapist?"

"Sure beat talking about my problems." He waggled his eyebrows. "Want me to be your therapist, babe? I've got a couch."

"Stop it. *Just stop it*. Every time I try to have a serious conversation with you, you turn it into a big joke. Is that all I am to you? A joke? I know I'm not brave like Tegan or quick-thinking like Logan or smart like Jed, but I'm a person, and I've got feelings. And I'm fed up with you running roughshod over them. I said I'd go out with Russell to help you, and I'm really scared, yet still you act like a total pig!"

The chair fell over as I shoved it back, and for one irrational second, I felt guilty for the crash. Then I remembered that Tegan slept like the dead, Miles had drunk all my wine, and the other two men were in cahoots with Ren and therefore partially responsible for my inability to sleep. I turned to run back inside, but when I tripped over a plant pot in my zombie-ish state, Ren's arm snaked around my waist and held me up.

"Get off me!"

Instead of letting go, he tightened his grip, and while my head kept protesting, my body made like a statue.

"Babe, I'm sorry."

His words slicked over my skin like caramel. Sweet, but bad for me. The apology sounded almost sincere, and if I hadn't known better, I might have fallen for it.

"No, you're not, because you keep acting this way."

"I'm sorry for that too." His arm loosened, but now the other one joined it, warm hands resting on my stomach as my pulse raced out of control. "You confuse me, cactus. The women in my life usually slot neatly into boxes. Colleagues I work with but keep my distance from. Friends I joke around with, but that I'd never invite to dance the horizontal tango. And women I fuck but nothing more. You? Every box I try to put you into, you don't fit. I want you in my bed, but I also want to be your friend. I want to send you far away from Luxor, and especially from Russell, but I can't because we need to find out what he's thinking. You're a puzzle, Taisiya Beaulieu, and one I don't know how to solve."

Wow. That was some speech. Possibly the most words Ren had ever said in one go, but my addled brain struggled to process them.

"I'm actually quite simple."

"You're anything but simple." How far away were his lips? An inch? A centimetre? The heat from his words felt like tiny firecrackers against my skin, and my pulse beat frantically in my throat. "Don't be scared. I promise I won't let you get hurt."

"Do you say that to all the women in your life?" And how many of them did he hurt himself?

"No, I don't promise them anything. And I never make promises I don't intend to keep."

"But I've never pretended to be a secret freaking agent before. What if I mess up?"

"You won't."

"But if I—"

One of his fingers came to rest on my lips. If his touch was supposed to soothe me, it had the opposite effect, and I shivered in spite of the heat.

"Shh. Not my first rodeo, cactus, and I've got faith in you."

Which was more than I had in myself.

"Why are you being so nice now?"

"Would you rather I made a joke about cowgirls? Because the words are just fighting to get out of my filthy mouth."

"Not really."

Good thing he'd moved behind me so he couldn't see my smile. Although being honest, I'd have preferred the wisecracks. Rude Ren was easy to push away. Sweet Ren made my stomach do backflips and sparky currents of electricity z-z-zap downwards through my limbs as though my body was desperately trying to ground itself.

And then I was in the air, cradled in Ren's arms as he carried me back into my apartment, my side pressed against his solid chest. Those muscles formed a barrier between me and the outside world, and just for a second, I wondered if he was right and things really would turn out okay. Then, as he laid me on the bed and pulled the still-damp sheet up over my body, I realised that not only would my life never be the same after Luxor, I might be in even bigger trouble than I'd previously thought.

"Houston, we have a problem," a crackly voice said.

Three p.m., and six hours since I'd called Russell to arrange dinner for that night. A meal at the Sheraton, he'd suggested. From what I could tell, well-off tourists mostly did the rounds of the eateries in the four- and five-star hotels in Luxor in the evenings rather than searching out the local places, and Russell was no exception. At least we'd be in public, and Ren was still in charming mode, reassuring me whenever my feet got chilly.

But now there was something wrong?

Logan held the phone to his ear, but the woman on the other end of the line was loud enough that I could hear if I strained. And her accent was British, which struck me as odd since Logan was American. Was it Miles's friend Emmy?

"How big of a problem?" he asked.

"About five foot six."

"Care to expand on that?"

"Bradley bugged my fucking office again."

Rather than frowning, Logan laughed out loud and clicked the phone onto speaker, presumably for Ren and Jed's benefit. "Oh boy, this is gonna be good."

"It's not bloody funny. He's furious. This is the guy who carries an abridged version of the Zen handbook in his purse, and he just threw a vase at me. And the TV remote. And a croissant."

"Wish I'd seen that."

"You'll get your chance. Right now, he's upstairs packing, and he reckons he's catching the first flight to Luxor, so he'll be your problem soon."

Logan paled under his beard. "Stop him."

"I can't."

"Sure you can. Just shoot him with a Taser or hit him up with etorphine."

"Nuh-uh. He threatened to quit. He can't freaking quit. Do you have any idea how much I hate shopping?"

"We can't have Bradley running around Luxor. He doesn't know how to do low-key."

"No kidding. He's got turquoise hair this week. But don't worry; I have a plan."

"What plan?"

"I'm gonna palm this week's job off on Ana or Fia, and then I'm gonna get the jet ready."

"Emmy..."

"This is all about damage control now. We'll be there tomorrow morning, your time. Can you send a car to the airport? Usually, I'd ask Bradley to arrange that, but he's refusing to speak to me at the moment and I'm sick of ducking."

Logan didn't bother to argue any further, just sighed. That worried me.

"I'll sort out a ride."

"Make sure it's got a big boot, yeah? You know what Bradley's like with luggage."

Ren muttered something that sounded suspiciously like "Fuck me." I'd have to decline no matter how much my nether regions might protest, but I understood the sentiment. The prospect of having a man who seemed somewhat hysterical thrown into our mess didn't exactly fill me with joy. And meeting other women, especially ones as authoritative as Emmy, made me nervous. I'd never been the most social of creatures. In fact, my spirit animal was a bear—fond of food, sleep, and my own company.

"Got it," Logan said. "What time will you arrive?"

"Not sure yet. I'll let you know. How's Miles holding up? Bradley's losing the plot because he's not answering the phone."

"That's because he's sleeping right now."

"Good. I'll pack the Valium, just in case. Anything else you need?"

All three men cut their eyes sideways towards me. Jed was the one who answered. "The usual. Maybe a set of body armour for Tai."

"Tai? Who's Tai?"

"To cut a long story short, she's Ren's next-door neighbour, who also happens to be dating our main suspect's brother. She can hear you, by the way."

"You invited her onto the team?"

"For her own protection. She didn't appreciate getting shot at this morning. Plus she's feeding us information."

"Fine. We'll talk when I arrive. Where are we staying?"

"I'll send you the GPS coordinates for Ren's rental property."

"That's the best place?"

"We've got all three apartments in the compound, and the wall around the place makes it easy to secure. I asked my contacts, but we can't find anything better for the moment. Ren told the landlord he's got some friends backpacking through, and he was fine with it."

"Miles lives in a second-floor apartment, so his place is out. Okay, I'll see you at Ren's." A shriek sounded down the phone. "Gotta go. I need to find my earplugs."

The line went dead, and we all looked at each other. Ren seemed vaguely uncomfortable, Logan rolled his eyes, and Jed just smiled.

"Uh, who exactly *is* Emmy?" I asked. "You mentioned some Blackwood thing?"

"She's Logan and Bradley's boss, and she part-owns

Blackwood Security," Ren said. "She's also Jed's ex-girlfriend."

"Ex-girlfriend? Isn't that awkward?"

Jed shook his head. "We get on fine. Plus she's the woman who overheard Ren making a comment about her ass and poured a jug of iced water into his lap. *That's* awkward."

Really? Hmm. I might actually have liked her if she didn't sound so scary.

"Bradley's Miles's boyfriend, isn't he? What did Emmy mean about him bugging her office?"

"Bradley's her PA, and she doesn't always give him as much information as he thinks he's entitled to, so he gets creative."

"Not that creative," Logan said. "He buys spy shit off the internet, and the tech guys always find it within a day or two, but sometimes we have unfortunate incidents like this one."

"Remember the time he overheard Mack and Luke discussing girls' names?" Jed asked.

"Mack and Luke are two of Emmy's crowd," Ren explained for my benefit. "Techie geeks. They're married."

Logan snorted out a laugh. "Yeah, Bradley got halfway through organising a surprise baby shower before someone told him they were thinking up a nickname for the new server at head office. Fuck. Emmy had better keep him under control."

"Have faith," Jed said, although he didn't sound totally convinced himself. "She'll do what she has to. Where were we? Who's going for dinner with Russell and Tai? We need two people in the restaurant, one outside in a vehicle, and someone with Miles. I don't want to put Tegan outside on her own. She's too much of an unknown quantity, skills-wise."

"I can go inside with Tegan," Ren suggested. "We could pose as a couple."

That shouldn't have made my gut twinge, but it did.

"Or me and Logan could have dinner in the restaurant and send you out a doggy bag," Jed said. "I like that idea better."

"In this country, a pair of men eating together at a table for two sticks out more than a man and a woman. Egypt's behind most of the world when it comes to LGBT rights."

"Aw, honey," Logan said. "Does that mean you don't get to feed me chocolate cake again?"

"We wouldn't have to act like a couple," Jed pointed out. "Would you rather sit outside in the SUV and sweat?"

"Good point."

"So, we've got two options," Jed said. "Ren has dinner with Tegan at the Sheraton, Logan can wait outside because he blends in better than me, and I'll babysit Miles until Emmy gets here."

"And what's the second option?" Ren asked. "You two go for dinner and I'm outside?"

"Yes. Tegan can watch Miles."

"Cactus, what would you be more comfortable with?"

There he was again. Considerate Ren. Although in a way, I wished he'd been his usual bullish self and made the decision because now everyone was staring at me.

Hmm... I quite liked the idea of Ren being in the restaurant—he was the man who'd already saved my life once, after all—but following our little heart-to-heart in the early hours, the prospect of watching him cosy up to Tegan left me cold for reasons I couldn't entirely explain. Would I rather have Logan and Jed nearby? Logan's quick save with the wine last night gave me confidence they knew what they were doing, but I didn't know them so well.

"Can't we just flip a coin?"

"That's not how this works, cactus."

"Fine. Then you make the decision. I'm all decisioned out for this week."

CHAPTER 26 - TAI

"YOU LOOK TENSE," Russell said as he topped up my glass of water. "Everything okay?"

No, everything was most certainly not okay. "Couldn't be better."

Where were Ren and Tegan? They were supposed to be there, but so far, I'd seen no sign of either of them, and I felt alone, vulnerable, even though I was in a restaurant full of people with a man who acted like the perfect gentleman. Was it just that? An act?

"Did you have a busy day?" Russell asked.

"Me? Oh, no, not at all. I spent the whole afternoon sitting in the garden with Tegan. Very relaxing. How about you? Did you hear any more from your brother after last night?"

"He called me."

"Oh? What about?"

Fish for information, that's what Ren had said. Ask open-ended questions so the target had to talk. The *target*. That's what he'd called Russell, and I felt awful for, well, not entirely lying, but definitely withholding information.

"What do you think of Finn?" Russell asked, neatly sidestepping my question.

A waiter slid a plate of poppadoms between us, together with a tray of colourful chutneys and a bottle of wine. Alcohol was the last thing I needed. My hands were trembling quite enough already, thank you, and if I got careless, I'd probably set fire to my sleeve with one of the candles clustered at the side of the table.

A couple walked past, providing a welcome distraction. A preppy guy in a button-down shirt and a slender brunette, the man's hand wrapped around his date's waist and one thumb stuck in the waistband of her wide-leg pants. Caring mixed with a touch of possessiveness, and I felt oddly envious.

Why was that?

Until I came to Egypt, I'd never really thought about what I wanted in a man, just fallen into bad relationships because I was flattered by the attention. Now I realised I deserved more, and if I couldn't have it, I'd rather have no man at all.

But what about Russell? If he had one fault, other than being related to a mass murderer, obviously, it was that he could be *too much* of a gentleman sometimes. Deep down inside, I wanted a man who protected me, who fought for me rather than merely opening doors and paying for dinner.

The host showed the couple to a table behind Russell, and I almost spat out the mouthful of water I'd just taken. It was Ren and Tegan. Ren had shaved off his stubble, slicked his hair back, and put on a pair of thick, plastic-framed glasses. Where had he gotten the makeover? He certainly hadn't brought that outfit with him. Not only that, his whole posture was different. Rather than his usual confident walk, he slouched forward and came across as altogether meeker.

And Tegan... Well, she must've been wearing a wig. Tendrils of chestnut-brown hair curled around her face, and my eyes were drawn to her lips, sharply outlined in a deep red. They'd both turned hipster, and when Tegan reached across the table for Ren's hand, a diamond sparkled on her ring finger.

If I'd felt nauseous before, now I felt positively sick.

"Tai?"

"Huh?"

"We were talking about my brother?"

Oh, right. What did I think of Finn? I thought shooting was too good for the man. Actually, hanging, drawing, and quartering was too good for him.

"Your brother... He seemed perfectly pleasant."

"Hmm."

"Hmm? What does that mean?"

"I don't really know how to put this."

"Put what?"

"It's a bit awkward..."

"Russell, just spit it out, would you?" Ugh, that sounded horrible. "Sorry, I didn't mean to be rude."

"No, no, it's fine. It's...well... Finn doesn't think you're good for me."

I knew the feeling well. That weird, hollow ache as though something was missing inside. A fault line. A void. Apart from my grandma and Paul, who came with his own problems, everyone in my life had rejected me at some point or another.

"Excuse me." I shoved my chair back and almost tripped over in my haste. Deep down, I knew I was being irrational, but the need to get away from the source of the pain was a visceral reaction I couldn't control. Call it self-preservation.

"Tai, wait."

But I was already scuttling towards the door. Where

the hell was the bathroom? With a weird sense of déjà vu, I recalled the last time I'd made a bathroom-related escape, at the Fellah's Tent, and started the wrecking ball rolling on this whole awful affair.

But today, I made it to the ladies' room without overhearing any dodgy antiquities-related conversations and ran into a stall. Except instead of the satisfying slam I'd been hoping for, the door bounced back with a thud.

"What the hell was that?" Ren asked, bolting the door behind us.

The walls of the tiny cubicle shrank further still as it filled with testosterone and aftershave. Something woodsy with a hint of sage underneath. I couldn't recall the name, but I might have sniffed it when I checked out his toiletry bag.

"Nothing."

"Cactus, your eyes are all wet." He wiped a stray tear away with his thumb. "That's not nothing."

"It's stupid."

"Okay, now we're getting closer to the truth. What's stupid?"

"Finn says I'm no good for Russell."

Ren raised one dark eyebrow. "Is that it?"

"I'm never good enough."

"Bullshit. You were doing great until you sprinted out of the room."

"But—"

"Finn's a professional liar, babe. He's probably just trying to keep you away from Russell because he wants Russell to leave the country."

"Do you really think so?"

"I wouldn't have—"

The outer door opened, and both of our heads snapped in the direction of the sound. In one smooth movement, Ren tucked me behind him, but when he realised it was only a pair of girls coming in to use the facilities, he twisted to wrap me up in his arms instead.

A Ren hug.

And like everything else, he was good at it.

My ragged breaths slowed as I felt the steady rise and fall of his chest, my own heart beating a wild tattoo as he kissed my hair. Last time I went out for dinner with Russell, Logan had stepped in to rescue me physically, and this time, Ren was fulfilling the role emotionally. I didn't know what to do with my arms, so I left them hanging limply at my sides as I turned my head to avoid dampening Ren's shirt. How long would it take for those women to pee? Secretly, I hoped a really long time.

"We've got you," Ren whispered as a toilet flushed. He lifted my chin so I was looking up at him. "Just keep going for a little longer."

I got this crazy urge to stand on tiptoes and kiss him, which was horribly wrong as I was on a date with another freaking man—one I actually sort of liked even if he had the family from hell—and also insane because ninety percent of the time, Ren drove me round the bend.

But there we were, pressed against each other, and I couldn't move away. Couldn't break the spell.

The second toilet flushed, and footsteps moved across the room. Water shooshed. A paper towel crumpled then landed in the bin.

"I've got faith in you, cactus," Ren murmured after the outer door closed. "Now go out there and knock 'em dead."

By the time I regained my faculties enough to stagger back to the table, Russell was on his feet, concern etched across his face, and Ren was already back at his table gazing into Tegan's eyes, much like he'd done with me such a short time ago.

See, Tai? It didn't mean anything. Ren's just a really good actor.

And so was Tegan. The way she giggled and smiled, I'd never have guessed she was undercover. The only indication she was watching me at all was the occasional flick of her gaze in our direction.

"Tai, I'm sorry," Russell said. "I shouldn't have been so blunt. And I should've prefaced the explanation by saying I completely and utterly disagree with Finn."

"It doesn't matter."

"Yes, it does. He made an unfair assumption about you being a gold-digger, and I set him straight. And can you believe he still had the gall to ask me to take his package back to London in time for mother's birthday next week?"

"Uh, did you agree?"

"I hung up on him."

Russell shrugged and nibbled on a poppadom, looking far more relaxed than I felt. Behind him, Ren reached over to brush a strand of fake hair out of Tegan's eyes, and I decided I'd much rather be having dinner with him than participating in this awkward conversation with Russell, no matter how convincingly Russell might dismiss his brother's opinion.

"Finn called me back," Russell continued. "Said he wanted to meet to talk things over."

What the heck was I supposed to say to that? "I

guess that sounds sensible. He is your brother, after all."

"By blood, perhaps, but he's behaving like an arsehole at the moment, even more so than usual. Part of me wants to cut him off, but against my better judgement, I said I'd go for dinner with him and discuss this properly."

What if Finn convinced Russell to stop seeing me? I'd be letting the rest of the team down. Although I still felt guilty for bending the truth with Russell, the prospect of failing to catch the men behind the massacre worried me the most.

"When are you meeting him?"

"I'm not. I suggested he meet me at the Winter Palace, but he insisted I go to his boat and wouldn't budge on that, so I changed my mind. If he won't put in the slightest effort, then I won't either. I'd much rather spend my time doing things I enjoy, which means having dinner with you. Anyhow, enough talk about my brother tonight. Let's enjoy each other's company and a good bottle of wine instead." He swirled the red around in his glass and took a sniff. "Okay, so it's a mediocre bottle of wine, but the sentiment's there. To us, and our time in Luxor."

I clicked my glass against his. "To us."

That was what I said, but as the words left my mouth, I had a strange urge to be drinking beer on the patio with Ren instead.

CHAPTER 27 - TAI

BACK AT THE compound, Ren greeted me with his hands up in a gesture of apology. He and Tegan had left the Sheraton while Russell was paying the bill and beaten our taxi back home.

"Don't yell, but we had to borrow your apartment again."

"I'm not going to yell, but why?"

"Logan's on his way from the airport with Emmy and Bradley. We figured Bradley and Miles would probably want some privacy when they arrive, which means they'll be in my apartment. The rest of us need to share with you and Tegan, at least for tonight."

I quickly counted up on my fingers. Me, Tegan, Ren, Jed, Logan, and now Emmy. "Six people in two apartments? But we only have two beds."

"True." Ren waggled his eyebrows, back to his usual caddish self. "Wanna share?"

My answer was automatic. "No way!"

But even as I said it, I couldn't help wondering what a night with Ren would be like.

Oh, wash your dirty mind out with soap, Tai.

"Suit yourself. What did Russell have to say tonight?"

"Finn's still being diff—"

I didn't get any further before a car door slammed

and feet slapped on the hard-packed dirt, running in our direction. Ren shifted his stance, and when I glanced down, I saw a gun glinting in the hand by his side. I froze as the gate crashed open with a metallic clang.

"Where's Miles? Where is he?"

The newcomer had turquoise hair and a crazed look about him, but Ren relaxed. "Bradley," he mouthed.

Logan appeared in the gateway with a blonde woman beside him. The two suitcases she was dragging looked as if they weighed a ton.

"Miles is asleep in that apartment," Logan said, pointing towards Ren's front door.

"And for fuck's sake keep it down," the blonde said.

Bradley just glared at her. "Miles almost *died*. Do you realise that?"

"Yeah, but he's still breathing. Don't stress about shit that didn't happen."

"Shut up!" Bradley shrieked as he ran to the door.

"Bradley still isn't taking this well?" Ren asked.

"What does it look like? He's barely speaking to me, and I had to pack my own fucking suitcase."

She spoke softly but confidently, and the don't-mess-with-me vibes rolling off her made me nervous. *More* nervous. Bradley must've had a steel spine to talk to her the way he did. Me? I began tiptoeing sideways, hoping to reach the safety of my apartment before she looked in my direction.

"You must be Tai?"

Too late. Dammit.

"Uh, yes?"

"Emmy Black."

She held out a hand for me to shake, and I hated

the way mine trembled when I placed it into hers. What must she think of my sweaty palms? Not a lot, it seemed, since she turned away almost immediately and focused on Jed, who sauntered through the gate in an *I Heart Luxor* T-shirt, a camera hanging over one shoulder. He flashed a grin in Emmy's direction, and she returned it, but only for a second. Then her expression hardened once more.

"So, what's going on?" she asked. "Everything under control?"

Not even a little bit, in my opinion, but Jed shrugged. "More or less."

"I put briefing notes on the server," Logan said. His unasked question: didn't you read them?

"I forgot my laptop charger, and the battery ran out. Do you need me for this jaunt, or shall I get some rest? How are we set for bedrooms?"

Jed took over. "Your input's always welcome, darlin'. Bedrooms... Yeah, we're short of those. Reckon you'll have to take Tai's."

My mouth opened to protest, but Ren pressed a finger over my lips.

"Explain later," he whispered.

Meanwhile, the others headed for my apartment as one, following some secret agent code of conduct that I wasn't privy to. As with so many things in my life, I felt like a spare part, an outsider, at least until Ren clasped my hand and pulled me along with them.

"What are you doing?"

"Going to get briefed. Rather be getting debriefed."

"With me?"

"Why? Are you offering?"

Aw, heck. Where did those freaking dimples come

from? I did my best to scowl back, but I'm not sure it worked, and little jolts of electricity rushed up my arm from my fingertips.

"Stop being so dirty-minded. I meant, do I need to come to the briefing?"

"Cactus, you're participating in the briefing. We need to know what went on tonight."

With Ren alone, I could cope, but now there were four virtual strangers, all of them self-assured and trained for this. Even Tegan had a steely resolve about her now, a resignation that she had to see this through to the end. Subterfuge was in her blood while my veins ran with custard.

Furniture was swiftly rearranged. Jed set his laptop on the coffee table, knelt in front of it, and entered a password longer than my address. Emmy sat in the chair-hammock, one toned leg crossed over the other, while Tegan squashed onto the two-seater sofa beside Logan's massive thighs. When Ren took the beanbag, that left me standing awkwardly, contemplating whether to perch on one narrow arm of the sofa beside Tegan. At least, until Ren tugged me down onto his lap.

"What the hell?" I squeaked.

"You looked lost."

I glanced around at the others, but nobody batted an eyelid at the seating arrangements, and before I could decide whether to scramble off or make the best of the situation, Jed began speaking.

"For Emmy's benefit, let's give a quick recap of where we are."

He went over the case so far, right up to my dinner with Russell tonight, and Emmy asked the occasional question, but mostly she listened.

"So we've got a missing treasure, a main suspect, and a relative who may or may not be involved, but who right now seems more like an innocent bystander. Plus there are other gang members we haven't identified yet," she summarised.

"That's about right."

"Where's the cartouche?"

"Safe," Ren said, and Emmy seemed to accept that. *His hand was on my freaking lap.*

"No leads on the other members of the gang?"

"Unfortunately not, other than the American Tai overheard. But I struggle to believe that Finn Weisz came up with this plan all by himself, and he also has a group of lackeys working with him locally."

"He must communicate with them somehow," Emmy said. "Have we tapped his phone?"

"It's in hand," Jed told her, "but there's nothing useful yet."

"Emails?"

"We're still trying to get at the rest of his electronics, but we're starting from scratch here. It's not like a terrorist network where we've got whispers coming from every corner and all we have to do is connect the dots. This came from out of the blue. But our people back at Langley are assisting, so we should start to get information soon. Nobody can stay invisible in cyberspace, no matter how hard they might try."

"*Soon?* Isn't that agency-speak for next year?"

"I've put a rush on it."

"Next month, then. It's so cute that you do things by the book."

"I know I'm gonna regret asking this, but do you have a better idea?"

"Of course I do."

"Care to share?"

"Simple. Rather than trawling through the web for one pinprick, we start with the endpoint and cast the net outwards. All we need to do is get hold of Finn's computer. Where does he live? I'll just pop over while he's out."

She said it so matter-of-factly, like breaking into someone's home was an everyday occurrence. Perhaps for her it was. She didn't seem the least bit concerned about committing a crime. Nobody in the room—well, except for me—seemed surprised by her plan either. But there was a flaw in it.

"You can't do that," I blurted.

She slowly raised one perfectly plucked eyebrow. "Oh?"

"Russell told me that Finn isn't going out at the moment."

"Really? Why not?"

"I don't know. I mean, I guess that maybe it's because he wants to lie low or something. You know, avoid attention. Russell asked Finn to meet him for dinner at the hotel he's staying in, but Finn said Russell would have to come to his boat instead."

"Finn lives on a boat?"

"Yes, on the Nile." Like there was any other water in Luxor. *Way to sound smart, Tai.* "Russell stayed there with him for a while when he first came to Luxor, but he said it was really cramped."

"Lying low... Hmm." Hmm? What was "hmm" supposed to mean? "Then I need to get on that boat. We've got three options. The first is some sort of evacuation, but that might raise suspicions. It'll be far easier if you call your boyfriend and persuade him to get his brother out of the way."

Easier? In what parallel universe? "Russell isn't my boyfriend."

"He thinks he is, and that's all that matters."

"What's the third option?"

"We could sink the boat, but that seems kinda drastic. Plus if there's anything on paper, it won't be easy to retrieve it from the bottom of the Nile intact. No, the second option's definitely best. You can call Russell in the morning."

"But—"

"He seems to like you by all accounts, so it shouldn't be too difficult to engineer something. Now, the sleeping arrangements. Who's taking first watch? Jed, I'll need you nearby when I'm asleep. Things haven't been too good lately."

"You rest first," Jed said. "I'll stay in here, and Logan can go outside with Tegan—one at the back, one at the front. You okay to take the second shift with Ren?"

"Sure."

"What about me?" I asked. "Do I need to take a shift?"

Emmy shook her head. "Get a good night's sleep. If you want to help, try to keep Bradley occupied tomorrow. That'd be doing us all a favour."

CHAPTER 28 - TAI

ALTHOUGH I UNDERSTOOD that I was in no way cut out to take on an intruder if one should appear, I still felt weirdly disappointed at getting sidelined. For a couple of days, I'd almost felt like I belonged on the team, a weird combination of fear and adrenaline mixed with camaraderie.

Now I was back to being the girl who got picked last for every single sports team at school. Awkward.

No, actually, make that super awkward, because I'd just walked into Tegan's apartment and realised the snag in the sleeping arrangements.

Two people.

One bed.

"Don't worry; I'll take the couch," Ren said from behind me.

Russell would have offered, certainly, but coming from Ren? The gesture was slightly unexpected. A pleasant surprise, but it wouldn't work.

"You're too tall. I'll take the couch."

As well as being better suited size-wise, it was the least I could do if Ren was going to be awake for half the night keeping us safe. He needed a proper rest, and he wouldn't get that if he was folded in half.

"It's a foot shorter than you too."

"I'll bend my knees or something."

"Nah, cactus, you won't. I may be an asshole, but I'm not that much of an asshole."

"I'm sleeping on the couch."

"Then we're both sleeping on the damn couch, and I'm not responsible for wherever my hands end up."

"Oh, this is ridiculous. If we're both going to sleep on the couch, then we might as well both sleep in the bed."

"You said it."

Before I could backpedal, Ren had pulled his shirt over his head and flopped back onto the mattress. Had he planned this all along? It wouldn't have surprised me. He always was several steps ahead, but he was also right—I'd made the suggestion, so now I had to go through with it, and besides, the sofa really didn't look comfortable.

But it did have a bunch of cushions, and I lined them up along the middle of the bed to keep Ren on his side. Did he snore? Please say he didn't snore.

It was weird sleeping in somebody else's bed, even with fresh sheets. Sayid's wife must've changed them earlier. And it was even weirder having another person next to me. How long since I'd shared a bed with a man? Months. No, not months. Years.

Guilt crept over me. By rights, it should've been Russell at my side. He was the man I was sort-of-dating, the man I'd contemplated seeing more of when I eventually went back home to England. But that was then and this was now, and everything had changed.

I lay down, tucking myself under the single sheet fully clothed as if a layer or two of thin cotton could protect me from Ren's wandering hands.

"Don't be upset, babe," Ren murmured from the

other side of my cushion-wall.

"I'm fine. Just stay in your half of the bed, okay?"

"I didn't mean about that. I saw your face when Emmy was handing out the orders earlier. She didn't leave you out on purpose—she assigns the best person for each role, that's all."

Mind reader. "I understand. I'm no Tegan, that's for sure."

"If Emmy had another of her own people with her, Tegan would've been bumped from night-watch duties too." He sighed. "Between you and me, I'm worried about Tegan. She might have the training, but when the adrenaline's not flowing, she lets the stress get to her."

"The stress is getting to me as well."

"You're weirdly calm in a crisis, cactus."

Calm? I begged to differ. Inside, I felt as if every nerve ending was going to implode, but I didn't want to admit that in present company. "Do you think Emmy was serious about keeping Bradley occupied?"

"Yeah. It'll be easier for you because he doesn't know you. He'll blame the rest of us for not telling him about the shooting, apart from Tegan, who'll need to rest."

That did make sense. "How am I supposed to distract him, though?"

"Ask him for make-up tips or something."

"Gee, thanks."

"Ah, fuck. I didn't mean that the way it sounded. What I meant is Bradley loves fashion and clothes and all that shit, and if you can get him to talk about it, he'll forget the rest."

"You really think that'll work?"

"Try it."

I covered a yawn, and it must've been infectious because I heard Ren suck in a breath as he yawned too. I felt bad for keeping him awake with questions, but not bad enough to stop asking them.

"Why did Emmy have to take my bedroom? And why is Jed with her? I thought you said they broke up?"

"They did, and they're both married to other people now. But Emmy has trouble sleeping from what I've heard, so Jed'll keep an eye on her to make sure she doesn't do anything stupid."

"Like what?"

"Sleepwalking. I don't know the full story, but there's a rumour she half-killed a guy once."

"While she was asleep?"

"Yeah."

"How? How on earth could she do that?"

"Someone comes at her wrong, and her subconscious just reacts. Like an automatic defence mechanism."

"But you'd be okay if she tried anything, wouldn't you? You're bigger than her."

"The guy she sent to the hospital was a Navy SEAL. Trust me, you don't want to mess with her. Just avoid her at all costs."

Holy hell. No, I definitely didn't want to mess with her. In fact, I'd make sure to keep right out of her way. She scared me a bit even when she was awake.

"Avoid her. Got it."

Ren took one of my carefully placed cushions and dropped it on the floor. Now I could see his face in the moonlight, and he gave me a small smile.

"Don't worry; she's on our side."

"How can I not worry? I have to call Russell in the

morning and convince him to do something he already said he didn't want to do. And I'm hopeless at persuading people. Back in primary school, I got put in charge of selling button badges for charity once, and I ended up emptying my piggy bank and buying them all myself."

Then Mum had yelled at me for wasting money while Peony laughed in the background. My protests that at least I'd helped homeless hedgehogs had fallen on deaf ears, my judgement criticised in a way that became all too familiar over the years.

"You've got more power than you think, babe."

"I'm not sure about that."

"What you don't have is confidence, but that can be learned. As I said, I've got faith in you."

That... That was the nicest thing anyone had ever said to me. So nice that a tear leaked out, and of course Ren noticed. I shrank back as his hand snuck through the gap to wipe it away.

"I'm not gonna molest you in your sleep, cactus."

"I know that."

"Then don't act so nervous. Either stand your ground or tell me to fuck off."

I couldn't possibly say that to Ren. Once, perhaps, but not anymore. It took an effort, but I straightened myself and stood my ground. Well, I was lying down, but you know what I mean.

"Better," he said. "Now get some sleep."

I closed my eyes, but my mind churned. My last thought before the darkness claimed me? That perhaps I wouldn't mind being molested by Ren after all.

"Shift change."

Tegan's voice cut into my dream, and I cursed under my breath. Both because the dream had ended and because I shouldn't have been having it in the first place. Not when it starred Ren, a bed, a lot of sweat, and hardly any clothes.

It took a moment for reality to seep into my consciousness, like a wave slowly rolling its way up a beach. Tegan had turned the lights on low. My carefully arranged line of cushions? Gone. The sweaty skin? All too real. My hand? Resting on... Oh, bloody hell. And Ren? Awake.

"Son of a biscuit!"

I bolted up as if I'd been electrocuted, but my feet tangled in the sheet and my ass hit the floor hard enough to send a shockwave up my spine. And worse, when Ren loomed above me to haul me to my feet, I could see right up his boxers to his supersized frank 'n' beans swinging overhead.

"Sorry," I choked out. "I'm so sorry."

"S'okay. I've been called worse."

"I didn't mean..."

Ren leaned in close, out of Tegan's earshot. "You can fondle my cock any day, cactus."

His obviously hard cock. It stuck out like a flagpole, bobbing about as he turned to go into the bathroom. Only when I heard the door lock click did I flop back onto the bed.

Tegan looked as though she was trying to suppress a smirk. "You and Ren? I thought you didn't like him?"

"I don't. I mean, I didn't. Honestly, I don't know how I feel about him anymore. He's just this massive presence, and most of the time I'm overwhelmed."

"I get that. My ex was the same—one big ball of testosterone and charisma. Never gonna fall into that trap again."

"It's a trap?"

"With Ren? Not in the same way, I don't think, but there's an unpredictability with that type of guy. I used to find it exciting, addictive, but after how it ended... No, if I ever date again, I'm going for Mr. Sensible. Oh, who am I kidding...? I spend my life running from non-extradition country to non-extradition country. I can't even have a relationship with a vibrator in case I get awkward questions from airport security."

"Where are you going to go next? After this is over?"

Tegan sank onto the bed beside me. "At the moment, I'm trying not to think about that. Before, I always used to plan ahead, but now... Sometimes, I wish I'd taken a bullet to the head at al-Nahas."

"You don't mean that."

She fell silent for a long moment, and I wondered if I should start worrying. Tegan had become a real friend over the last few weeks, and I had precious few of those.

"I'm not suicidal or anything," she said softly. "I guess...it would just have made things easier, that's all. Although..."

"Although what?"

"I'd have missed out on this. The teamwork. The challenges. I loved it once, and even though I'm freaking terrified, it feels good to be a part of something again. Does that sound crazy? The loneliness, the lying... It's been eating away at me, and it's such a relief being myself, even if it's only for a few days."

"No, it's not crazy. And I know what you mean about the loneliness. Maybe we could travel together after this is over?"

"Are you serious?"

"The police want to talk to me in England, and I'm... I'm..." I didn't want to say the word.

"Scared?"

"Yes."

"I don't want to trivialise what happened at work or anything, but they're not gonna extradite you over corporate theft. Probably if you went in and explained, everything would get dropped."

"But what would I tell them?"

Honestly, the only benefit I could see to a police interview would be if they realised I was clearly too dumb to pull off any kind of fraud.

"Just tell them the truth. I doubt there was any big conspiracy in your case, so they'll investigate and clear you. I can help out with what to say if you like? I've been on the opposite side of the table enough times." When I hesitated, she gave my hand a squeeze. "Think about it, okay? It doesn't have to ruin your life."

She lay down and rolled away from me onto Ren's side of the bed. Through the doors, I saw Emmy walk out of the apartment next door, relaxed as she settled onto a sunlounger and fiddled with the gun in her lap. The freaking *gun*. Ice formed in my veins, taking the edge off the heat kindled by Ren earlier. Every time I began to hope we might get out of this mess intact, I got a horrible reminder of the truth. This was a war against an unseen enemy.

Ren reappeared from the bathroom, minus the bulge—I couldn't help looking, okay?—and crouched in front of me.

"It'll be all right. We'll fix this, I promise."

How did he always know what I was thinking?

"I want to believe that," I whispered.

Instead of answering, he leaned forward and kissed my hair the way he had in the toilet stall earlier then disappeared out of the door, leaving me more confused than ever.

Tegan's whisper came from the other side of the bed. "I think he likes you."

CHAPTER 29 - TAI

"IS THAT MY toothbrush?" Jed asked.

Emmy stood on the patio with her phone in one hand and the blue toothbrush in the other. She'd tied her blonde hair up in a messy bun and knotted an oversized T-shirt at her waist, somehow managing to look effortlessly cool while I felt as though I'd been dragged backwards through a briar patch. Logan was doing push-ups in a pair of shorts while Tegan stared into a mug of coffee, and Betsy scrabbled around in the dirt, clucking. Just another regular day chez Sayid. The new normal.

Emmy paused mid-stroke. "Hush, dude. We've swapped saliva enough times in the past."

"That was different."

She managed a frothy grin. "Yeah, it was, but your wife and my husband would kill us both if we tried that again."

Jed rolled his eyes as she leaned over and spat toothpaste into the bushes.

"Spitting?" he muttered. "First time for everything."

Logan finished his push-ups and jumped to his feet in one smooth motion. "Hey, is that my T-shirt?" he asked Emmy.

"Well, it certainly isn't mine. Gimme a belt and I could wear it as a dress."

And if I wasn't mistaken, I'd seen those shorts in Ren's suitcase too. Didn't she bring anything of her own to Egypt?

Seemed as though Ren had had the same thought when he materialised beside me.

"You brought two suitcases. What the hell did you pack in them?"

Emmy glanced in my direction, then focused back on Ren and smiled unnaturally brightly. "Stuff."

"Stuff?"

"Yup. Stuff. Life's little essentials. It's amazing what you can carry with a private jet and a couple of decent backhanders. Besides, they're far more interested in what's leaving the country at the moment. Want a croissant? I just got back from the bakery."

"You shouldn't be eating those," Bradley said, hands on his hips as he walked around the corner of the building wearing a pink silk dressing gown and fluffy slippers. A matching eye mask was pushed up on his head. "Toby said you have to eat egg white and spinach omelettes for breakfast this week."

"Well, Toby's not here."

"Who's Toby?" I whispered to Ren.

"Her nutritionist."

Bradley glowered as she tucked the toothbrush into Jed's hand then picked up a pain au chocolat and a mug of coffee and strolled into my apartment. I didn't know whether to admire the woman's confidence or hate her.

But when Ren nudged me in Bradley's direction, I remembered I had a job to do no matter how I felt about Emmy. As Tegan had reminded me last night, it was good to be part of a team.

"Hi, I'm Tai. We didn't meet properly last night."

Bradley squashed the breath out of me with a hug. "Miles told me a lot about you."

"Uh-oh."

"Don't fret, doll, it's all good. Did you honestly walk out of your job?"

"I just couldn't stand it any longer. Have you ever had a boss you wanted to push off a bridge?"

Bradley glanced in the direction Emmy had gone. "Yes."

Oops. Wrong thing to say. *Quick, Tai, think.* Ren's words came back to me. "Uh, I love your eyeliner. Whenever I use it, I end up looking like a raccoon."

Or at least I had on both occasions I'd tried. Me and make-up didn't really mix. Imagine Dame Barbara Cartland crossed with Marilyn Manson and you'll understand why I avoided those fancy counters in department stores. A smear of lip balm was pretty much my limit.

But Bradley seemed unfazed. "I can teach you some little tricks that'll leave you red-carpet-ready." He looped his arm through mine. "Come on, Miles is making French toast for breakfast."

"Hey, hey. Wait." Jed stepped into our path before we could escape. "Not so fast, Picasso. Tai needs to make a phone call first."

Dammit. I'd hoped that if I avoided the problem for long enough, it'd go away. How on earth was I supposed to persuade Russell to lure Finn off his boat? I had no idea, but with so many eyes watching, so many people counting on me, I couldn't chicken out. Not now. And especially not after Ren had said he had faith in me.

"Gosh, I almost forgot." Five faces stared at me expectantly. "Uh, I'll call from my apartment." Except Emmy was in there. "From Tegan's apartment," I corrected.

Ren followed me inside like a faithful puppy. I'd always wanted a dog, but the closest I'd come was the stray I'd found three days before my thirteenth birthday. A tiny terrier, a Jack Russell maybe. I'd begged Mum to let me keep him, promised I'd never ask for anything else, but she'd complained about house-training and shedding hair and sent him to the shelter the next morning. Betsy was the only pet I'd ever had, and making sure she had water and corn in the mornings was oddly satisfying. Some living, breathing creature *needed* me.

"Thought you might want moral support," Ren said.

"Admit it—you just want to hear me screw up again."

"If the conversation isn't going your way, don't panic. Back off, regroup, and try again later."

"But that takes time."

"Then it takes time. Better than blowing the operation or putting yourself in danger."

"I'm not cut out for this secret agent stuff."

"You're doing better than you think. Want to practise the conversation with me first?"

I gave my head a hurried shake. The only thing more painful than bumbling my way through this ruse would be having to do it twice. My mouth was dry, and attempting to swallow led to a coughing fit. Silently, Ren fetched me a glass of water while I dialled.

The phone rang on speaker once. Twice. My heart slowed infinitesimally as I wondered if Russell might be busy, but then my luck ran out.

"Tai? You're up early."

"I couldn't stop thinking about you."

It wasn't a total lie.

"Really? I've been thinking about you too. And dinner."

"Last night's dinner? The food was amazing. When you suggested going for Indian, I thought it would be a poor imitation, but the samosas were so light and crispy. And I loved the saag paneer. And the kulfi. What was your favourite thing?"

What was I even waffling about?

"The company."

"Oh."

"Let's do it again tonight. Any restaurant you like."

Something chimed, and I checked my phone. Nope, no messages. Did the noise come from Russell's end?

"I'm still finding my way around Luxor. I'm sure you're far better at picking out a place to eat than me." No answer. "Russell? Are you there?"

"Sorry. My brother just tried to call again. That's the fifth time this morning."

"What does he want?"

"Who knows?"

"You haven't answered?"

"No. Quite frankly, I'm sick of pandering to him and my mother. She smothers me, and Finn's been a control freak from the moment he was born, constantly demanding attention. I've tried my best to keep them happy, but enough's enough."

The fragile hope that I might be able to enlist an unwitting Russell into our plan skittered away. What if he wouldn't lure Finn off the boat? Would Emmy really go with one of the other options?

"I'm sure he only means well. Take his idea of coming to Luxor—didn't you say you were enjoying yourself?"

"I'll concede I needed a holiday."

"And the night before last, he only wanted to send a gift to your mother, even if he was a bit pushy in trying to make you take it."

"I guess."

"I promised I'd have dinner with Tegan tonight, so why don't you meet with him and talk things over, and we can go out tomorrow instead?"

I held my breath, then almost swallowed my tongue when Ren leaned forward and squeezed my hand. A coughing fit ensued, and I totally missed Russell's answer while Ren thumped me on the back.

"Sorry, what did you say?" I choked out as soon as I was able. "I didn't hear."

"Are you okay?"

"Perfect. I just, uh, I think I swallowed a bug. Maybe a mosquito."

A mosquito? *Good grief, Tai.* I desperately needed to improve my lying game. When I was seven, a teacher described me as pathologically honest in my school report, which sounds like a compliment, but it only arose after I fussed about having my photo taken with the visiting mayor. When he asked why I wouldn't smile, I told him he smelled like old socks. Needless to say, Mum hadn't been thrilled by that response either.

"Try drinking a glass of water," Russell suggested.

"I'm fine now, honest. What did I miss?"

"I said that you're right. Finn's life can't be easy either, not since tourism slowed over here, and I should cut him some slack."

Really? Wow. My words had worked. They'd actually worked.

"Why don't you offer him a compromise?" I was on a roll now. "He wants you to go to his boat, and you want him to come to the Winter Palace. Why don't you suggest meeting halfway? Somewhere near the boat but not on it? That'd be fair."

"That's not a bad idea at all. And you'll go to dinner with me tomorrow night instead?"

"Absolutely. Sounds wonderful, and I'll come up with some restaurant ideas in the meantime."

"I'll pick you up at seven. Tai?"

"Yes?"

"I'm really glad we met. For the first time in ages, I'm looking forward to life outside of work."

"Me too. Not the 'outside of work part,' obviously, because I don't have a job, but meeting you has changed the course of my life." Aaaaaand I was going to hell for leading Russell on. "You've given a stupid, impulsive trip meaning."

Ren grinned, and Russell cleared his throat then gave a little chuckle that was part surprised, part pleased.

"I'm glad you feel that way, darling."

"So, I'll see you tomorrow?" I needed to end this call before the cold band around my chest constricted so much I couldn't breathe.

"I can't wait." A second passed. "You're still there."

"So are you."

"Well, uh, bye."

Ren hung up for me.

"Hey! Why did you do that?"

"Because you were about to get into the whole 'you hang up, no, *you* hang up' thing, and my balls would've shrivelled in protest. You did good, cactus."

"I did?"

"Couldn't have done it better myself."

"Well, of course not. Your voice is too low and rumbly."

Ren just stared at me.

"Sorry, that was a terrible joke."

"Humour in a crisis? We'll make an agent of you yet. C'mon, let's tell the others what's happening.

By lunchtime—a meal I felt too sick to eat—I'd texted innocently back and forth with Russell, and it seemed that Finn had agreed to compromise. They'd be meeting for dinner at Wok's the Story, a Chinese restaurant that, according to Ren, was within sight of Finn's boat.

"Do you think he planned it that way on purpose?" I asked.

"Undoubtedly."

"Then how will you get on board? Won't he see you?"

"It'll be dark, and Emmy's good at this shit."

"She's the one who'll get on the boat?"

"Yup."

"On her own?"

"Me and Logan are gonna play lookout, and Jed'll join the Weisz brothers in the restaurant."

"What about me? What should I do? I could help out like Tegan did yesterday."

Heat spiked through me as I thought back to Tegan and Ren's "date" to the Indian restaurant, the flames a dangerous mix of jealousy and longing. Dangerous because Ren had wormed his way under my skin enough that I'd put myself in harm's way to act as his fake girlfriend for a few hours. My hand still tingled from where he'd squeezed it earlier, and I came to the horrible realisation that I liked him. As in, really liked him. In the most stupid way possible because we were a world apart and had nothing in common but a shared hatred of antiquities thieves.

Why couldn't I have liked Russell in the same way? He ticked every box, on paper at least. Smart, well-off, successful... A week ago, I'd fallen asleep hoping that our holiday friendship might last until we got home to England. I'd dreamed of dates to the Natural History Museum and West End musicals and the fancy eateries around Windsor Castle, all the places I'd never go alone.

But I knew now that we'd never work out. Not just because I was working to put his brother in jail, but because I'd had a taste of Ren, metaphorically speaking. Felt that shiver when he came near, the rush of fire when he brushed against me. The heady lust I'd tried so hard to ignore.

I couldn't settle for second best, even if first was way out of my reach.

Even if he gave me the brush-off.

Which was exactly what happened.

"Nah, you stay here, cactus. We'll have enough to worry about."

Enough to worry about without waiting for naïve, cowardly Tai to screw up. Oh, he didn't say the words,

but I knew what he meant, and I won't deny it stung
But I smiled even as tears threatened to spill out.

"And Tegan?"

"She'll stay with you."

A babysitter. Brilliant.

"What if something goes wrong?"

"Tegan's got a gun, and she knows how to use it."

"I meant with snooping on Finn's boat."

"Have faith, babe. We've had plenty of practice a
this. All you have to do is relax and keep Bradley calm
I'd make a comment about keeping the bed warm if
wasn't scared of losing my balls."

At the mention of the word "balls," I had a sudder
flashback to that glimpse I'd got of Ren's earlier and
choked on my tongue.

"Hey, I was only kidding. I'll sleep on the couch i
you want."

Swallow, Tai. Breathe. "No, it's fine. This is ar
awkward situation, and we both have to act like adults.

"Good girl. We're gonna head out soon."

"Uh, I guess I should say good luck, then."

This time, I got a kiss on the forehead when
longed for so much more.

"See you later, cactus."

Ren said he had faith in me, and now I had to
return the favour, no matter how difficult it might be
Even though I didn't exactly have him, I still couldn'
bear to lose him.

CHAPTER 30 - TAI

"ANYTHING?" I ASKED Tegan as we sat at the table on the terrace.

The others had been gone for three hours, and dusk was approaching. They weren't due back yet, I knew that, but surely it wouldn't have been too much to ask for them to call with an update occasionally?

"In these situations, no news is usually good news. Look on the bright side—we haven't heard any sirens or gunfire."

Oh, that was comforting.

Bradley walked out with a tray of drinks. And when I say drinks, I mean cocktails. Colourful concoctions decorated with fruit and tiny umbrellas, ice cubes clinking as he walked.

"Pre-dinner apéritif?" he asked.

"Dinner?"

"Miles is cooking. Mango chicken with rice and a vanilla soufflé for dessert."

"Cooking? At a time like this?"

"It helps him to relax."

"I guess I can understand him wanting to keep busy, but how can he eat? Emmy's about to walk into the lion's den if she hasn't already."

"Don't worry about Emmy." Bradley waved dismissively, and colourful bangles jingled on his wrist.

"She's just the Terminator with better hair. I should know; I style it. And speaking of hair, there's enough time for me to fix yours before Miles serves dinner."

"What do you mean, fix my hair? What's wrong with it?"

"What's *right* with it?" He ticked off the points on his fingers. "The length is meh, it's got no body, the split ends go halfway up, and the colour's drab. Now, only brought a small bottle of bleach, but it'll be enough to do highlights, and Miles has some leftover foil from cooking the chicken."

Bradley was halfway inside before I came to my senses. "Wait. Wait! Have you lost your mind? We're in the middle of...of..."

What did I even call this situation?

"A job," he offered. "They call it a job. But it's fine; Emmy's careful, so things hardly ever go wrong. The time her house got blown up by an assault team was a total one-off. Can you find a spare towel?"

I was going to pretend I didn't hear the second-to-last sentence. "You're not dying my hair."

The beginnings of a headache pulsed through my skull, a dull throb that reminded me of its presence with every breath. I had a packet of pain pills in my pocket from my last Ren-induced migraine, so swallowed a couple then washed them down with one of Bradley's concoctions.

"But you'd look so much prettier," he said. "Aren't you supposed to be going on another date with that computer hacker from London?"

"Russell isn't a hacker!" Didn't hackers steal information? Russell wasn't a criminal, no way. "He does...something with software."

"Yes, he hacks into it. I heard Emmy say so. Now, hurry up or dinner'll get burned."

"Tai's right." Oh, thank goodness. Tegan was backing me up. "If we do need to run for any reason, she can hardly do that with foils in her hair. It'll get damaged if she doesn't rinse out the bleach in time."

Bradley twiddled one diamond earring as he thought. "Fine. Just a cut, then. It'll take fifteen minutes."

"But—"

He pointed towards Tegan's apartment, where the tiny dining table and two chairs waited near the door. "Sit."

In all honesty, it was easier to let him cut my hair than argue. And I knew he was right about the state of it. I looked at the straggly ends in the mirror every morning, but I'd been too nervous to try and find a hairdresser in Luxor in case something got lost in translation and I ended up getting a crew cut. And Emmy's hair looked amazing, all bounce and shine and long wavy layers.

If Ren had a girlfriend, she'd have hair like that. Not a wild tangle of frizz that looked boring on a good day.

"Maybe just a quick trim..."

Bradley beamed at me. "You won't regret it, I promise."

I didn't regret getting my hair cut—Bradley had chopped layers into my tangles and given me a sweeping fringe I'd never have been brave enough to try on my own—but I did regret the cocktails. And the chicken. Yes, it had tasted delicious, but I ate too much of it, and when I stepped outside to get some fresh air Betsy clucked at me. I swear she knew I'd just eaten one of her relatives.

There was still no word from the boat team, and needed more painkillers. Fortunately, I'd stocked up right after Ren arrived because he had the incredible ability to give me a headache like no other.

Bradley had found a radio from somewhere, and the faint sounds of Egyptian pop drifted out as fetched a fresh packet of paracetamol from my bathroom then slumped into a chair on the patio. While the others bopped around inside Ren's apartment, breathed in the warm air and tried to block out whatever the rest of the team was doing. This was the hardest part. The waiting. I wished I was with them, no matter how scary it might have been. Anything was better than sitting there not knowing what was going on.

I swallowed two pills dry and stared at my phone screen. I knew I couldn't call Ren, but I really, really wanted to hear his annoying voice tell me everything was okay. A *bang* sounded in the distance, and I almost jumped out of my skin. Was that a gunshot? I listened for sirens, for running feet, but everything carried on normal. Perhaps it had just been a car backfiring?

Then my phone rang. Why was Russell calling? Wasn't he supposed to be with his brother?

"Hello?"

"Tai Bowloo." The stranger said it as a statement, mangling my surname in a thick Arabic voice. "Listen to me."

"Who the hell is this?"

"That doesn't matter. What matters is that I have your boyfriend here with me, and unless you do exactly as I say, he's going to lose his head."

Of all the thousand things I could have said, what fell out of my stupid mouth was, "Which one?"

"What?" the man snapped. "He only has one head."

"I meant, which boyfriend? Ren or Russell?"

"You have two boyfriends? You Western women are all the same with your loose morals."

"It's not like that..." I started, but then the rest of his words sank in. "What do you mean, lose his head?"

Sweat popped out on the back of my neck, and it was a good thing I was sitting down because my knees would've given way otherwise.

"Russell is tied up in front of me, and I have a gun pointed at him."

I shouldn't have felt relief. But I did, and I hated myself for it. Hated myself for being grateful that it wasn't Ren whose life was at risk.

"Let him go! He hasn't done anything!"

Was this why nobody had heard from Ren and his team? Because the whole job had gone horribly, horribly wrong?

"We can't let him go. Not until he's helped us to find the cartouche that you and your friends stole from us. You think we are stupid? Aqueel told us you didn't go straight back to Luxor after you arrived at al-Nahas."

Oh, shit, shit, shit! "But Russell is nothing to do with this. He doesn't know where the cartouche is. I don't even know where the cartouche is, I swear."

"I believe you. No man would be stupid enough to trust a woman with that information."

"How dare you—"

"Shut your mouth! Russell is running out of time. You must bring us your *other* boyfriend's laptop, and Russell will help us to break into it. Then we will get the information we need."

"But—"

"The laptop—bring it. We know you are at home. There is a man waiting outside your gate, and you will hand the laptop to him. Stay on the phone while you do it, and if you try to alert anyone, the next thing you will hear will be the gunshot that kills your friend."

What should I do? Ren's laptop was encrypted, I knew that much. And it was sitting on the coffee table in my apartment. But could Russell crack it? And what did Ren have on there? He was in the CIA, that much I was certain of from the snippets of conversation I'd overheard, so surely this wasn't the only covert job he might have details of lurking on his hard drive. What other problems could arise if terrorists somehow got access to that information?

Or... Or what if I gave the man *my* laptop? Would he be able to tell the difference between the two? Passing a laptop over would buy me time. Once I'd done my part, I could hang up and call Ren straight away. He'd be able to fix this, I knew he would. He'd promised.

The only other alternative was to hide out in my room and not give the man a laptop at all. He might be bluffing. Mightn't he? My stomach flipped. What if he wasn't?

I longed to be able to talk to Tegan, but I couldn't, not with this sick freak listening in. Could I write a note? Perhaps if I grabbed a pen and paper...

"The clock ticks, Tai. You have fifteen seconds to get that laptop out of the gate, or Russell dies. I'm not messing around here. You know we've already killed many other people."

My heart threatened to give out, but if I died from a coronary, Russell would be shot for sure. *Think, Tai. Think!*

What should I do? *What should I do?*

CHAPTER 31 - TAI

I RAN DOWN the path with my own laptop, picking the
"Grl Pwr" sticker off the back as I went. Ren certainly
wouldn't have one of those, especially in hot pink. *Keep
breathing, Tai.* If I didn't lie convincingly, it could cost
Russell his life. The man would undoubtedly realise my
deception when he turned the laptop on and found my
emails instead of Ren's, plus a file of recipes I'd never
got around to making and the world's largest collection
of cat memes, but it would buy Russell time. Time that
I could use to call Ren and get him to save Russell the
way he'd saved me at al-Nahas.

"Five seconds," the man on the phone said.

"I'm coming, I'm coming."

My hands were shaking so much, I could barely
undo the gate, and I waited for the sound of a gunshot,
but then the bolt shot back and I tumbled out into the
street, almost landing on my bottom in my haste to
save Russell.

Sure enough, there was a man in a white robe
standing just outside, half-hidden in the shadows of a
mango tree. A pickup idled alongside, no doubt waiting
for him to grab Ren's laptop and make a quick getaway.

"Here." I held the laptop out at arm's length, hating
the thought of touching the enemy. He was a thief. A
murderer. "Here's what you wanted. Now let Russell

go."

He snatched the laptop out of my hands, but rather than answering, he laughed, a dry cackle more suited to an old crone. Or a witch. Or a warlock.

"This isn't funny!"

He just laughed harder.

"Hey, we had a deal."

"Women are all the same. So stupid."

"How dare—"

I never got to finish the sentence.

An arm wrapped around my throat from behind, and then the world faded away.

CHAPTER 32 - REN

EIGHT O'CLOCK, AND Ren Fontana leaned back in the plastic lawn chair and exhaled a cloud of shisha smoke. When in Egypt, do as the Egyptians do, and that meant puffing on a shisha pipe, drinking black coffee, and cheering every time The Pharaohs scored against Tunisia.

Except Ren was anything but relaxed. Rather than listening to the TV commentary, he concentrated on the two sets of chatter coming through his earpiece—Russell and Finn in the café opposite, courtesy of Jed's microphone, plus Logan and Emmy as the latter searched Finn's boat.

She'd snuck on board half an hour ago, thanks to a stroke of luck and Finn's tendency to act like a dick. As the two brothers had walked from the boat to the café, a teenager shot out from behind a car, bumping Russell hard enough for him to stumble off the kerb. Finn tried to grab the kid, but he twisted out of his grip and ran off, laughing as Finn's shouts followed him along the street. Emmy took advantage of the distraction to scoot along the jetty and down the gangplank, and now she was skulking around on board the *Lucky Star*, taking care to duck below the windows. What had she found so far?

Four dead cockroaches, three live cockroaches, two

dirty socks (unmatched), and a crispy tissue.

No mask.

She still had half the boat left to search, but from her tone, she wasn't hopeful. The mask of Ay wasn't some trinket that could be stuffed into the back of a drawer. So where the hell had Finn hidden it?

And after a brief discussion where Russell offered to pay for a courier to take his mom's birthday gift back to England, a suggestion Finn had seemed less than impressed with, the conversation in the café turned to childhood memories and talk about people both brothers knew back home. Did Finn know that Kate and Bruce Fortherington-Bennett had gotten divorced? No, but he wasn't surprised since Bruce had kept a stack of gay porn magazines in his locker at school.

Magazines? That was it? Ren had once stashed a naked cheerleader in his fuckin' locker. A hot little brunette who'd worn glasses in class to make herself look smarter. What was her name again? Brittney? Tiffany? Something like that. Ren hadn't exactly taken notes during his high school days. Then his father died in an accident at work, his mother married the slimy fucker she'd been having an affair with, and Ren found himself at college with two choices—either knuckle down and make something of himself, or stay bitter at the world and waste the rest of his life.

Between studying for his bachelor's degree and working shifts as a bartender to pay his rent, he hadn't had time for women. A major in psychology and a minor in Middle Eastern language, literature, and culture had taken the majority of his focus. Then he'd graduated, and working abroad for the CIA, he needed to be careful who he fucked around with. And speaking of fucking around, what the hell was he doing with Tai?

Ren couldn't deny he'd woken with a smile on his face when he realised her hand was on his cock, and yeah, he might've left it there on purpose just to see what she'd do when she noticed. Her reaction didn't disappoint. Tai was that delicious combination of spunk and naïvety that made him hard, and even though he absolutely shouldn't have been thinking of her that way, he had to plead guilty to jacking off to thoughts of her in the bathroom a time or two. Since college, he'd always gone for the innocent ones. The quiet ones. The ones who didn't try too hard with their make-up or squeeze themselves into three pairs of Spanx for a night out. There was nothing less sexy than trying to peel off control underwear for a quickie—he'd been there and tried it.

Jed always kidded that if there was a librarian within fifty yards, Ren would be there checking her out, and it wasn't so far from the truth. He'd been with a librarian once, and all that primness was just for show.

Plus Tai was an enigma. When Ren wound her up, she sniped right back at him, but there was a hint of nervousness there. Like she'd been hurt by a man in the past and wanted to avoid it happening again. Ren wanted to avoid it happening too.

Which was why he had to *stay away*.

Stay away from Tai and get this job finished. And sell his soul to the devil, also known as Emerson Black, so he could beg her to find out who the fuck had sent the police after Tai in England. Because Tai was no thief. Anyone who'd spent five minutes with her could see that, and she deserved to go home without getting arrested.

Somebody scored a goal, and a groan rippled through the crowd—a sentiment Ren could agree with. Where was the damn mask? They needed to find it so he could get back to Langley for a rest. This hadn't exactly turned out to be a vacation, had it?

Until that moment, Russell and Finn had been talking quietly in the background, but suddenly, Russell's voice rose ten decibels.

"No, I didn't leave it in my hotel room. I know I brought it with me."

Brought what? What was he so concerned about?

Ren shifted in his seat to glance through the plate-glass window opposite and saw Russell first patting his pockets and then stooping to check under the table. Had he lost his wallet? His phone?

"Can you call it?" he asked his brother.

His phone, then.

Finn pulled out his own phone and dialled, and the two men stood still and listened. Jed pretended to ignore them and carried on reading his guidebook.

Nothing. No phone.

Ren had seen that panicked look before, on one of the geeks at work when he accidentally left his smartwatch in the locker room. The heart-wrenching fear of a man separated from a part of himself. The guy had even given his laptop a name, for fuck's sake. Anabella. Ren preferred his women breathing and sentient.

"Maybe I dropped it outside?" Russell said, and headed for the door without waiting for an answer. Finn threw a handful of notes on the table and hurried out after his brother.

Ah, shit.

Jed couldn't give himself away, so Ren mirrored Finn by leaving cash for the waiter, then vanished from the soccer crowd in a puff of shisha smoke.

"Emmy, get off the boat now. Russell and Finn are heading in your direction."

"They've got line of sight," Logan said after a second. "You can't go up the gangplank."

"Understood."

Ren hadn't worked with Emmy personally before, but he wasn't surprised that she remained utterly calm. In the secretive world of intelligence and security, her reputation preceded her.

"Well, that's the boat searched. Fucking mask's not on board anyway. How long do I have? Can anyone cause a distraction for me to get the hell out of here?"

"Thirty seconds," Logan told her. "Hold on."

He stepped out from between two parked cars and body-checked Russell, but it was Finn who stopped with a mouthful of abuse.

"What the hell was that for? Don't you idiots look where you're going?"

"Russell's still coming," Ren said as Logan held up his hands in apology.

"Fuck." A pause, and Ren imagined Emmy's mind whirring, thinking up options and calculating the odds of their success. More than once, he'd heard her referred to as the ice queen, and even in the searing Egyptian heat, she stayed cool. "Okay, I'm going into the water. Someone get the car and pick me up by that cluster of feluccas to the north."

She'd be soaking when she got out of the Nile, and nothing would bring more attention than a dripping blonde woman strolling along the Corniche during the busiest part of the evening. Ren had the spare key, and he was closest to the SUV.

"I'll drive."

He forced himself to stroll rather than jog, just another tourist out for an evening meander. Training made him stop in front of a shop window, pretending to peruse the rainbow of T-shirts on display as he checked for a tail.

The shopkeeper was at his side in seconds. "You want T-shirt? Good price?"

"*La, shukran.*"

Every tourist learned enough Arabic to say no thanks. Otherwise hawkers followed them down the street, trying to sell everything from clothing to camel rides. *No tail.* Ren quickly moved on.

One minute and thirty seconds gone.

He hadn't seen Emmy slip into the water, which meant the two brothers most likely missed her escape too. They'd walked up and down the street and were on the boat now, Logan reported. Had Russell found his phone? Talk about a stroke of bad luck—Emmy had been twenty seconds from getting caught behind enemy lines. A close call, too close for comfort.

Ren started the car and waited for a horse to trot past, brass medallions jingling as it pulled a caleche full of tourists.

Two minutes gone.

When Ren pulled up by the steps to the dock, a couple was standing at the top, giggling as they tried to take a picture of themselves and the boats with a selfie stick. Great fucking timing.

"Aw, it's not long enough," the girl complained, checking the screen.

That wasn't a phrase Ren heard often.

The guy started fiddling with the settings. "We should use the timer. I told you we should use the timer."

Ren scanned the water. No sign of Emmy, but she'd be appearing at any moment like a swamp creature rising from the deep. Who the hell knew what was in that water? No one in their right mind even dipped a toe in.

"Want me to take the picture?" he offered.

They both swivelled their heads, and the girl's face lit up in a smile.

"Oh, awesome!"

She passed the camera over while the guy scowled. *Shoulda had a bigger stick, buddy.* Ren gritted his teeth while they shuffled into position, then snapped off a burst of photos.

"Those look great." He added a wink just because he could. "You're model material, babe."

The guy grabbed her hand and tugged his girl out of Ren's clutches, throwing a dirty glare over his shoulder as he did so. Mission accomplished.

Five minutes gone.

"I'm in place," he told the others.

But where the hell was Emmy?

Chapter 33 - Ren

REN HOPPED OVER the chain at the top of the steps and took them two at a time down to the jetty. Eight feluccas bobbed gently in the current, and the reflections of streetlights danced in the ripples as a gentle breeze stirred the surface of the water. He pulled a pack of cigarettes from his pocket and lit one. No, he wasn't a smoker, shisha excepted, but stand someplace you shouldn't be with a lit cigarette and nobody ever questioned you.

Six minutes gone. Seven.

Finn's boat wasn't far from the jetty, only a hundred and fifty yards, and Emmy should've arrived by then. The current was with her, and by all accounts, she was a strong swimmer.

"She's not at the jetty."

"I'm coming along the sidewalk from the boat," Jed said. "There's no sign of her here either."

Logan chimed in. "She'll be swimming underwater, but with that distance, she'll have to come up for breath at least once. Probably twice."

"How long can she hold her breath?" Ren asked, half joking, half worried. She'd been gone for eight minutes now.

"Eight minutes? Nine? I forget her exact record."

Nine minutes? Holy shit.

"But that's if she's just sitting there," Logan added. "I'd give her maybe two minutes swimming if she's going with the current. I'm still near the boat, and there's no activity in the water here."

"What if her clothing got snagged on something below the surface? Does the Nile have rip currents?"

"She's careful." His tone stayed light. "Relax."

Relax? Right. At times like this, Ren regretted becoming a spy instead of a linguist or a translator. "Did Russell find his phone?"

"Nope. But remember that kid who ran into him earlier? I reckon he took it. He had something in his hand when he ran off."

Another minute ticked past, and Ren couldn't speak because another handful of tourists stopped to admire the view. At this rate, they'd be looking for a damn corpse. Emmy Black was meant to be Wonder Woman, and she couldn't manage a simple swim?

Tick, tick, tick. Why did time always pass so slowly when you were on the lookout for a body?

"Guys, do you think we should borrow one of these feluccas and go search for her?"

"Nah," Logan said. "She'll be pissed when she turns up and we're not where we're supposed to be."

"But—"

Jed cut Ren off. "Stop being a pussy and wait Emmy's basically immortal. Someday, Marvel'll write a comic book about her."

How had Jed ever dated Emmy? Ren couldn't take the stress. This was yet another reason he preferred sweet girls over superheroes. Would Tai vanish into the Nile like that? No, she wouldn't.

Twenty-five damn minutes had passed, and Ren

vas on the verge of saying to hell with Jed and Logan
ınd stealing a felucca anyway when he saw it. A pale
pot in the water, too still to be a reflection. Was that...?
ʾuck, it was. It was Emmy, fifteen yards offshore. What
he hell was she doing? Why didn't she simply swim the
inal stretch?

"I think she's close. She just came up to take a
ʼreath."

"Took her fuckin' time," Jed said. "Pick me up
ʼutside the mosque?"

"Sure. Logan?"

"I'll stay here and watch our boys."

Another minute went by before Emmy bobbed up
ıgain, this time right in front of Ren. The gleam in her
ʼye was at odds with the disgusted look on her face.

"This outfit's going in the incinerator," she
ʼrumbled as she hoisted herself onto the jetty. "Don't
ıelp or anything."

"Where the fuck have you been?"

"Take a wild guess, dude."

"Why did it take you almost half an hour to swim a
ıundred and fifty yards?"

"Do you want me to answer that before or after I
ıaul this tchotchke onto dry land?"

"What tchotchke?"

"An educated guess? The mask we've been looking
ʼor."

The mask? Was she serious? For the first time, Ren
ʼealised she was holding something in her hand. The
ʼnd of a thin rope, dark-coloured paracord by the look
ʼf it, its tail disappearing into the murky water. He
ʼidn't bother to ask questions, just grabbed the rope
ʼnd heaved while Emmy dripped half the Nile onto the

wooden boards of the jetty. A puddle spread out arou
her while he slowly hauled the dead weight of whatev
she'd found to the surface. Was it really the Mask
Ay? They'd have to wait until they got to the villa
find out.

But it was certainly heavy. At least ten kilos—may
even fifteen, Ren estimated as the water drained aw
—stuffed into a canvas hold-all that had once be
cream or light grey but was now a dirty green colo
About the right size too. He'd seen Tutankhamu
mask in the Egyptian Museum in Cairo a few yea
back, and it'd been half a metre tall.

"Hey! What's going on?"

Shit. More damn tourists. A middle-aged cou
this time, British judging by the man's accent. Bo
wore wedding rings and slightly concerned expressio

Before Ren could answer, Emmy burst out gigglin
"I want to swim, but he won't let me. Meanie." She ga
Ren a half-hearted shove and tripped over her own fe
"Aw, babe, why won't you let me go back in the water'

Ren gave them a helpless look and shrugged. "l
too much to drink," he mouthed, wrapping an a
around Emmy's waist. "Let's go, honey."

"Go? Go where? Back to the hotel bar?" Emmy to
a wobbly step forward, holding out a hand to t
woman. "Why don't you come with us? We can
friends."

The woman grabbed her husband's arm and too
step backwards, concern morphing into distaste. "\
have somewhere to be."

"And so do we," Emmy muttered under her brea
"Although a hotel bar doesn't sound like a bad idea."

Ren picked up the sodden bag and jogged up t

steps with Emmy following. Good thing he'd only rented the SUV because she fuckin' stank. He'd gladly forfeit his damage deposit for some other schmuck to shampoo the upholstery.

"Is this what I think it is?" Jed asked when he climbed into the back seat.

"Dunno. I didn't exactly stop to open it ten metres down. But whatever it is, Finn cared enough to hide it under his boat. It was tied onto one of the mooring lines."

Jed gave a low whistle. "Good thing Russell lost his phone when he did, eh?"

"Yeah, mostly. Do me a favour and run into the pharmacy, would you?"

"What for?"

"Praziquantel. I'm ninety-nine percent likely to have the shits tomorrow after what I've been wading through, and I'd rather not get schistosomiasis as well."

"You carried the mask along the riverbed?"

"Well, I wasn't going to leave it behind, was I?"

If Ren had learned one thing tonight, it was that the stories were true. Emmy really was an unnerving blend of insanity and smarts and determination all wrapped up in a pretty package. Which gave him hope. Hope that she and Blackwood could get to the bottom of Tai's so-called crime back in England and clear her name. But how should he broach that subject?

They pulled up outside the pharmacy, and Jed strode inside.

"What's our next step?" Ren asked.

"I need to take a shower."

"I meant with the mask."

"Yeah, the mask... It belongs to the Egyptian

people, and we'll need to give it back, but not yet. Finding it's just the start."

Unfortunately, she was right. Their job wasn't done yet. Until they caught the thieves, the mask, the cartouche, and the rest of the treasure, which had been moved away from al-Nahas by a contact of Emmy's in the Egyptian military, wasn't safe.

"Someone needs to round up Finn and his accomplices."

"Yes, they do. But unless Finn's more devious than me, which is unlikely, he didn't mastermind this. And there's a buyer involved further up the chain. I've got a friend who's involved in art theft—preventing it, not carrying it out—and if there's one thing I've learned, it's that nobody steals a piece like that on spec."

"True. And how did Finn find out about the mask in the first place? Only seven people knew it had been discovered—Miles, an American who worked on the dig, the Minister of Antiquities, and four others who are dead. Seven people, and one of them talked. Miles keeps saying it wasn't the American, but he's hazy on the details."

"It wasn't the American."

"How do *you* know that?"

"No motive. The American's a professor called Vernon Martelle, and Miles has known him since he started digging shit up. Vernon lives in trenches, and his claim to fame is that a decade ago, he unearthed the biggest trove of Viking treasure ever found in the UK. And do you know what he did with the three-million pound finder's fee?"

Ren shook his head.

"He donated it back to the museum so they coul

build a children's educational centre. Trust me, Vernon wasn't behind this, not on purpose anyway."

"What do you mean, not on purpose?"

"*I* knew about the mask. Miles told Bradley, and Bradley told everyone in the house and bought cupcakes to celebrate. None of my people would've breathed a word, but if Vernon or the minister let the find slip in the same manner... Plus Miles is flakey, and he's an academic, not a spy. Someone could've overheard him on the phone."

Ren swallowed a groan. "So our pool of suspects just got bigger?"

"Yup. We need to talk to Finn."

"Talk?"

She shrugged. "I'm good at asking questions."

Her tone said she wasn't planning to play quiz show host.

The door opened, and Jed slid into the back seat clutching a paper bag and an economy-sized package of toilet paper. "What'd I miss?"

"Emmy wants to talk to Finn."

"Good idea. Then we can sort out this mess and go home. When d'ya want to pick him up, darlin'?"

"Sooner rather than later. If he spots the mask's missing, he's either gonna go rent a set of scuba gear or run."

"Logan's watching him."

"Good. Let me get cleaned up, then we can go and have a chat."

The sound of "Despacito" filled the cabin, and Jed sniggered. "New ringtone?"

"Some clown in the office changed it again. Nate, probably. Still, the phone survived its swim, so that's good news."

Or was it? When Emmy answered, Ren wanted to consign the damn phone to a watery grave.

"OMG, she's disappeared and Miles is freaking out and we can't find her and dinner's burning and—"

"Bradley, calm down. Take a breath. Who's disappeared?"

"Tai! She's gone!"

Tai? Ren's chest constricted in an instant, and when he tried to inhale, sucking in air took an effort. How could Tai have disappeared? She was supposed to be in his apartment with Bradley, Miles, and Tegan, and it only had three rooms.

"What happened?" he asked. "Tell me."

Bradley had gone from not breathing at all to hyperventilating. "She...she... She went outside for fresh air, and she's gone."

"You've checked the other apartments?"

"Tegan did. She's not here!"

"Have you tried calling her?"

"Her phone's turned off."

"We're on our way," Emmy told him. "Turn the stove off and stay inside."

Ren's earlier words about sweet girls being less stressful than superheroes? He took them all back.

CHAPTER 34 - REN

WHO CARED ABOUT speed limits? Ren dodged around pedestrians and horses and dawdling taxi drivers, ignoring blasts of the horn and angry shouts.

"Are you trying to kill us all?" Jed asked, hanging onto the grab handle above the door.

No, but if Tai was in trouble, then every second counted. Why hadn't he stayed behind? Tegan was an ex-cop, not a bodyguard. Had someone abducted Tai from right out of the compound?

"We need to get back fast."

"Not with a camel as a hood ornament, we don't."

"We've got airbags."

Emmy didn't say a word, just tapped away at her phone until they were almost at the villa.

"Stop!"

When Ren didn't respond instantaneously, she yanked on the handbrake, sending the car into a skid.

"What did you do that for?"

"You were about to drive over a potential crime scene."

Ren's blood ran cold. A fucking *crime scene*. If anyone had hurt his girl...

Well, not *his* girl exactly, but they'd shared a near-death experience and last night she'd felt him up in her sleep, which gave him a certain amount of responsibility. He leapt out of the car and ran through the gate.

"What happened?"

Of course, Bradley had ignored Emmy's instruction to stay inside, and flashlight beams crisscrossed the yard as the three musketeers poked through the bushes near Betsy's coop. The chicken squawked every time one of them got too close.

"I don't know!" Tegan didn't just sound scared, she sounded terrified. "One minute she was here, and she stepped outside to get some air—like, right outside the door—and then she didn't come back."

"Didn't you hear anything?"

"The music was on too loud," Miles said, hanging his head, guilty. "We should've left it off."

"When did you last see her?"

"About half an hour ago. Perhaps forty minutes?"

"Forty minutes?" Now anger simmered in Ren's veins. "Tegan, what the hell were you doing?"

"I'm sorry. I'm so, so sorry. I thought she'd gone to the loo, and by the time I realised she hadn't... And then we were looking for her... I'm sorry." Tegan began sobbing as her mask finally cracked. "I'm so sorry."

Jed put an arm around her shoulders. Mr. Hearts and fucking Minds. "What's done is done, and we need to focus on finding Tai. Can you tell us exactly what went on? Every detail, even if you don't think it's important."

"While you discuss that, I'm gonna take a shower," Emmy said.

Bradley wrinkled his nose. "What happened? You stink."

"I went swimming." She pointed at the bag in Jed'